Struck

by

J. M. Davis

This is a work of fiction. Names, characters, places, and incidents are either the product of the author's imagination or are used fictitiously, and any resemblance to actual persons living or dead, business establishments, events, or locales, is entirely coincidental.

Struck

COPYRIGHT © 2016 by Jillian Davis

Cover Art by *Angela Anderson*

The Wild Rose Press, Inc.
PO Box 708
Adams Basin, NY 14410-0708
Visit us at www.thewildrosepress.com

Publishing History
First Black Rose Edition, 2016
Print ISBN 978-1-5092-0582-0
Digital ISBN 978-1-5092-0583-7

Published in the United States of America

"Nik," I start, casting my eyes to the creamy column of his neck. I can see his pulse throb against the hollow of his throat. "We can't—"

He dips his head and crushes his lips to mine before I can finish. My eyes grow wide, and I grab onto his shoulders and try to push him away. His hands are still on my face, his long fingers reaching behind my ears, touching the vine of Marks that coil behind them. They respond eagerly to the touch, flaring with a warmth that arrows straight to my core.

I gasp beneath his expert lips, and his tongue slips past my teeth. He explores the depths of my mouth, and it sends a shiver down my spine. I lean my trembling body against him, relishing the way I fit perfectly against his firm frame. The kiss is desperate, passionate, tender, and absolutely all consuming.

His strong hands refuse to let me go, his palms hot on my already flushed skin. I synchronize my lips to his movement, and our kiss deepens until I feel as though I'm going to burst into a quivering pool of nerves. His body reacts to our kiss as well, sending me into a frenzy of wild, squirming desire. *God, this feels so good.*

My insides erupt into a lightning storm. Spangles of rippling currents flow through my veins. *No!* I try to pull away before it reaches my lips. But I'm too late. It tingles as it passes through our kiss. Nik trembles from the raw power. *No! Please god no.*

Nik breaks our kiss. When he lifts his face, his eyes blaze with something unnatural, and I know it's *my* dangerous electricity coursing through him. *I killed him...*

He stares, deadpan into my eyes and declares solemnly, "I've been struck."

Other Books by J. M. Davis

The author's debut novel, *THE DEVIL'S WINGMAN,*
was published in April 2015
by The Wild Rose Press, Inc.

Dedication

To my husband, Alex.
For not only being struck by me,
but for always sticking by me.

Acknowledgments

To Shannon Ford for simply being my #1 fan.

To my children, Garrett & Lexi for talking in hushed
voices at the library while I researched for this book.

To my CP, Bethany Shaw, for reading this in its first
draft and offering invaluable suggestions.

To my parents for constant love and support.

To my editor, Lill Farrell, and The Wild Rose Press
for accepting me into the publishing family
with open arms.

Prologue

I watch from the sidelines as Trevor makes the final score of the game, sealing the win for the Mepelo Mustangs. Though I despise soccer, I'm a good girlfriend, dutifully attending each of his home games, rooting and encouraging him on.

I cover my ears as the crowd goes wild in the stands, erupting into excited cheers. Some jump to their feet, clapping, while others whoop like holler monkeys. Soccer games are a bit of a big deal in our hometown, but then again, so is baseball, basketball, and football. Pretty much anything that involves sweat, a ball, and too much testosterone.

I pull my gaze from the stands, searching the field for Trevor. I find him fist-pumping his way through the throng of teammates, rushing to give him high-fives. Not wanting to invade on their high of winning the state tournament for Mepelo High, I wait patiently, feeling awkward as I dig my toe in the dirt of the freshly cut grass of the soccer field. The sun is still high in the sky, which makes for a warm wait. Beads of sweat work their way down my back, making my T-shirt stick to my skin. I reach into my back pocket to retrieve my poetry book, something I often carry with me to pass idle time. It's worn, and some of the lyrical verses are highlighted for me to revisit and commit to memory. Before I could crack it open, I hear someone say,

"Abby."

I look up, noticing Trevor sprinting toward me. Perspiration has his normally loose curls smashed flat against his forehead. He's grinning, obviously still soaring from the excitement of his big win. He sweeps me into his arms and swings me around. Not having time to tuck it safely away, I keep a tight grip on my beloved poetry book.

"That was an awesome score!" I hug his neck, feeling the stickiness of his skin, which makes me cringe a little. *Ew. Sweat.* I move my hands to his shoulders, feeling his warm skin beneath the damp uniform. Suddenly aware of the potent smell of sweat and grass that wafted from him, I wrinkle my nose.

"Now if I could only score *off* the field." Trevor looks down at me smiling, then gives me a playful wink.

I giggle, and swat at him with my book. Trevor and I have been dating off and on since the eighth grade, but it wasn't until three weeks ago that we decided to take it seriously. We met in Algebra class, and as I struggled to multiply numbers with letters of the alphabet, he excelled in it. Mrs. Newton eventually forced our relationship to go from simple classmates, to tutor and tutee. I frowned at the pairing. Trevor was a jock, and insanely popular, and I was…not.

I *was* and still *am* a moody person, so it was easier for me to stay hidden amongst the shadows of my classmates. Peering over my books at them in class, or peeking around restroom stalls as the cheerleaders slathered on fruity-smelling lip-gloss and tossed their hair until it was perfect. Labeled "Abby Angst" in high school, I was often found in the library, pouring over countless books of poetry. I preferred to hang with Poe, Hughes, and Frost. As a matter of fact, some days, I still do. After eight weeks of tutor sessions, I passed Algebra with a B minus and gained a friend in the process.

In ninth grade, Trevor and I dated fleetingly during the summer, and then again, for about a month before Christmas. I always broke it off first, feeling too overwhelmed by his popularity and too intimidated by the glares I often received from the other girls in school. By the middle of our tenth grade year, Trevor insisted that we try it again, and as I stared into his big brown eyes, I relented. We even made a pact to make a conscience effort to partake in each other's hobbies. I'd attend his soccer games, and he'd go to The Grind, the local coffee shop, to listen to poetry readings.

"At least a celebratory kiss," he says as his laughter dissipates, and is replaced by a seriousness that makes me squirm in his arms. Trevor and I have never kissed before. Our relationships were the briefest of affairs, never warranting anything more than a lingering hug. We told ourselves that we'd take things slow, to make sure our relationship was solid this time around, and not just an adolescent infatuation.

I gaze up at him, catching my bottom lip with my teeth as I think about it. *Our first kiss. It's supposed to be special.* He has dirt smeared across his forehead, and his cheeks are pink with exertion. Though he appears out of breath and exhausted, his eyes still glimmer with keen interest. His mouth is so close to mine, and when he squeezes me a little tighter and says, "Come on, Abby. I've been dying to kiss you since I was thirteen," I become jelly in his arms. "You gonna let me or not?"

Screw the ideal moment, and to hell with poetic advances, I'm going to let him. I incline my face to his, and close my eyes. His lips brush faintly against mine, and I give a soft moan. This only leads to him pressing harder, deepening our kiss and adding a flick of his tongue along the seam of my lips. Then I feel something. A searing heat blossoms in my chest, and like a lightning bolt zigzagging its way across the sky, it courses through my veins, spidering out through my limbs and up my throat. I feel it push past my lips and force its way into Trevor's. And it's not just the spark of excitement of my first kiss, but something *different.* Something dangerous. Something deadly.

With a choked gasp, Trevor backs away from me. He clutches at his chest before falling heavily to the ground. I watch, shocked into complete silence when he lands with a sickening *thud.* I drop to my knees and touch his face.

"Trevor?"

I scan the length of him, his legs are sprawled, and his arms are lying limp at his sides. His eyes are still wide open, as if in disbelief, but the depths of the molasses pools are ghastly vacant. My fingers tremble as I lower them to his neck. *Please be okay. Please be okay.* Tears prick at my eyes, and fear grips my heart like a fist as I press my fingertips to his pulse. Nothing.

Then, I scream until my vocal cords are raw.

Chapter 1

Eight years later

"Damn it!"

"Shhh!" hisses Barb, the eldest and bitchiest librarian, James O. Davis Library has ever employed. I scowl at her as I bend to retrieve the stack of DVDs that nose-dived off my cart. *Guess I need to slow down around curves,* I think. I shove them back onto the cart and grip the handle, tossing Barb the fakest smile I could muster before trudging to the movie rack. *Why do people even borrow movies from the library? They're always scratched and are usually ancient. Libraries are for books for God's sake.*

I finish filing the DVDs back to their rightful spot, then head to the returned books pile. I glance around for Barb as I load my cart. The old bag is always hovering around me, just waiting for me to screw up enough to fire me. I don't know why she hates me so much. I do as I'm told, and more. Perhaps that's why she has it out for me. She's old school. All card catalogs, and Dewey Decimal System, while I consider myself a "high tech" librarian. I pioneered the great wi-fi movement, as well as organizing the historical logs of the library's conception. I even made a display of the yellowing blueprints, a piece of the original floorboard, as well as the family tree of the founder, James O. Davis. Barb hated that. After all, she'd been employed here for over forty years and never thought to exhibit such items.

With Barb nowhere in sight, I push my cart across the room and turn down the first non-fiction aisle, returning a book about writing resumes to its proper place. I hum to myself as I work diligently, slowly working my way through the pile. As I weave my way deeper and deeper through the rows of books, I grow more and more relaxed. I like the way the room grows darker in the far corner of the library. The lighting never harsh over the aging books. It was like a storm cloud had permanently taken residence in that end of the library. The book shelves seem to be perpetually shrouded in shadows and cool air. It's comforting; at least it is to me. Maybe it's the solitude it brings. The way I can get lost amidst the aisles, and towering shelves, lost in the countless spines of old novels, new novels, encyclopedias, atlases, and every other book in between.

I lift the next book from my cart and in a natural reaction, bring it to my nose, and inhale. I love the smell of the brittle paper from timeworn books. It's my second favorite smell on earth. My first is rain. Two scents that are complete opposites. Dead trees that have been harvested and processed into paper, and the crisp aroma of freshly fallen rain. *Well, maybe they aren't so different after all. Technically both are scents of nature.*

Sighing, I push the leather bound book into place, and reach blindly for the next book. As I scan the title, my heart catches a beat. Lyric Poetry of the Early Twentieth Century. I don't know why, but I flip through it, skimming the index for a single name. *Primsdale.* My chest tightens when I see it, but I find the author's page anyway. Taking a deep breath, I read the poem that still haunts me after all these years. The poem, though written decades before my existence, resonates with me. I could have written it myself.

> *I know nothing of love,*
> *So why do I pretend,*
> *To agree tis a powerful drug,*
> *Deadly enough to seal my lover's end.*
> *If our hearts were meant,*
> *If our lives to be laced;*
> *Then shall I regret this kiss*
> *That puts a frown upon my lover's face.*

I don't know how long I stand there, my eyes closed, still seeing those words as if they were tattooed across my eyelids. The images they stir deep within me also beget tears, hot tears that burn my eyes and leave warm trails down my cheeks.

I choke back a sob, clutching the book to my chest, my shoulders sagging from the weight of the memory pressed upon me. And again, like so many times before, I find myself recalling the night Trevor died. Staring into his lifeless eyes, disbelieving that he was really gone, but at the same time, entirely convinced that he was, because how could someone with a beating heart look so...*still*. The tang of bile bit at my throat when I realized that was our first, and *last* kiss.

As ambulance workers carted his body away, I remained, still crumpled on the ground, hugging my knees, crying until my head pounded and my eye sockets ached. The sirens eventually faded in the distance, and the stadiums emptied. A few people strayed, touching my shoulder, offering condolences and murmurs of concern before they left, but I barely heard them. Their words just background noise, din that one could overlook, tune out.

Instead I sat, my eyes transfixed on the spot of grass that lay crushed with the imprint of Trevor's body. My chest feeling as though it were imprisoned within someone's iron grip, their clutch ratcheting tighter and tighter, slowly crushing my ribs and spine. And not just from grief, but also from guilt. I knew then, just as I know now…I killed him. Everyone thinks he died of heart failure, brought on by the exertion of the game. But I know the truth. *I killed Trevor.*

I lean against the shelves for support, not trusting my knees to keep me upright without the help of the solid steel behind me. And still, the memory hacks away at me, leaving me feeling raw, like an exposed nerve. I can still smell the damp grass as a fine mist of rain blew through the air, and settled upon the ground. As I cried into the crook of my elbow, the rain picked up, pattering across my back like cool, massaging fingers. The back of my head became saturated, my long hair heavy against my neck.

"Why?" I asked, though I knew I was alone. "Why?" As if in answer, a rumble of thunder bellowed, and the rain came down in angry sheets, matching my own tears and tortured wails. That day, the sky cried with me, or so it seemed.

The dirt where I sat quickly turned to mud, the seat of my pants drenched, soaking through to my panties. Eventually my discomfort won out, and I lifted my head. I sniffed, and wiped my nose with the back of my hand, before dragging myself upright. The sky was hazy with rain, but even still, I was able to catch a glimpse of my poetry book. It was only a few feet from me. In the chaos I must have dropped it, and there it still lay open on the ground. I forced my legs to move forward, though the task seemed impossible. They were tingly, and sore from being made to endure an awkward position for over two hours. I cursed myself for not shaking them out when they pleaded for me to do so.

I bent, picking up the book, being careful with the sodden pages. My eyes fell upon the blurred letters, the words still readable though the black ink was smudged. That's when I read those haunting words. The words that seemed to be fated for me to read that day. Words that burned within my soul, forever reminding me of what I did. Reminding me of the cruelty I had bestowed on poor Trevor. The evil I unleashed, using the kindest gesture in the world to do it. *Our kiss.*

Again, I read the poem, though I'm not sure why; I could recite it on command. My heart catches on the lines that hurt the most. *I know nothing of love. Deadly enough to seal my lover's end. Then shall I regret this kiss. That puts a frown upon my lover's face.* Grinding my teeth, I inhale sharply, trying to cleanse myself of the foul memory, ridding myself of the gut-twisting guilt that consumes, even if just for a moment. *That's all I need. Just a moment.* Just long enough to get a grip on my sanity, just long enough to finish my work, and hustle myself out of here. I shove the poetry book into place, and quickly restock the final items on my cart.

"Is there anything you need done before I leave?" I ask Barb with a smile, though I'm silently praying she says no.

"You put away all the returned books?"

"Yes."

"And the DVDs?"

I fight the urge to roll my eyes. "Yes."

"Audio books? Magazines? Organized the Info-Board?"

"Yes, yes and yes." I retrieve my purse from my assigned cubby and turn to face her, a smile still plastered across my face, but I arch an eyebrow, daring her to find some unnecessary task to keep me here a moment longer.

She frowns and folds her chubby arms in front of her. "I suppose that is all I need from you for today. You're free to go."

"Are you certain Barb? I mean, if you need me to help you with the evening rush, I can stay. I mean, I wouldn't want you to get swamped with all these clamoring customers."

I make a show of looking around us, my eyes wide as if the four people in the library have suddenly become one hundred busy bodies. I look at them, but they're each lost in their work. One is sitting at a table quietly reading, another is looking up something on the computer, while the last two teen girls pick through the magazine rack. The silence in the room delivers my point home.

She dismisses me with a curt humph, and marches away.

I smile to myself, adjusting the strap of my purse as I walk through the automatic doors and out into the balmy evening air. I take a deep breath, but it does little to pacify the anxiousness that is built up within me. The memory of Trevor is still livid within my head, still sucking away at my sanity, evaporating my energy with each step I take. *I've got to get home.* I need a hot shower, or even better, a long soak in the tub to clear my mind. This is common, this overwhelming wash of guilt.

It comes each and every time I recall that night with Trevor, over eight years ago. It used to be debilitating, so much so that I would crumple into a fetal position whenever the memory presented itself. Sobbing until the tears ran dry, or the ache in my head became too intense to continue. Now, I can keep the episodes at bay, though it takes a great deal of control.

I unlock the door of my car, and slide behind the wheel, thankful to be off my feet. I toss my purse into the bucket seat beside me, and start to roll the window down. I still have manual windows, so I work hard to wind the handle, lowering the glass just enough to allow the night air to permeate the staleness of the cab. I pinch the bridge of my nose, taking long drags of breath through my nose, releasing each one slowly through my mouth. It takes several minutes of repeating this routine to get comfortable enough to drive.

I pull the strap across my lap and snap the seatbelt into place before starting the ignition. The engine sputters for a moment, as if woken up from a long sleep, then rumbles like an angry bee caught in a jar. I pull out, and slowly creep my way across the security lit parking lot. I turn onto Sycamore and lay into the gas pedal, stoking the engine into further annoyance. It grumbles at me as we roar down the quiet road.

I stroke the steering wheel, and say, "It's okay Pete. It's good to have your motor run hard every now and then. Reminds you what it was like when you were in your prime."

The car is vintage, built in the early seventies, and is considered cool by the standards of old men and car enthusiasts. However, to most people, it's a pile of junk. Not that I can blame them. To the untrained eye, those rust spots are blemishes, as are the tattered seat covers, drooping roof lining, and stained floorboards. But to those who appreciate the beauty of a classic, with original parts and interior, this car is a diamond in the rough.

Someday, when money and time are plenty, I will chip away the dust that has long covered this old jewel. *Yeah, someday,* I think as I ease the car to a halt. As I wait for the light to turn green, my phone rings. I fish through the contents of my purse, pushing past my small journal, and dozens of receipts and napkins that bear my scratch work. I often use whatever's handy to pen my musings. Thoughts that will someday turn to lyrical poetry.

The ringing stops. *Damn.* I think about giving up my search, but the ringing starts again. I frown at this, because it can't be good if someone is calling repeatedly. I continue to tear through my purse, until finally my fingers find the blaring cellphone. *Aha!* I pull it out and glance at the screen. It's Lora, my best and only friend, unless you count my cousin, Mo. He's a year older than I am, and we basically grew up as siblings. My mom died just minutes after I was born. Her heart simply gave out after the eighteen hours of excruciating labor. Dad raised me with the help of his sister. God bless Aunt Blair. She was there to fix my crooked pigtails, teach me how to apply makeup, and help me buy tampons.

I hit the accept call button and lift the phone to my ear.

"What's up?"

"Abby." Her voice comes out haggard, and strained, like she has a bad case of laryngitis.

"Lora? What is it?" Something about the way she sounds makes my senses go on high alert. *Something's not right. I just know it.*

"Can you come over?" She sniffles, then blows her nose into the receiver.

"What's wrong?" My stomach dips with apprehension, and I whip the car around, turning it toward the edge of town, where Lora lives with her prick of a husband, Tony.

"Oh Abby. I made—" She begins crying, barely able to croak out the words in between her sobs. "I made him so mad this time."

I'm instantly furious, feeling the heat flare into my cheeks. "What did he do?"

"Just hurry. Please. I don't want to be alone when he gets back." She hangs up and I'm left with a dull silence. I've always disliked Tony, even back in high school. I thought he was a pompous dick who cared more about the notches on his bedpost than Lora. When she agreed to marry the asshole, I threatened to disown her, but that was an empty promise, and she knew it.

Lora was the only person in school who tried to befriend me. I'll never forget the day we met. She walked in on me in the bathroom, though I wasn't actually *using* it, it was still embarrassing. I was hunkered down in the last stall, reading Edgar Allan Poe, while nibbling on beef jerky. She pushed open the door, which I forgot to latch, and found me sitting there in all my pathetic glory. I still remember what she said.

"Beef jerky, huh? That's definitely a po' man's meal."

We both laughed, and the rest is history.

After Lora and Tony married, his true nature was revealed. Turns out he holds fast to chauvinistic ideals like women are terrible drivers, men are the kings of their homes, and their women should remain slim and sexy, even after having several children. Then last year, the mother of all douchebag qualities came out. He's a wife beater. And for that, I despise him. On his drunken binges, he gets off on pushing Lora around. Once, he gave her a black eye that she hid behind her designer sunglasses. I often wonder what the women in her yoga classes would do if they found out Lora's secret. Would they try to help? Would Lora become the topic of gossip and curious stares? Just thinking about a room full of whispering, tongue-clucking chicks in spandex pisses me off.

I race toward Lora's house, my blood pumping so much adrenaline that my veins feel like they're on fire. As the car headlights swing across Lora's garage door, I scan the front lawn. Nothing seems out of sort. A few stray toys litter the grass, and a plastic pool is set up, a rubber duck still floating lazily across the surface. Lora's prized roses are trimmed to perfection and scaling their way up the trellis. I kill the engine, and step out onto the driveway. The porch light is on. I pick my way up the sidewalk, stepping over a plush bunny rabbit, before I find myself standing on the welcome mat. I steel myself for what's behind the door. Will she be bruised? Bleeding? Before I can knock, the door creaks open.

"Abs?" Lora's voice is broken. *Whatever went down tonight was bad.* She usually puts on her "tough girl" persona whenever he does this, and it pisses me off. She protects him by saying stupid shit like, "He's just drunk. He doesn't know what he's doing" or, "He doesn't mean it. He always apologizes the next day."

I slip through the gap of the door, and instantly wrap my arms around her. She clings to me, burying her face in my hair, and I just let her cry. I hold her until her quaking shoulders still, then I pull back and look at her. Her normally tight curls are unruly, dangling across her forehead and into her eyes. I push them back, hooking them over her ears, and inspect her closely. Her face is red and splotchy from crying, and her eyes are bloodshot. Her entire right cheek is an angry crimson, and bluish-purplish bruises are already starting to overtake her pretty face.

"Oh, Lora." I pull her close again; hugging her with a fierceness that I hope will keep me grounded. If it doesn't, then I fear I will fall apart right here. But right now, I must remain strong, for Lora.

"What happened?"

She steps back and wraps her arms around herself. It's her defensive pose, and I know it well. She often does it whenever she has to explain Tony's drunken antics. But this time it's different. This time, she seems so small, so vulnerable, so *scared*. I swallow on a dry throat, and say nothing, waiting for her to speak.

She rubs her arm, and that's when I notice the handprint across her bicep. It's obvious Tony's brute strength has left multiple marks across her body. I wonder where else she bears evidence of his rage.

"He'd been drinking…"

Of course, isn't he always? I can't help but think it, but I grind my teeth to keep from saying it out loud.

"Mason was playing outside, and parked his bike

too close to his car. It fell over and scratched the paint…Tony went ballistic."

She shivers, and closes her eyes for a beat. I wait, clenching and relaxing my fists, formulating my own conclusions. *If he touched Mason…I'll kill him.*

"Something in me just snapped Abs. I tried my best to protect him, I did. But…"

"But?" My gaze sweeps around the room, finally noticing the shattered glass that lay broken on the floor. "But, what Lora?" I grab her arms to shake her, but release her when I see her wince. "What the hell happened?"

She sobs, thrusting her fist against her mouth to stifle it. I break away from her and tear down the hall, sprinting past little Ella's nursery until I reach Mason's room. I stand at the door, my breath sawing past my dry lips, my hatred taking a backseat for the genuine fear for what lays beyond this door. I turn the knob, and push it open. The glow of a nightlight shines dimly across the room. It barely illuminates Mason's tiny body curled up on the bed. He's sleeping, though not soundly, his feet twitch and he whimpers softly. I cross the floor and arrange myself gently on the bed beside him. I touch his small shoulder, but I don't want to wake him.

Lora steps up behind me. "I won't let this happen again Abby. I can't." I turn to look at her over my shoulder. Her face is serious, her lip trembling as she stares at her son. Tears rim her eyes, but she refuses to allow them to fall. She angrily wipes them away.

Mason stirs and rolls over. I try not to gasp, but fail miserably.

Chapter 2

I cover my mouth with my hands as my stomach lurches into my throat. His bottom lip is swollen, and a reddish bruise blossoms at the corner of his mouth. *Poor baby.* I rake my fingers through his fine blond hair, fighting to keep my own tears at bay. With a renewed hatred for the man responsible for this, I lift myself from the mattress and turn to face Lora.

"So what are you going to do?" I hold my breath as I watch her, wondering if she's going to feed me some bullshit line about how Tony will change, or how she has to stay, for the kids' sake.

"I'm leaving him." Her hazel eyes hold mine, as she says it again, but this time with more resolve. "I'm fucking leaving the bastard."

I'm elated, and can't help but wrap my arms around her. *Finally! Finally she has enough guts to leave! Thank you God!* She leans into me, and together we gaze at Mason as he snores lightly, his angelic face all but blemished by the hideous marks left by his father.

A loud rumble of a motor shakes the house, and I feel Lora stiffen beside me.

"He's home," she whispers, her tone edged with absolute terror.

"Just get the kids, and come home with me." I pick up one of Mason's book bags and unzip it. "I'll start packing Mason's things, you get Ella."

She nods, then says, "First, I'm going to go talk to him. Tell him I'm taking the kids and staying with you for a while. You stay here, or else he'll feel like we're ganging up on him."

I groan. "You're doing it again." I want to scream at her, but I don't. Instead, I punch the book bag, though it does little to ease my rage.

"Doing what?"

"Making excuses. Quit making excuses for that asshole." I gesture to the door, indicating the piece of shit that hovers just outside.

"I'm not," she counters. "I just know what pushes his buttons. And *you,* Abby, push his buttons."

I scoff, but knowing that I piss him off, actually makes me rejoice a little on the inside. *Good,* I think. *I'm glad the fucker dislikes me. The feeling is mutual asshole, and I'm glad to be taking Lora away from here. Away from you...*

"Fine," I say. "I'll stay and get Mason's stuff together...but so help me Lora if he starts any shit with you..."

"He won't," she assures me. She plants a kiss on Mason's forehead before turning to leave. I watch her disappear down the hallway, then I set to work on packing Mason's clothes. I hear the front door open and close, then some light murmuring between Lora and Tony. I strain to listen, but can only make out muffled voices. I move to the doorway and peer down the hall. The soft light from the frosted glass sconces wash the walls in a buttery glow. Although I know I shouldn't, I tip toe down the hall, edging closer and closer to the living room, where Lora and Tony stand arguing. Their voices raise, and it doesn't take long for their discussion to become heated. He grabs her by the forearms, and shakes her, her hair whipping wildly back and forth. She looks like a pitiful rag doll in his arms. So frail, so helpless. He flings her across the room, where she stumbles and lands on the couch. He quickly strides over to her, and backhands her across the face. I'm sickened, torn on what to do first. Help her? Call the police?

"You think you can just *leave*!" He looms over her, his chest heaving with anger. "You belong to me Lora. Forever. There *is* no getting away from me!"

He swings again, and this time Lora shields her face, tears streaming down her bruised cheeks. Through her splayed fingers, I notice her eyes are wide, and full of fear. His fist connects with her temple, and she falls back in the seat cushions, completely knocked out. *Lora!* Seeing her lying there unconscious and bleeding is the deciding factor for me. My vision turns red as I hurl myself at him, wielding my arms like whirling weapons, my fists pounding against him blindly as rage consumes me. He whips around, startled, but easily keeps my flailing fists at bay by seizing my wrists.

"You stupid bitch," he snarls. "You're half the trouble around here. Putting fucking ideas in her head and turning her against me."

"You did that yourself asshole," I hiss, fighting with every ounce of strength I have to wrench myself free. He holds fast to me, and I become desperate, so I do the only thing I can do. I lift my leg and kick him squarely in the nuts. It's enough to loosen his grip, so I scramble back, staring at him as he folds in half, wheezing as if all the air has been ripped from him. He lunges, and like a linebacker, tackles me to the ground. He straddles my waist, his weight is immense, and restricting, and it doesn't take long before I am struggling for the tiniest intake of air.

"She's my fucking wife!" he screams. "You stay the hell away from her or I'll break your fucking neck!" The veins in his neck are bulging and his eyes are half-crazed with anger. For a moment, I'm utterly speechless. Scared straight to the marrow of my bones for my life. His hands find my neck, and this scares the shit out of me. I claw at him, frantic to keep his fingers from cinching around my throat. *If he gets his hands around my neck, he'll strangle me.*

"You're nobody, Abby." His hands circle my neck, and I can feel his thumbs pressing hard against my windpipe. I thrash wildly, like a rabid dog in a cage, but remain pinned beneath him, my back pressed into the floor. He clamps tighter on my throat, and my vision grows spotty. "You're a fucking nobody, so do yourself a god-damn favor and stay the hell away from my family. No one wanted you in high school, and nobody wants you now, you stupid whore."

His outburst slices deep, evoking a fury so dark, and menacing, I am no longer worried about *my* life…instead I'm concerned about *his*. I glare at him. My body bristles as it understands how dire my situation has become. My muscles ratchet tight, and my heart pounds within my ears. All I know now is survival. I clutch Tony's wrists, forcing myself to take even and shallow breaths. *I have to get out of this alive.*

A heavy rainfall begins to beat against the roof, and a thunderclap shakes the house. The electricity flickers a few times, then goes out completely. *Shit.*

Could things get any worse?

Tony barely acknowledges it, his hands still securely around my neck.

Lightning flashes outside the window, illuminating the room for a second before plunging us back into the darkness. In that moment, I am able to see the tension in his arms, as well as the bitter determination to kill me. I need a new strategy, as I will never be able to compete with brute strength. My mind is a flurry of incomplete thoughts. I can hardly think for lack of oxygen. Again, the room is lit up by lightning, and again he's glowering down at me, his lips pulled into a tight grimace. Then, I attempt the most far-fetched, repulsive tactic I can come up with.

I cough, trying to gather my voice, but with his strong fingers digging into my trachea, I'm only able to croak out, "I...I'm sorry." The words burn my tongue as I say them. *Like hell, I am,* I think.

My eyes have finally adjusted to the darkness, and I'm able to see Tony above me. Though he's shadowed, I can still make out the details of his face. His brows pinch tight in confusion, but his hands stay firmly in place. I forge on, my stomach souring at the prospect of where this plan would ultimately take me.

"I only did it..." I sputter before finishing by saying, "I only did it because I wanted you." *Ugh.*

Tony's hands loosen just a fraction, but it's enough to allow a long drag of air to enter my lungs. I inhale greedily, savoring each breath as it clears my foggy head. He studies me for a long moment, then the corner of his lip curls into a wicked grin.

He's going to fall for it! I'm relieved and revolted. He fell for it, just as I thought he would. He's egotistical enough to think anything with tits wants him.

"I knew it," he says. "I fucking knew you were hot for me." He leans close to my face, his breath stale and potent with alcohol. I wrinkle my nose, and do my best to ignore the stomach-retching scent. It's a cross between perspiration, cheap cologne, and booze. It's nauseating. "How long you been sweating me Abby?" He finally releases my neck, but I can still feel the imprint of his hands on my skin. I gasp, and choke back my sobs. *I'll be damned if he'll see me cry.* His fingers graze my shoulder, then move to my chest. I seize up, bile collecting in the back of my throat as he fondles my breasts. *Oh God, please help me get through this.* I try to glance at Lora, but I can only make out her foot, dangling over the couch cushion. *She's still knocked unconscious.* My heart squeezes for her, and I want badly to reach out and touch her. To make sure she's okay.

"What about Lora?" I ask, pretending to be concerned about my friend's feelings, should her husband and I engage in an adulterous situation.

"She'll never have to know," he answers. "Hell, we can make this into a ménage, if you're up to it." The thought of being intimate with this vile man is enough to make me want to vomit.

The electricity kicks on, though it flickers a few times before the air conditioner and fans whirl back to life.

"Daddy?" Tony looks over his shoulder. Mason's tiny voice sounds strange, as if still dazed from sleep.

"What the hell are you doing out of bed?" Tony's booming voice echoes off the walls. I can't help but get instantly pissed. *He's just a kid for God's sake. Why do you have to be such an ass?*

Mason steps closer. His hair is disheveled, and he's rubbing his sleepy eyes with his small fists. "Are you guys wrestling?" His brown eyes lift from us and settle upon his mother. My stomach sinks as I watch his face fall. For being so young, he easily comprehends the trouble he walked into. "What's wrong with Mama?" He moves to go to her, but Tony throws his arm up, blocking his path.

"Get your ass back into bed," he growls. "Now."

"But Mama…" Mason tries to push past his father's strong arm, but it's futile. "I want Mama!" He stamps his feet, and this infuriates Tony.

"I. Said. Get. Back. In. Bed." He pushes the boy, making him stumble backwards.

"No," Mason says stubbornly. "I want Mama."

I cringe at this, knowing that the situation is about to get completely out of hand. Not that it hasn't already.

"Boy," he says, snatching Mason by the hair. "You just earned yourself an ass-whooping."

My chest tightens, and my heart sinks in unison. The rain outside is steady, the patter of it against the windowpanes drowns out everything except for the beat of my thudding heart as it picks up speed. *Please God no. Don't let him hurt Mason.*

Instead of swatting Mason on the rear-end, as some parents may have done, Tony starts wailing on the boy, too enraged to care that I'm still sprawled beneath him. I'm jostled roughly as he begins beating the boy along his back, arms and thighs. It's brutal, and I can't bear to watch it another second.

"Tony," I purr. "Save some of that for me." I give

him the sexiest smile I can manage, and run my finger along his abs.

He does a double take, releasing his hold on Mason. He smirks and leans down, placing his hands on the carpet, one on either side of my head. I feel caged in, which makes me panic, but I push on with this revolting charade. "I like it rough." Then I peer at Mason from over his father's shoulder. He's weeping, his face red and wet with tears. "Mister Fluff is scared, you better go give him some cuddles." Mister Fluff is a stuffed moose I gave Mason on his first birthday. The two have been inseparable ever since. The child sniffles, but quickly takes up the opportunity to get away. He flees, his little feet carrying him as fast as they will go.

Tony burrows his fingers through my hair, then grabs a handful, yanking me roughly. I stifle a gag as he trails his lips up my neck, which still throbs with pain. "I can't wait to see if you're an animal in the sack," he says against my ear. "They say the quiet ones always are."

"What if Lora wakes up?" I question, pretending to be breathless, which doesn't take a lot of effort. His weight is pressing, and the stench that clings to him makes my stomach turn.

"Then I'll knock her senseless again." He says this with such an eerie air of nonchalance, that I can't contain my tremble as it zips up my spine. Tony mistakes it for lust and growls as he works at the button of his jeans. *This is it,* I think. *No turning back now.*

"Do you think she'll leave you, if she finds out about us?"

He laughs sharply, and it cuts me to the quick.

What a fucking dick! The humor he finds in the idea appalls me, and I flex my fingers to keep from scratching his eyes out. "Lora isn't going anywhere, unless I tell her to. The only way she'll get away from me, is if one of us dies." He tosses a disparaging glance at Lora's still body. "And by the looks of it, she'll be the one severing that tie before I do."

Anger flares deep within me, sparking adrenaline through my bloodstream. I can't do it anymore. The farce is too great, too awful to allow it to continue any further. But I *must.* To keep Lora, and Mason safe, and little Ella too...I *must* go on.

A crackle of lightning clashes instantaneously with a boom of thunder so great it vibrates the walls. I feel Tony startle, but I remain stoic, barely blinking as the thunder rolls away, taking its angry growl with it.

He lifts his head, and his face is close—too close— to my own. There's perspiration across his upper lip, and along his hairline. "Ready to play rough?" He rears back and smacks me across my cheek, snapping my head to the side upon impact. The pain shoots across my skin and rattles my teeth. He covers my mouth with his hand, and it tastes of grimy sweat and salt. He leans down again, and we are now nose-to-nose. "You said you liked it rough babe, so be prepared to have your insides beaten just as hard."

My stomach churns and I swallow back the bile that stings my throat. I pry his fingers from my mouth, and gather all of my courage. *Please let this work.*

"Kiss me," I urge breathlessly. He doesn't hesitate, plunging his mouth down onto mine. He's rough, nearly suffocating me as he feverishly paws at my clothes. I wait, listening to my body and praying that it will respond the way I hoped. Nothing happens. I feel his tongue push past my teeth, and I heave, wishing I could shove him off me. *Please. Please. Please.* I begin to question myself. Perhaps Trevor's death was coincidental. Perhaps I've lived with the guilt all this time for nothing. Maybe, just maybe, I am normal.

Then, it happens. Just like it had eight years ago. The spark deep within my core, bursts to the surface, and flashes through my parted lips. Tony gasps and withdraws, his mouth frozen in an awkward sneer. He's wide-eyed, and stares at me incredulously, as his body wavers back and forth.

"See you in hell, mother fucker," I say firmly, glaring at him as he takes his last breath.

Tony keels over, his body slumping into a pile of elbows, knees, and rolled eyes on the carpet. With his weight off me, I can finally move my legs again, but I just lie, unmoving for a long time. *Oh my God.* I killed *again.*

Chapter 3

I feel like a black widow spider, devouring the life of any man unfortunate enough to get close to me. *I'm a freak of nature. Too dangerous for anyone to love.*

I hear a groan behind me, so I quickly sit up, which makes me sway. The ache that radiates from my cheek filters down across my jaw and into my gums. My teeth are sore, as if I just had oral surgery without anesthesia. I reach up to my neck and wince. It's still tender, and raw, like a blistering sunburn. Another low moan comes from the couch, so I drag myself into a standing position so I can assess Lora's condition. She's touching her temple, her eyes screwed tight as she probes at the misshapen welt that protrudes from her hairline.

I sink into the cushion beside her and run my fingers through her hair, pushing it out of her eyes. *Oh Lora.* She blinks, then squints as she studies my face. Tears rim her big, hazel eyes, and her lips quiver as she says, "I'm so sorry." She touches my face carefully, tracing her finger over the swelling. I do my best not to cringe, but it hurts like hell.

"It's okay," I say, even though it's not, as I lean my forehead against her shoulder. She smells like soap and strawberries. I inhale, trying to let the scent take me back to sweeter days. Like our sleepovers. When we'd stay up all night, making mixed CDs, slurping on milkshakes and talking about boys. Granted, she mainly gushed about Tony, while I obsessed over fictional characters in my favorite novels. *The good old days. Back when we were innocent. Before the beatings. Before the deaths.*

We both begin to cry, though I'm sure it's for different reasons. I still mourn Trevor, and not because he was my great love or anything. Not to sound crass, but we were only kids. I mainly mourn for his life—taken too soon. Taken by *me.* I also cry for Lora's broken heart. Though it was long crushed by Tony's callousness, her stubbornness to see their relationship through had healed it time and time again. Or maybe it wasn't healed. Maybe it had grown used to the abuse? I know why Lora is crying. She grieves for the life she wished she had. The perfect marriage. The loving husband.

We stay that way for a long while, just letting the tears come as they may, which is hard and unrelenting. My ribcage feels as if it's restricted in a corset, and I have a splitting headache. It isn't until I feel her tense, that I lift my head. I know what she's about to ask.

"Where's Tony?" I lean back, my gaze sweeping across the floor to where he lays dead. Lora pushes herself upright, her eyes lighting on his still body. Her lips part in a surprised gasp, then her hands shoot up to cover her mouth. I think she's going to be sick in her lap, but instead she lets out an agonized scream. I wrap my arm around her shoulder, allowing her to collapse into me. She feels like delicate porcelain, able to be crushed with just the slightest of pressure so I am sure to hold her gently. Her voice hiccups as she asks, "What happened?"

I bite my lip as I consider her question. Though she knows the guilt I carry about Trevor's death, she has no idea to what extent. Lora has always thought that I shouldered the blame just out of responsibility. For being with Trevor as he died. She didn't know the truth. That his death was stained upon my own hands. That I killed Trevor. With a kiss.

"I came in after he knocked you out. We fought…" My voice falters, forcing me to swallow though my throat is parched. "Mason came in—"

She cages my wrist with her slim hand and squeezes. "Mason?" She searches my face, and I can see the fear in her eyes as she waits for me to answer.

I nod, and lick my lips. They are so dry they feel like brittle leaves, cracking beneath the sun. "He beat him Lora." There was no way to soften the blow, no way to sugar coat the ugliness of what had occurred within her home. "He *beat* him."

Her eyelids flutter closed, and she whimpers, like an injured dog. I know she's breaking. Her fragile cast is splintering, and soon the fissures will be so great that they will evolve into permanent scars. I could only hope that she will come out stronger because of it. Like the loss of my mother. Though I never knew her, I have to believe that her death has played a part in molding me into the woman I am today. I have to believe that or else her death was senseless, and in vain. And what's the point in life at all if it hasn't served some purpose?

"And Tony? Is he…?" she whispers, her gaze peering through her parted fingers.

"Yes," I say firmly. I don't need to check his pulse to know that he lies dead upon the floor. The pang of guilt not hampering me this time as I recall the crackle of power that pulsated from my lips, as I sealed his fate with my kiss.

Her hand comes up to cover her mouth as she gags. She runs down the hall, and I hear the bathroom door slam shut. I close my eyes, and exhale. *I'm sorry Lora.* When she doesn't return, I go to check on her. The door is open, but the bathroom is empty.

"Lora?" I don't say it too loud, for fear of waking Ella. I glance down the hall and notice Mason's door is ajar, so I step up to it and peek inside. He's sleeping, and Lora is standing over him. I keep my footsteps as quiet as possible, tiptoeing over scattered toys and books. I stand beside Lora, but say nothing. I gaze at Mason, sleeping in his bed, clutching Mister Fluff tightly in his tiny hands. His blankets are mussed and shoved to the end of the bed. *When did he finally fall asleep?*

"I loved him you know," Lora says through her soft weeping. "Even at his worst, I still loved him."

Irritation splinters through my veins. "He beat you black and blue Lora. How could you love him? He's a monster. He ran around with half the chicks in town, and yet you stayed. He drank away half your savings and gambled away the other half. How in the hell could you love a man like that? 'Cause he sure as hell didn't love you." I curse myself as soon as the words leave my mouth. *Way to go Abby. Pour some salt into her already open wounds.*

"He did." She tries to say it with authority, but instead it comes out weak. Pathetic. "He just...he just had some demons that he couldn't tame I guess." She turns and briskly shoulders past me and hustles herself out of the room. I go after her, my steps hurried, and I catch up to her in the living room. She stops short when she sees Tony's body.

I grab her arm, whirling her to face me. "Oh my God! Are you serious?" I shake my head and laugh, but not out of amusement, but out of complete disbelief that here she is, still making excuses for him. I begin to pace the floor, then fold myself into a squat near Tony's limp body. "Lora. This man has been nothing but heartache for you since day one. If you're going to keep *protecting* him, then I can't help you. You have to see him for what he is."

"*Was,*" she quietly corrects, then wipes a lone tear that trails down her bruised cheek.

I close my mouth, suddenly lost for words. *Was.* I close my eyes and touch my forehead, feeling the pent-up frustration bloom into a dull ache behind my sockets. *Damn it.* I stand and walk to her, and take her hands into mine. "Lora. Although I don't understand it, I know you loved Tony. It's not my place to tell you who to give your heart to. But those kids in there…" I point to the other rooms. "They need you to love them *more.* Loving Tony was hurting them, and hurting you. You see that, don't you?"

She nods. "I know that Abby. That's why I was going to leave. He'd always left the kids alone before, but when I saw him…" She pauses, blinking back tears as she collects herself. "When I saw him hit Mason that was it for me. I knew I had to get out." Her gaze sweeps back to Tony, and her voices catches as she says, "But I didn't want him to *die.*"

I squeeze her hands, pulling her attention back to me. "We have to call the police." I stare into her eyes, willing her to understand my plight. That I am responsible for his death, and there's a strong chance I may get arrested. She only returns my exchange with a half-hearted nod. I sigh and reach for the phone in my back pocket. As I dial nine-one-one, my hands shake, and I think I may drop the phone. It rings only once, quickly answered by a pleasant dispatcher. The woman greets me with a professional, "Nine-one-one, what's your emergency?"

As I explain the situation to the woman on the other end of the line, my chest compresses and breathing becomes difficult. Relaying the horrific details is taxing, and my muscles feel taut with anxiousness. I hang up and collapse into the sofa, my stomach twisting into tight knots. *This is it. They will find out that I did it. I killed Tony.* "The police are on the way," I say as I stare straight ahead, looking at nothing really. I stay that way for a long moment as I contemplate how to frame my next few words. *How can explain to my best friend that I killed her husband with a kiss of death?* Unable to find another way, I growl in frustration, as I slide my gaze to hers and blurt out, "Lora. I killed Tony."

Before I can say anything more, I hear sirens approaching in the distance. Lora just stares at me, dumbfounded no doubt. Not that I blame her. I just told her I killed her husband. It's shocking news to hear from anyone, let alone your best friend. I feel uneasy under her intrusive gaze, so I stand and head to the front door. I open it, and step out onto the porch. It's difficult to remain calm as I stand there, waiting for the cops to arrive and haul me away. After the horrendous scene that took place inside the house, I am thankful to be out of it. I revel in the fresh air, drawing in deeply and letting it fill my lungs. Usually bookworms such as myself, relish the dank odors often found in libraries, but I also love the scent that lingers after a rainstorm.

The earthly aroma of sodden dirt and grass, infused with the crisp airy breeze soothes me like a lullaby. I let it wash over me, too afraid to acknowledge that if I am arrested, I will no longer be able to bask in the warm sunlight. Or listen to the steady drone of windshield wipers on glass as they wipe away raindrops. Or snuggle down deeper into my scarf when the winter air proves to be too harsh. I try not to dwell on it, but the realization has a profound effect on me. My knees wobble, and I must sit down, so I sink into a plastic lawn chair.

"Abby? Are you all right?" Lora touches my shoulder, but it does little to comfort me.

I shake my head, but say nothing as a panic attack surges through my body. It kicks my heart rate up, and stifles me as if I were trapped in a small box. I want to scream, but instead I press my lips together to keep it in. Just the simple task of breathing is proving to be strenuous, so I worry yelling will take away what little air I have left. I close my eyes as vertigo sets in.

"You couldn't have killed him," Lora says gently. "How could you? You don't have a weapon."

I clamp my eyes tighter. *If you only knew,* I think bitterly. The police sirens blare. *They are here.* My eyelids spring open, expecting to find them parked in the lawn, spilling from the car as they descend on me. But they aren't. Not yet anyway. It only takes another three rounds of labored breathing before they are.

I grip the armrests until my knuckles turn white. The thought of being imprisoned petrifies me, and not because of the obvious. The fact that I'll be in jail, with my freedom removed *is* terrifying. And knowing that the only way I'll get to see and talk to my dad is through a panel of glass makes my heart ache. But it's the restriction from experiencing the weather that sends a pang of unshakable dread through me. Such an odd thing to miss, but for me, it's the most upsetting.

Two cops climb out of the marked sedan. Their blue uniforms are starched and perfect. One looks laid-back, his arms swinging loosely at his sides as he crosses the lawn, while the other sidles up to us with his fingers gripping his belt buckle. The calm officer smiles as he approaches, and seems friendly enough. But his partner…he's all shifty-eyed and twitchy, like he's either jittery or trigger-happy so I remain still so as not to give him a reason to draw his weapon.

"Evening ladies," says the nice one. "My name is Officer Frank, and this is my partner, Officer Dingle. Do you mind telling us what has happened here tonight?"

I open my mouth to speak, but my throat seizes. I lick my dry lips and swallow, trying to wet my mouth enough to talk, not croak like a frog.

"My husband," Lora says. I glance back at her, surprised that she's speaking so clearly. Her arms are crossed in front of her, hands clinging fiercely to her elbows. I know it's just a ruse. She's merely put on her tough girl mask again. When it's all said and done, she'll break down again, and it won't be pretty. "He came home drunk, and things got a little out of hand."

It takes immense power not to scoff. *A little?* God. She's always been oblivious to Tony's wayward antics, but surely she can see that things got more than just a *little* out of hand. I frown as I recall all the late night calls from her. *"I found a phone number in Tony's pocket. Tony hocked my graduation ring. Tony never came home last night."* As I gaze up at her, watching her talk to the two policemen, I think, *God, Lora. What is wrong with you?* Her hair is wild around her petite face. Her pale hazel eyes contrasting with her rich coffee-colored hair. Her fair skin usually resembles an expensive porcelain doll, smooth and bearing not a single blemish. But not tonight. Tonight it looks like spilled ink upon a beautiful canvas.

The officers ask her a series of questions, but their words are lost on me as I gaze at Lora, my thoughts piling up on one another clumsily. I wonder how she feels when she looks in a mirror.

Does she cry? Does she get angry? My eyes linger across the yellowing purple smudges of bruises that mar her beautiful complexion, and I think, *what goes through her mind*? When she sees her battered face staring back at her, does she ever regret the decisions she's made? Does she curse her heart for ruling her head? They say love is blind, but in Lora's case, it's also deaf and mute.

The coroner arrives a few minutes later. The slim man steps out of a black SUV and strides across the lawn. His eyes are sharp, taking in the scene around him, before nodding a professional hello to the two officers. "The vic inside?" he asks as he jerks his chin toward the front door.

Officer Frank answers with a nod and says, "Living room. Haven't been inside to check the scene yet."

My heart lurches. *Vic. Scene.* The words sound so ominous, so final.

The coroner checks his watch. "My shift is over in an hour, so I'd like to wrap this sitch up ASAP quick." Then he sets off to enter the house with the two officers right on his heels, their questioning obviously over for the moment. Lora and I follow suit.

Wrap this sitch up ASAP quick? Sitch? As in situation? This may be just another "sitch" to you dipshit, but to us, it's our life.

I can't help but glare at him as he assesses the living room. He may be conditioned to death, but most of society isn't. Although there certainly is no love lost between me and Tony, it's still unnerving to see him sprawled across the carpet, his body completely frozen in death. The coroner reaches in his pocket and pulls out a set of latex gloves. He wriggles his fingers in them, snapping them into place before kneeling beside Tony. He touches two fingers to his pulse, reaches into his front pocket, removing a pen and small notepad. He scribbles something, then looks up at Officer Frank.

"Time of death?" he asks.

"They claim about thirty minutes ago."

My eyes dart to the policeman. *They claim?* They treat us like we're suspects. Perhaps I am, but Lora is innocent. She's hurting and she's the true victim here. *Treat her with some damn respect.*

A rumble of thunder rolls in the distance, and I wonder where the storm is heading now. Maybe Chion, which is south of here. Given its steady speed, I'm sure it's at least two or three towns over by now.

"I'd say that's pretty close," says the coroner. "Help me load him up, and I'll have his autopsy report on your desk in no time."

"No foul play?" questions Officer Dingle.

"There's no physical evidence of any, unless they slipped him something." He eyes us for a second, then adds, "but by the looks of them, I think the man just wore himself out wailing on them. Did he have any heart conditions? High cholesterol? Heart disease in the family?"

"Not that I know of," answers Lora, who's standing in the farthest corner of the room. Dark circles ring her lower eyelids, and her face is pale, as if stricken with illness.

"I'm confident this is a medical issue, but I won't know until we perform the actual autopsy." He stands and shoves his notepad back into his front pocket. He slides his pen behind his ear, and says to the two men, "I'm going to get the gurney. You get everything you need?"

"We just need to get a statement from each of them," says Officer Frank.

"Well then, let's get him zipped up and headed to the lab," the coroner says hastily.

He barely acknowledges the gasp from Lora, or her soft weeping as he exits the room. I move to the window so I can stare at the yellow letters spelling out CORONER across his back. *Does the man have an ounce of compassion within him?* He strolls across the lawn to the SUV and flings the door open. He leans in, rummaging around for something but I turn to look back at Lora. Her eyes are cast down, and she's sniffing as she hovers in the empty corner. *Poor Lora.*

The coroner returns pushing in a squeaky gurney topped with a black bag. *A body bag.* My head swims and I lean against the wall for support. Lora darts out of the room, disappearing somewhere.

"Can I get a hand?" The coroner arranges the bag just so, then stands at Tony's head. He bends and sticks his hands under Tony's armpits, and waits.

"Barry, you think you can give him a hand, while I get a statement from the wife?" Officer Frank asks his partner.

Barry? I almost laugh. *Barry Dingle? Swap that around and you have Dingle Barry. Wow. No wonder the man is a ball of nerves. He must have been tormented all through school, college, and not to mention the Police Academy.*

Officer Dingle purses his lips, but does as he's told. He squats and collects Tony's ankles into his hands. Together they lift his lifeless body and sling him onto the gurney. The coroner tucks Tony's limp arm into the bag and draws the zipper up over his waist, then chest, then face. I hold my breath as he seals the bag completely. It's the single most disturbing experience I've ever experienced.

Well, seeing Trevor being carted away by paramedics as they steadily worked on him, almost to the point of obsession was heart-wrenching. But seeing a body be sealed into a glossy, oversized piece of luggage is jarring, and leaves you feeling dumbfounded. You just stare at the bag, thinking what has this person's life become? An item to be hauled? An inconvenient, oversized piece of deadweight that needs to be concealed because no one likes to look at death?

I drag my hand across my face. *When is this nightmare of a night going to be over?*

Officer Frank is nowhere to be seen, so I assume he caught up with Lora, and is busy taking her statement. I remain stationed against the wall, not trusting my legs to behave long enough to get to the sofa. The coroner pushes the gurney past me and out of the house. I breathe a sigh of relief when I hear his SUV start up and pull away.

Officer Dingle returns, brandishing a notebook and pen. His gaze quickly lands on me, and he approaches, but doesn't stand too close.

"I need you to tell me everything that happened tonight, Miss…"

I give him a look of disinterest and say, "Cox. Abby Cox."

He makes a note, and goes into full-on cop mode. "Can you describe the events that occurred here tonight?" He narrows his beady eyes over his pad at me, his pen poised and ready to document everything I'm about to say.

I roll my eyes and launch into my recount of the night's events, starting with the phone call from Lora. When I finish, he jots his final notes and looks up from the pad. "Thank you. Mrs. Jones will be notified of the autopsy results within seventy-two hours. If you should need our assistance with anything, please just call the precinct and ask for Frank and Dingle." He tucks the notebook and pen away just as the other officer rounds the corner with Lora.

"We are done here, unless either of you ladies have any questions…?" Office Frank's gaze shifts from Lora's to mine, his brows expectant as he awaits our response.

"So, now what?" Lora asks, her voice small and pitiful. "What do I do now?" Her eyes sparkle with impending tears, and for a fleeting moment, I wonder how many more tears can she shed? Does the body ever run out of tears?

The officers exchange a terse look. Officer Frank looks sympathetic, while the dingle berry just stands there, apparently oblivious on how to handle a grieving widow.

Officer Frank walks up to Lora and places a hand on her shoulder. "Now, you move forward ma'am. There is nothing else to do, but move forward." He gives her a sympathetic smile, then turns away. The two men leave, taking with them the strange, surreal-like state I have been floating in. *They didn't arrest me.* In fact, they didn't even suspect me. A *medical issue*, that's what the coroner said. I frown. The results of the autopsy are expected within seventy-two hours, and that's when it will happen. That's when they will discover his cause of death, then they will have no choice but to arrest me…

Chapter 4

I gather Lora into my arms, and lead her to her bedroom. It's illuminated with a tall, wrought-iron lamp, shining a dull light across her vanity, which is lined with expensive perfume bottles, and other collections of feminine toiletries.

The room is bright, and cheery, with its buttery yellow paint and sunflower artwork. A complete contradiction to the mess that just occurred, which lurches my stomach into a nauseating churn.

After I settle her into bed, I retrieve some pain medication for her headache, an ice pack for her bruises, and an entire box of tissues for her never-ending tears.

"I'm going to stay with you tonight, okay?" I ask, handing her a glass of water.

She gazes up at me from her pillows, her pale yellow comforter pulled up to her neck. Her eyes are so swollen and pink; my own hurt just by looking at them. "Thanks Abby," she says before tossing her head back and swallowing the pills. She chases them with a mouthful of water.

I take the glass back and set it on the nightstand. "I'm going to run home and grab a few things. I won't be long, I promise."

"I'll be fine," she says, drawing her blanket tighter.

"Call if you need anything." I bend down, and

wrap her in a hug, squeezing her gently. "Hisses and kugs."

She smiles a little at that. It's been our parting words for the past five years. During Lora's bachelorette party, one of her cousins hired some lame exotic dancer, who showed up wearing a construction worker's outfit, and toting his own bottle of booze. He was already half-lit when he arrived, so once the ladies fed him a few shots and allowed him to lick alcohol from their navels, he was rip-roaring drunk and ready to get wild. Buck wild.

By the middle of his routine, he was wearing nothing but a tool-belt and a smile. After he grinded and dry-humped everyone in the room, he stumbled up to Lora and brought her hand to his lips, trying to be chivalrous, which was laughable after he just shook his bare ass in our faces for the past hour. He squinted at her, no doubt seeing double, belched quietly then slurred, "Hisses and kugs to the bea-you-ful bride to be." It was pathetic, but absolutely hilarious, and has been in our vocabulary ever since.

I smile back, then make my way out of her room, pulling her door partially closed behind me. I peek in on Ella and Mason, both are still asleep, which is good because I think I have just enough energy to drive home, pack a few things and drive back. I'm hoping I can muster enough strength to crawl into bed when I get back.

I trudge across the lawn and collapse into the driver's seat. I'm so exhausted I consider staying and just borrowing clothes from Lora. *No,* I scold myself. I need to feed Jack, my cockatiel. The bird needs fresh water, as well as a scoop of sunflower seeds. *Sunflower.*

I think of Lora, lying alone in that sunflower-filled room, and my heart squeezes. I hang my head as the weight of everything bears down on me.

Tears collect, but I blink them back fiercely. *No. I will not cry. I don't have time for that shit.* I start up my car, and back out of the driveway. As I turn onto the main road, I recall every last detail of the day. From my mundane day at work, to Lora's frantic phone call, to Tony slapping around his own wife and son. All leading to the inevitable ending, which I could not change.

I'm on auto-pilot as I drive, and as I let myself into the house and shower. In a sleepy daze, I rifle through my closet for a change of clothes, and some pajamas. I glance at my bed and I'm tempted to slip into it. The fluffy pillows and goose-down comforter is inviting, but instead I continue with the task at hand. I pack a small bag full of necessities, and snag my poetry book from the nightstand. *Now all I have to do is feed Jack.* I rinse out his water bowl and refill it, then give him a scoop of mixed seeds and a sprinkle of his favorite snack; sunflower seeds.

"I'll be back tomorrow," I tell him as I close the door to his cage.

He cocks a feathered head at me, and squawks. I smile at him, then grab my bag, heading back out into the never-ending night. I slide behind the wheel of my car, and again the day catches up with me. *Was there another way?* Perhaps there was. We could have gone to the police. Had a restraining order put against Tony. She could have divorced him. *I could have stayed the hell out of it...*

With a shaky hand, I start the engine, and head back to Lora's house across town. I continue to obsess about it. Tony threatened to kill me. *"You stay the hell away from her or I'll break your fucking neck."* He threatened my best friend's life. *"Lora isn't going anywhere, unless I tell her to. The only way she'll get away from me, is if one of us dies."*

Anger and regret swells and churns within me like a hurricane at sea. It's overwhelming, and before long, I find it hard to see through the haze of my tears. To make matters worse, rain begins to fall yet again, and my windshield wipers aren't the best. *What is up with the weather today? I guess the storm clouds insist on sticking around.* The constant whirl of the wipers as they drag across the glass drowns out the radio, but it isn't enough to muffle my own sobs. Lightning flickers, illuminating the sky in an eerie flash of golden light. I jump at the sudden roar of thunder that follows it. The wind picks up, and shoves my car across the lane and into the patch of grass along the highway. I scream, bumping along the uneven path, the tires unable to find their proper footing. I grip the steering wheel, and through my blurred vison, I swerve back onto the road. My chest heaves as I right the car, thankful to be the only person traveling on the wet roads tonight.

I glance in my rearview mirror, then back through the windshield at the sheet of constant rain that pummels my car. It falls heavy on the roof, filling the cab with a raucous banging. I can barely concentrate on the road with the deafening hammering. *Damn.* The storm picked up quickly. *Too quickly.* I check my speed, and decide it's too fast for the slick roads and let off the gas.

Lightning twinkles in the distance, and for a moment, I think the rain is letting up. When a jolting boom of thunder crashes overhead I tense up, my fingers wrap around the steering wheel as if my life depends on it. My emotions start to overtake me. Bleak thoughts swirl within my brain, much like the howling wind that cuts across my car. Memories of the kiss with Trevor surfaces and refuses to be ignored. I purse my lips, as if to quell the deadly power they possess. *Why am I this way? Why am I a freak?*

For some reason my mind flitters back to middle school, when the kids teased me for clinging to my books, rather than joining them on the playground. Then to high school, when they dubbed me "Abby Angst." Though the kids mostly ignored me, it still stung. It sucked to be considered weird, pathetic, or nerdy. But what really hurt was being just plain *unwanted.*

A loud pop and snap send me slamming on the brakes. A second later, a tree smashes across the road just a few feet away. *Shit!* My heart is pounding wildly within my chest, and all I want, is to get back to Lora's safely. With my heart in my throat, I ever so slowly creep the car around the fallen tree and get back on course.

A steady roaring, like a jet plane flying overhead builds, getting increasingly louder and louder until it becomes unbearable. I wince, and flick my gaze back to my rearview mirror and notice a funnel-like shape blazing its own trail behind me. *A tornado!*

Debris and dust whirl around it, as it picks up lawn chairs, street signs, and mailboxes and hurls them through the air like feathers on a breeze. Fear prickles my scalp, but I can't seem to tear my eyes off the menacing cone of destruction. *Oh shit!* I try to recall the safety measures that have been beaten into my head since elementary school. Get to cover. Cover your head. Get out of your car…

I scan the surroundings, searching for suitable cover. *Come on! There has to be something!* I spot a modest church. At this time of night, I am positive the doors are securely locked, but it at least has a doorway. Then I notice a bricked archway that encompasses a walking path around the side of the main church, leading to an additional building. *Even better!*

I pull off the road, and throw the car into park. I gulp, trying to gather my courage, but right now I'm flooded with adrenaline, and fear. With my heart pounding, I fling my car door open and scramble outside. My legs feel like sand, but somehow, I will them to cooperate. I take a quick look behind me, just as the tornado skips across the grass and begins barreling straight for me, screaming like a banshee. I can't shake the thought that I'm being hunted. That I'm in the cross hairs of the twister's sights, and it's ready to pull the trigger.

I dash across the street, rain pelting me so hard I cry out and shield my face from it. I can barely see through the sheet of rain as I cut through it. It's cold even in the summer night air, sending goose pimples across my skin. The howl of the tornado chases me relentlessly, refusing to surrender until it's driven me mad. And it must have succeeded because I imagine the tornado as a hired assassin and I'm its next victim. I shout for help, though I know I'm all alone.

I plow through rain puddles, splashing water out around me as I pound across the pavement, praying that I reach the archway in time. My clothes are completely saturated, sticking to me like a wrinkly second skin.

The streetlight behind me creaks, and for some stupid reason I pause. It bows and leans as if pulled by an invisible magnet. The glass shatters, and I'm on the move again, tossing a quick glance back as the entire post is sucked into the air, careening through it like a launched missile. It disappears into the gray swirling clouds of the tornado, and my stomach sinks into my soggy shoes. The tornado twists with maddening fury, hopscotching its way across the ground. It's gaining on me…and fast. I crouch slightly as I run, trying to duck the flying debris, but a niggle of uncertainty gnaws at me. *I'm not going to make it.* The archway and all the protection it promises is yards away. *I will never make it. It's too far, and I'm so exhausted…*

I stagger, though I know the tornado is raring up on me like a tidal wave. It's screeching like a wet cat, and unleashing its claws in the form of debris sailing at a wickedly dangerous speed. *I cannot out run it.* I almost feel like giving up, deciding it would be better to just stop and allow it to swoop in on me, rather than giving myself false hope that I actually stand a chance of surviving this night. *This night. This grueling, heart-crushing, gut-wrenching night. I just want it to be over…*

I stumble; my body is giving out on me, my muscles burn with exhaustion. I land on my knees and the heels of my palms. The asphalt bites into my skin, and when I turn my hands over, I see the welling red blood as it tries to pool within my palm. The rain washes it before it has time to collect. I look up, and up and up at the massive tornado bearing down on me. *I'm going to die,* I think. It reminds me of a monster, hovering over me with a gaping mouth. *It's going to slurp me into its gut, chew me up and spit me out.* I scream, and scramble off the pavement, my feet slipping, my waterlogged tennis shoes, having zero traction against the slick asphalt.

The thunderous growl of the tornado rattles me, making it difficult to think of anything except the certain death that surrounds the twister like an ominous aura. I am suddenly stricken with immobilizing fear and realization all at once. *This is it. I am going to die.* My chest hurts from the exertion, and my heart feels as though it's breaking. Perhaps it is, because I feel betrayed. I adore weather, in all its various forms. And now it's out to kill me.

I feel my body being pulled, like I'm on the outskirts of a whirlpool, my hair whipping around my face. I run again, but hit a wall of fierce wind that sends me stumbling backward. A gush of air tosses me to the ground, and I land flat on my back. My head bangs against the pavement shooting pain across my scalp. I cling to it, wincing when I touch the oozing scrape through my wet hair. I have no time to dwell on the sight of blood on my fingertips because my body slides across the ground toward the screaming tornado. My jeans scrape across the gritty pavement as I watch as my feet swing forward, drawing me closer, and closer to the dark vortex. The twister is dragging me by my ankles, and I furiously try to grab onto the street. My fingernails tear as I struggle, and I cry out, desperate to escape this churning mass of destruction. *Oh God, please! I don't want to die!*

A plastic yard flamingo flies through the air, and I try to duck, but it smacks me with tremendous force on the side of my head. I grow dizzy, and my vision wavers in and out as if someone is waving a flashlight back and forth in front of my eyes. I grow still, and I'm not sure if it's from the force of the impact, or the acute awareness that in a moment, it will all be over. Maybe both.

My body lifts gently off the ground, and I think, *Maybe it's not going to end so horribly. Perhaps I will drift into unconsciousness, and then the winds will cradle me until I die.* I am okay with this, because as the tornado looms over me, shrieking like a wounded animal, my eyelids flutter closed and I feel weightless.

Then all is black.

Chapter 5

I wake to an eerie silence. The rain has lulled to a faint mist, and the night sky is clear of clouds. The moon emits silvery rays, highlighting the street in a sparkling shimmer. I'm propped up against the wheel of my car, my legs stretched out in front of me. I turn my head slightly, taking in my battered vehicle. It looks no different, and I can't help but chuckle.

Through a tornado, the bucket of bolts holds up, but the minute you hit a pothole, the hubcaps fly off. I wince at the pain my laughter brings. My ribs ache, and my head pounds as if I'd taken a brick to the skull. I remember the flamingo, and bring my hand to my head, my fingers parting my damp hair to find the wound. Tears prick my eyes as I probe it. It's not deep, but it's definitely raw.

I look out across the open road. The tornado is gone. All that is left is a whirling breeze, and the scattered debris left in its wake. *I survived.* It's hard to believe, but I did. *I survived.* I can easily dredge up the frightening moments when the twister was swooping in on me, like a hungry shark. It's open mouth ready and eager to ingest me whole. I shiver. *I need to get back to Lora's.*

I try to stand, bracing myself on the car.

"I wouldn't do that just yet," says a man's voice.

I slump back down to the pavement out of shock.

My whole body stiffens, shouting obscenities at me for falling so heavily to the ground. Everything aches. My eyes. My muscles. My bones. I hold my head, attempting to steady the spinning surroundings as I try to find the man behind the voice.

"Who's there?" I call, though it sounds weak and small. My heart thuds rapidly as uncertainty creeps in. *Who said that?* I worry it may be a carjacker, a robber, or worse. I'm in no condition to run or fight back. I'm not even confident I can scream, since my throat still burns like an extinguished fire from nearly being choked to death by Tony.

A man steps into my field of vision, and at first all I see are his shoes. As my gaze lifts higher, I notice he is wearing dark denim pants and a gray jacket. It's unzipped, revealing a wet T-shirt, stuck against muscular abs. He's easily six feet tall, and I feel dwarfed by his size. Especially as he looks down at me, regarding me attentively, as if I were a flight risk, and he's been ordered to keep watch. I grow uncomfortable, not to mention vulnerable at this position, so again I attempt to stand on two feet. He watches, but does not move to help as I drag myself upright, leaning against the car for support.

"Who are you?" I ask, though it comes out like a pant.

"Nik." He says no more, as if that explains everything. I study him, trying to make out the details of his face in the moonlight. Although he reeks of stark detachment, his eyes say otherwise. They're tender, and a beautiful blue, like the sky on a clear day.

"What happened?" I swallow, and take a tentative look around. Street signs, roof shingles, and broken limbs lay scattered as far as the eye can see.

"I pulled you to safety before the tornado claimed you." He looks out in the distance and says, "The destruction was minimal, given the size and intensity of the storm."

I follow his gaze, noticing the nearby houses and buildings are all still intact. A little battered, but at least they are standing. I think about Lora, and wonder if her house fared just as well. *What if it didn't?* My stomach sours at the prospect that it could be leveled. The ache in the back of my skull throbs, keeping time with my pulse. I touch it, and briefly close my eyes as I ward off a wave of nausea. *I need to check on Lora.* I open my eyes to find Nik staring at me. He's taken a step closer, and in this proximity, I note a sweet scent lingering in the air. It reminds me of honeysuckle and rain. *Is it him?*

"You should have that looked at," he says , as he shoves his hands into his pockets.

Of course it's not him, I think. *Get a grip Abby. That head wound is really messing with you.*

I tuck my hair behind my ears with determination just to prove a point. "I'm fine." I make my way to the car door, and open it. I look over my shoulder, and say "Thanks, for um....saving me." The words sound ridiculous, like I'm a heroine from a romance novel. But I'm far from the gorgeous protagonist. *I'm more like the nerdy sidekick,* I think bitterly.

"You were lucky," he replies. "That tornado was chasing you like it had a vendetta." The corner of his mouth curls into an *almost* smile, and it's enough to send warm fuzzies tickling across my skin. If just a quirk of his lips makes me melt, I wonder what a full-blown grin would do....

Then something about what he said draws me out of the musing. *"That tornado was chasing you like it had a vendetta."* My eyes latch on to his, and I say, "What do you mean?"

His brows furrow a fraction, and he examines me closely, as if he's trying to figure out a complex math problem. "The damn thing never strayed from your path. For a moment, I wondered if you had it on a leash." His observation is terrifying, and it knocks me back a step. I know it's silly, but somehow this proves what I felt all along. *It was out to get me. Me. Just me.*

My blood runs cold at the thought, and I can't quell the shiver coursing through me. I clutch the door, and blink a few times, taking care to breathe through my nose, and exhale through my mouth, the way you're supposed to when you're about to completely lose your cool. *I'm being ridiculous. Tornados don't target people.*

I can't hide my shaking, so I grip the car tighter and close my eyes. *This is all too much. I'm going stark raving mad.*

"Are you all right?" I open my eyes, and he's cocked his head to the side. His eyebrows are pinched, and I think he may start to back away, like I'm diseased or something. *I wouldn't blame him.*

"I just need to sit." I plunk down in the seat of my car, staring at the ground beneath my feet. A pool of rainwater has collected, and on the surface swirls a small rainbow of oil. No doubt from my clunker. I stare at it, finding it almost poetic the way even something crude, and potentially toxic can be beautiful if mingled with nature. I recall the time Trevor's soccer team was forced to play a match in the rain. Snippets of lightning flickered through the clouds as I hunkered down with an umbrella, watching from the metal bleachers, praying I'd make it the entire game without getting electrocuted. By the end of the game, Trevor's white and green uniform was entirely brown, caked with mud. His sodden hair was matted against his forehead and chunks of grass took up residence on both knees. He was filthy. Like pig-wallowing filthy. He jogged over and gave me a breathtaking smile. His perfect white teeth practically glowed amongst his dirt-streaked face. I thought then, no matter how messy, how stinky or covered in grit, Trevor would always be handsome.

Then I think about me. Though I don't find myself to be beautiful, Trevor would insist that I was. He'd often say, *"Your eyes drive me crazy."* He got a kick out of my gray eyes, swearing that he had never seen such a shade before. I never thought twice about the color of my eyes until he mentioned how they'd change, like a mood ring depending on my frame of mind.

Most of the time they're stone-gray, but they darken to nearly black when I'm angry. When I'm excited, or extremely happy, they lighten. Trevor once described them as, *"shiny gray pearls."* I want to smile, but can't. I think of how a vile, dangerous power surges through me, and the only way I can deliver it, is through a kiss. A beautiful thing, a kiss, except when given by me. Then, it's cold and deadly.

All the memories of Trevor, and what I did to him, begin rallying like an outraged mob within my mind. Yanking on me, trying to drown me as they always have before. My throat seizes, and breathing becomes increasingly difficult. I look up at Nik, and he's still standing there. *Why?*

"You can go," I say waving him off. "I'll be fine."

The drizzle of rain picks up and storm clouds crowd out the moon. Nik lifts his head, his eyes cast upward at the sky. A terse frown creases his lips, and his eyes tighten, almost as if he's studying every raindrop that falls. His hands come out of his pockets and he holds out his open palms. The rain splatters across the planes of his outstretched hands, then he curls them into fists, and takes a deep breath. His gaze lowers to my neck, surely settling on the marks left by Tony, before lifting back to meet me square in the eye. "You sure? You don't seem *fine*. In fact, I think you're far from it."

I raise my hand to my throat, covering the contusions that flare angrily upon touching them. I wince. "I said I'm fine," I reply through clenched teeth. "Thanks for saving me, or whatever, but your little act of heroism is over, okay? Just go." I glare at him, wishing he would just leave me be. I want to be alone. I want to curl into a ball and cry through the painful memories. Tears pool, and I try to blink them back, but it's too late. Again, I'm crying and again I find myself asking, *does the body ever run out of tears?* After all that I've shed in the past eight years, I begin to think the answer is no.

I feel my cheeks heat from embarrassment, as I lose it in front of Nik. A stranger. I grow irate that he's still there, watching me as I choke on my sobs, my body wracking with each wail. I angrily scrub at my face, glowering at him through tears as I shout, "I said go, god damnit!"

Nik looks taken aback by my outburst, his eyes wide with surprise, but instead of fleeing like I hoped he would, he crosses his arms in front of him and says, "Like hell I will."

I grow infuriated, and as I jump to my feet, a clap of thunder breaks loose above us. Nik's eyes flick upward, then settle back on me. His stare becomes intense, pinning me into place, and rendering me speechless.

"Funny how the weather seems to match your mood." His brow lifts, daring me speak. When I purse my lips into a scowl, he continues by saying, "But that's bullshit right? No one can have that kind of effect on weather."

What? Why would he say that? I glower at him for a long time, my lips so tight I can only breathe through my nose. I feel my heated breaths sawing in and out of my nostrils. He only stares back, matching me glare for glare.

"I saved your life. I think I deserve more than just a 'thank you, now fuck off'."

I groan. "What do you want from me? A pat on the back? Money? Or how about I call the evening news and rave about how you rescued little ole me?" I smile tartly, then curl my lips back into a rigid sneer.

A frown plays at his lips. "Just a simple thank you and a hand shake will be enough."

"Fine!" I reach to take his hand, but he quickly dodges my advances by taking a step backward. This irritates me, my ears burn and I growl, "What's your problem?"

"If you don't mean it, don't do it." He holds his hands up in surrender, his eyes lifting to the sky when a low grumble of thunder rolls over. A smirk spreads across his face. "See what I mean?"

I force myself to look up, and I notice it's no longer raining. Gray clouds churn slowly across the span of sky above us. There's not a star twinkling in the blanket of darkness, just fluffy storm clouds that seem to be lolling around lazily. I look back at Nik, whose watching me with curious eyes. *What's with this guy? People can't control the weather. Pure coincidence.*

"I have to go. It's late, and my friend is probably worried about me." I say this with a forced, neutral voice. "Thank you very much for saving me." I extend my hand, watching him, waiting to see if he'll take it. He eyes it for a second, and gives me that almost there smile.

"You're welcome." He clasps my hand with his, and my lips part slightly as a tingle of electricity runs through me. The fine hairs along my arms stand on end, as if charged with an energy. We're palm to palm, and it's a connection that seems to radiate straight to the apex of my thighs. *God...what would those hands feel like on the rest of my body?* My cheeks warm at the thought, and I cast my gaze down at our linked hands. His skin is warm, and it feels good against my chilled skin. The tension in the air begins to disintegrate, and the weight that's been riding upon my shoulders that night, lightens just a little.

"I owe you one," I manage to say, looking up into his sparkling blue eyes, our hands still entwined.

"I'm going to hold you to that."

This chokes me up a little. *What does he mean by that?* The insinuation that our paths will cross again makes my heart skip a beat. *That's silly. He probably meant nothing by it.* The sun is starting to peek over the horizon. A mist of fog hugs the ground, sprinkling dewy kisses across the grass. *I can't believe it's morning already!*

"Well, you take care," he says, letting my hand go. He draws his hood over his head, and it frames his handsome face in soft gray flannel.

"You do the same Nik." I sink into my car, and pull the door shut. I take my time as I buckle myself in, adjust the mirrors, and start the ignition. For some reason, I'm finding it difficult to drive away from him, though just moments ago I wanted so desperately for him to leave and allow me to wallow alone in my own misery. This stranger who risked his own life, to save mine. I give him a wave as I slowly pull away.

He calls out to me, so I hit the brakes, finding myself oddly elated. *Stop that,* I scold myself. I rein in my giddiness, and arrange my expression into vague indifference. *What does he want?* He hunches to my level and taps on the window. I quickly roll it down, curious. As soon as the glass parts, I smell it. Rain and honeysuckle. *It's heavenly.*

"I didn't catch your name," he says peering through the open window.

"Abby," I answer, unable to resist giving him a smile.

"Abby," he says, testing the name on his palette. Then he smiles, and this time…God, *this* time, it's electrifying. Dimples plunge deep in his cheeks, making his face look chiseled, like a statue carved to precision. Now I truly understand what Aunt Blair means when she says; "*Dimples are angel kisses.*" With that heart-breaking smile, and those eyes as clear as precious gems, Nik could have been handcrafted by God himself.

"Good." His smile gives way to a more serious expression. "Now I can say…someday, I'll owe my life to a girl named Abby."

What? I gaze up at him, captivated by the intensity within his eyes, and flummoxed by his odd choice of words. I want to ask him to elaborate, but I can't. The way he's staring at me stirs something fiery within my core. *No. I am not allowed to feel like this.*

There is only way to douse the fire that spreads through my veins, and that is with space.

I eke out a quiet goodbye, and pull the car away, leaving Nik standing there. His hood loosely frames his strong, angled face as he watches after me. Through the fine mist of rain, he looks mysterious. Like that elusive shadow in the night, whose origins go undetected.

Chapter 6

As I put distance between us, my phone rings. I glance at the passenger seat where it lays, blaring and blinking. I check the ID screen. *Lora.* My heart compresses in fear, and I quickly snatch the phone and connect the call.

"What's wrong?" My gaze flickers to the rearview mirror. Nik is gone.

"Abby? Where've you been? I've been calling you all night! Are you okay?"

"Huh?" My eyes keep darting from the road before me, to the review mirror, searching for Nik, but he's nowhere to be found. *Where did he go?*

"I've been up worried about you. I thought something happened to you damn it. Don't do that to me. I can't lose you too."

Guilt quickly grounds me into a clear focus. *Forget about Nik and concentrate on Lora. She needs you.* "I'm sorry Lo. I'm fine, a little shaken up, but I'll explain everything when I get to your place. Everything okay over there?"

"Yes." She hesitates, no doubt finding it tough to say everything is okay. When indeed it is not. I can still hear the bleakness in her voice. She's like a creaky dam, constantly clearing her throat, as she desperately fights back a raging flood of emotion. "You swear you're all right?"

Of course I can't swear to it. A tornado nearly swallowed me whole. The only reason it didn't was because of Nik. *Nik.* I picture his messy golden hair, and those eyes that rival any pristine stretch of ocean…

"Abby? Hello?"

Lora's voice jars me back to reality. "Um, what?"

"Never mind. Just drive carefully and I'll see you when you get here."

"Okay." I disconnect the call, and drop the phone into my lap. I squeeze the back of my neck, hoping to relieve some of the tension that's collecting there. It helps a little. And so does thinking of Nik. The warmth of his hand still lingers on my skin, and I touch my cheek, wishing it were his hand caressing me.

But that will never happen. I'm bound to a life without love, all because of this unwanted power within me. I came to terms with my life of celibacy a few years ago, though it wasn't without tears, and ample screams ringing off my bedroom walls. *Why me?* I kept asking. *Why me?*

I felt it was unfair to bestow such a burden on someone like me. Someone who yearned for love from a mother, who craved acceptance amongst peers, and now…now I'm to be tortured for the rest of my existence, marked by evil with a kiss of death upon my lips? *Wow,* I think. That last thought was actually poetic. When I pause at a stop sign, I'm sure to jot it down on a scrap of napkin I find in my glove box.

I begin to wonder what Lora's neighborhood will look like in the aftermath of the tornado. Will there be trees down? Power lines? Destroyed homes? *Thank God Lora's house was spared.* As I draw near, I grip the steering wheel, steeling myself for disaster. As I maneuver the car through the streets, I see no sign of damage. Not a trace of destruction other than muddy lawns and branches hanging low from the weight of wet leaves. *What the hell?*

The tornado must have changed course, which is common. They are unpredictable, blazing a trail anywhere they damn well choose. I look down the road as far as my eyes can see, and still...no damage. Everything seems normal. I scan the trees that line the backyards, and see nothing that indicates anything is amiss. It's highly probable that the tornado changed course. And thank God it did. If it hadn't, Lora and the kids could have been injured. Or worse.

I shudder as I start rehashing every detail of last night. The grim aura that clung to the darkness, the deafening howl of the tornado as it barreled down upon me. The blatant pursuit that ensued after the storm chased me out of my car, and into the night. My chest tightens at the memory. *If it wasn't for Nik, I'd be dead.* His words emerge from memory, nagging me like an overly concerned grandmother. *"The damn thing never strayed from your path."* But that's ridiculous, not to mention entirely implausible. Tornados do not hunt people.

Another question suddenly pops into my mind. *What happened to it? Where did it go after Nik rescued me?* Looking around at the surrounding neighborhoods there's not a single trace of the tornado. *Did it simply vanish?*

I pull into Lora's driveway, searching the house and yard for damage. There is none. *Thank God.* As I emerge from the car, I hear an ear-piercing screech. My head snaps up at the sound, finding Mo, my cousin running full speed across the lawn toward me. *Oh shit.* He slams into me, wrapping my neck in a fierce hug, practically choking me.

"Easy there big guy," I say, reaching up and untangling myself from his grasp.

The screen door bangs against the frame, and I flick my gaze to the house. Lora is crossing the yard, her hands up in surrender.

"Sorry Abs. When you didn't come back, I got worried and called Mo. I thought maybe you went to his place."

"Hell naw," Mo says. "This heifer's trying to give someone a heart attack or something. Staying out all night. Not telling a single soul. Girl, what's wrong with you, you been drinking or something?"

I roll my eyes. "No."

He brings his hands to his hips and leans forward. His dark brown eyes study me, and he sniffs the air around me. "Well you don't smell like a man, so you weren't answering a booty call."

I scowl at him. "Of course not, jerk off." I slam the car door shut and push past him. Mo knows about my death kiss, but he doesn't take it seriously. I confided in him once, figuring if I had to choose between him and Lora, telling family would be better. Family is supposed to love you no matter how fucked up you are. After I told him, he said it was impossible to be able to kill someone with just a kiss.

He told me, *"this is real life Abby. You ain't Rogue from X-Men. You can't kill a man with your touch."* I argued with him till I was breathless, but he wouldn't budge. He seems to think I've carried so much guilt, that my mind rationalized it by convincing me that I was entirely to blame for Trevor's death.

Sounds like a bunch of shrink talk to me. Pointing a rhetorical finger to my brain for creating this irrational belief that I killed Trevor. But I know better. I felt it. I have *felt* the strange power surge through me, crackling with intensity as I deliver a lethal dose of it through a kiss.

"So then where the hell have you been Miss Priss?" he asks. His long legs easily keeping stride with me.

"I went home to get more clothes and stuff. Then the weather got bad. There was a tornado in Prescott County. Did you hear about it?"

"Hell yeah," says Mo. "Everybody is talking about it."

"I saw it on the news this morning," adds Lora. "They say it's the biggest tornado ever documented." I feel sick. *Biggest tornado ever documented?* I stared fate in the eye last night, and there is only one reason I didn't become a death toll. Nik.

I picture his dimples, deeply notched in his creamy skin, and his sky-blue eyes. I begin to question the past few hours. How was he able to save me? How did we escape such a menacing tornado, that seemed hell bent on destruction? How are we both not dead? Mo snaps his fingers in front of my face, bringing me out of my thoughts.

"What?" I ask, irritated, pushing his hand away. I stalk across the yard and join Lora on the porch. I try to study her without being overly obvious, doing my best to keep my face slack of any reaction. But it's damn hard when she looks this way. Livid, dark bruises outlined in sickly jaundice-like colors, clash against pale skin. Her eyes are bloodshot, and tiny pinpricks of broken capillaries sprinkle her right cheek.

"I said, yo ass is lucky," Mo says with the exaggerated accent that heightens whenever he gets worked up. That's the second time I've been told *I'm lucky* in less than five hours. Nik told me the same thing just after I gained consciousness.

I bristle at this because I've always felt I were the second unluckiest person on earth. The first being the man foolish or naïve enough to get too close to me. But I've always believed that I'm cursed to be loveless for my entire existence, thus being the second unluckiest person in the world. So to be told how *lucky* I am bodes about as well as flames below a bookshelf.

"What is up with you?" Mo frowns, scrutinizing me for a moment before turning to Lora. "She ain't acting right." Lora shrugs.

"Does she ever?" She nudges me with her shoulder, and gives me a lackluster smile. She's trying so hard. Trying hard to be her old-self. The old, carefree, fun-loving Lora, but I know it's an act. She's putting on her brave face for me, and it makes me feel like shit. Here we are, wasting time and energy discussing me, when clearly we should be talking about Lora.

"How about you?" I ask. "How are you holding up?" She lifts a shoulder, then hugs herself. I suspect she's either attempting to ward off discussion, or holding in her emotions. Maybe both. She looks at her shoes.

"It's all too much to take in, you know? I was going to end things with Tony. I was. I was actually ready this time." She glances up at me fleetingly, then fixes her gaze back to the ground. "But having it end this way…it's just devastating. How am I supposed to explain this to my kids?"

Before Mo or I can answer her, a little figure emerges at the front door. Mason stands there in his pajamas, clutching Mister Fluff with one hand, and scrubbing at his tired eyes with the other. "Mama?" he says quietly from behind the screen door. Lora touches her fingertips to the corners of her eyes, wiping away her tears, before she turns around.

"What's up buddy?" She goes to the door, and opens it. Mason lifts his arms and she hoists him onto her hip, pressing a tender kiss to the top of his head.

"I have boo boos." He touches various parts of his body, his lip quivering as though he's about to break out in tears. It is Lora's undoing. She starts sobbing, leaning her forehead against his.

"I know baby." She hugs him close. "I know."

I can feel my heart squeeze painfully in my chest. *Poor Mason. Poor Lora.* Then my blood turns to ice water as I think of Tony. *To hell with him. He's the reason they're hurting.* Mo rushes over, and wraps a slim arm around Lora, and then gestures for me to come closer. When I'm within arm's reach, he pulls us into a tight huddle.

"Listen, the both of you. We are gonna get through this…together. All right?" We give half-hearted nods, and let Mo lead us into the house.

Lora sets Mason down, and barely chokes out, "I need to check on Ella," as she scurries down the hall, sniffling the entire way. I kneel in front of Mason, looking into his big brown eyes.

"I see you've kept Mister Fluff safe." I take the stuffed moose and hold him to my ear, as if he's whispering to me. I nod and smile. "He says you're very brave."

Mason grins at this. "That's 'cause I'm a super hero."

"A super hero huh?" I muss his hair. "What's your super power?"

He thinks about it for a beat, then says with definiteness, "Saving mommies."

I nearly fall over. "Saving mommies?" I glance up at Mo, who purses his lips together, and looks away.

"Yeah." His eyes sparkle with excitement. His smile reveals a tiny row of teeth. "I saved Mommy from Daddy all the time just by walking in the room." He bows out his little chest proudly. Then he pauses, his brow furrows, and he gives me a small frown. "Except...this time I couldn't save her." He shakes his head, his lips pucker as though he's about to cry.

"You did though Mason. You *did* save her." I take his small hands into mine. "And every day...you'll continue to save her."

Chapter 7

Though Lora is hesitant to go to the doctor, we finally convince her that after the blow to her temple, she needs to be thoroughly examined. It's decided that Mo will take her and the kids to their family doctor and pediatrician. I wanted to take them, but Lora was adamant that I not miss work on account of her. So after a shower and a short nap, I drive into town and start my shift at the library.

I'm forced to wear a scarf, which I've knotted into a stylish loop around my neck to disguise the ugly bruises that ring my throat like a necklace. I somehow make it through the workday. I even successfully dodge Barb, and kept my sharp tongue in check when a lady got a little mouthy when I charged her for a grossly damaged book she tried to slip past me in the book return.

Like a mechanical toy, I move automatically, clocking out and strolling across the parking lot. I get into my vehicle, and head to Lora's. I go through the motions woodenly, and when I pull into her driveway, I blink a few times. I'm so exhausted I barely recall the drive. *Did I drive through any stop signs?*

I climb out of the car and slam the door shut, finally noticing the van that is parked in the yard. *Shit. Tony's mom.* I collect myself for a quick moment, preparing for the next step of this horrific ordeal. Judy is all right I suppose, but she's always seemed oblivious of her son's behavior, though I don't think it's out of denial. I truly think she just sees the world differently than most people.

Like it's all sunshine and roses, when in fact, it's more like rain and thorns. I cross the lawn and knock once on the door before I let myself in. I find Lora sitting on the sofa, Ella in her lap, sucking happily on a pacifier.

Judy is hugging Mason to her chest, her eyes glossy with unshed tears. Mo is standing in the archway that connects to the kitchen. Clearly keeping his distance, yet sticking close enough should Lora need him. All eyes turn to me as I enter. "Hello," I say, dropping my messenger bag to the floor. I study Lora to ensure she's okay. She gives me a faint smile and swallows before turning her attention back to Ella,who's wriggling in her arms. Mason pries Judy's arms off him and races to me. He wraps my legs in a tight embrace and I pat his mop of brunette hair that seems to be more cowlicks than anything else.

"Nice to see you again Abby," Judy says, dabbing a tissue to her round cheeks.

"Same here. I'm sorry it's on such upsetting terms." Mason takes my hand and together we move further into the living room. She nods and blows her nose.

"I never thought I'd have to bury my child." She fondles the wad of tissues in her lap. "It's heartbreaking."

We all remain quiet, and in order to fill the silence, Judy begins to ramble. "They say the good die young, and now I see how true that statement is. He was such a good boy. So handsome. So giving."

Yeah, he was giving all right, I think. *He gave Lora nothing but heartache.* "I know he's flying high in heaven right now. Probably palling around with his Grandpa Mitch…"

I look up to the ceiling and bite my lip to keep from scoffing at her lame words. Who am I to damper her fragile spirits? I let her continue, even though the thought of Tony in heaven is absurd. *Any man who beats his wife and toddler son has a special place waiting for him in hell.* Of course I don't say this, instead I allow her to paint Tony in false glory, which seems to bring her some comfort.

"Lora," she says turning to her, fisting her tissues in her hand. "Have you given any thought to funeral arrangements?"

Lora gives a small shake of her head. Her thick hair swinging softly around her face.

Judy chokes up a little, but presses on. "I'd like to do it, if you don't mind. It's the last thing I can do for my son."

Lora looks at me, shell-shocked. She hadn't given any thought to the funeral, I can tell. Forget living day by day. She's just trying to get through hour by hour. I lift my brows at her, indicating to her to take Judy's offer. Preparing a funeral is the *last* thing Lora needs to worry about.

"Of course Judy," she finally says.

"Oh thank you Lora. It will be a beautiful dedication to him. All you have to do is come." Judy lifts her eyes, shifting them from Mo to me. "All of you." She raises herself from the couch, adjusting her ankle length floral skirt. She collects her purse and slings it over her brawny shoulder. "I'll call you with the details."

She traces a finger down Ella's cheek, then gives Lora a quick hug. "Be strong honey." She turns and walks to Mason. She kisses the top of his head, and looks into my face. "Take care of her Abby. She's hurting."

I want to scream. *Of course she's hurting! You can see the bruises on her face for God's sake! How do you think they fucking got there?* Instead I just say, "I know."

She pats my arm and leaves, pulling the door closed behind her. I look to Mo, who is shaking his head in quiet astonishment. From the tight purse of his lips, I know we're both thinking the same thing. *Can she be so fucking blind that she doesn't see the bruises brought on by her own son's fists?*

I think it's best to ignore discussing the funeral, or Judy's visit, so I ask, "How did the doctor's appointment go?" I look from Lora, to Mo, to Lora again.

"Mason has some deep bruising, but other than that he's fine." The pain and guilt she bears is apparent in her eyes as she gazes at him. I smile down at him, wishing I could erase the past twenty-four hours from his memory. To wipe away the last image he has of his father, which is sure to leave a permanent imprint on him. Something he'll carry all through life, influencing his decisions, and shaping him as he grows.

I can only pray it molds him into a strong, loving man who respects those he cares for. I lift my head and look to Lora. "And you?"

She pushes her hair from her ear and tilts her face.

Her right ear is wrapped with bulky white bandages. "Blood clot in the ear. They had to make an incision to drain it." She looks sheepish, like she'd just damaged her parents' car during a late-night joy ride. "The rest is superficial." She glances away and lets her hair fall, concealing her bandages. Staring at the brutal wounds that cover my best friend and her sweet little boy, I'm angry at Tony all over again.

I hate him for what he did. And I'm glad he's dead. I want to say as much but instead, I swallow down the biting words and say, "I'm glad that's all it is, and that you both are all right." I force a smile and sit beside her on the sofa. "I'm going to run home and check on Jack," I tell her. "Will you be okay while I'm gone?"

"Abby," she protests. "I'm a grown woman. You don't need to baby me." She taps Ella on her nose playfully. "Ain't that right?" The squirming baby giggles and thrashes her tiny fists in the air. "Go home Abby. Get some rest. I'll be fine."

I glance up at Mo, unsure if I should believe her. Is this the true Lora? Or brave-face Lora who's as brittle as parchment paper behind the tough-girl act?

My cousin strolls through the room and takes a seat beside us on the arm of the couch. He smells of sweet perfume, though he should be wearing cologne. But, Mo is far from conventional. Unafraid of stares, or judgment, Mo often wears bowties with skinny jeans. Out of boredom or acting on a whim, he's been known to dye his normally dark hair bleach blonde. My eyes linger on the single freckle that sits at the corner of his eye.

Born Morrison Floyd Cox, my cousin has always been attractive. He was an adorable baby, and as a kid, his cheeks were perpetually pink from all the pinching and constant gushing from old women. In school, he was every teen girl's crush, and even now in his twenties, he's officially crossed into what heterosexual women call, "*a waste*."

His eyes meet mine, and he gives me a knowing smile as he reaches across the space to touch my shoulder. His hand is tender, not to mention immaculately manicured. I look down at my own battered and chewed nails, wrinkling my nose at their neglect. I curl my fingers into my lap, and gaze at Mo. He's always been polished, which has been our on-going argument since we turned fourteen. He complains that I'm *"smothering my hotness"* which usually earns him an eye roll.

He swears that even hair models would envy my thick auburn hair, if I would take the time to deep condition it. He also fusses at me for my lack of fashion sense. He often clucks his tongue in either disbelief or sympathy at my choice of clothes, saying, *"girrrl, did you get dressed in the dark this morning?"*

"I'll stay with her," Mo says. "You go on home. You could use a shower and some beauty sleep." He winks at me, and I can't help but smile. Mo talks with a rolling accent that he miraculously acquired sometime in middle school, around the same time he developed a liking for Latin boys and Broadway musicals. It's no secret that Mo is gay, and it's a fact that we've never openly discussed. I always knew he was gay, and I accepted it. Mo is Mo, and labeling him as gay wasn't, and still isn't necessary.

"You sure?" I ask.

"Yes, damn it." He stands and grips me playfully

by the arm. "Do I need to haul your ass out of here?"

I swat at him, laughing. "Okay okay."

Mo grabs my shoulders and pulls me into a hug. He holds me there as he whispers against my ear, "She's going to break down as soon as you leave, you know that don't you?"

"Yes," I mutter, just before he holds me at arm's length and says, "Get out of here and get that mop you call hair washed. It stinks." He curls his lip into a disgusted sneer. "Seriously."

I look at his own, perfectly arranged messy spikes and reach up to touch the bun that sits at the nape of my neck. Sprigs of loose hair hang around it, and I feel a flourish of embarrassment shoot through me as I realize that it's being held with a regular office rubber band. *Jesus. I am a mess.*

Mo notices this, and smiles. "Like I've always said, just because you're a librarian doesn't mean you have to look like one."

I stick my tongue out at him, and look over at Lora. "I'll check on you later, okay?"

She nods and reaches for my hand. "Thanks Abby." She squeezes my fingers, and I squeeze firmly back. I find myself wishing I could remove her pain, just as I wanted to do for Mason. To fix everything, and give her back her innocence. To restore her to the girl she was before she became a survivor of domestic abuse.

I look around the room at the tiny, broken family and my heart hurts for them. They deserve better. They certainly deserved better than Tony, and now that he is gone, they can mend the severed pieces of their lives and thrive. The dark thoughts worry me, and for a

74

moment, I question my humanity. *How can I be so callous? The man is dead, and I killed him.* I impulsively reach for my neck, recalling the crushing pressure as he tried to choke the life from me one intake of air at a time. *There was no other way,* I think. *Given the chance, he would have killed me.*

I shake the grim memory away, and decide it's best to take my leave now, before I start to relive the entire night again. I bid goodbye to everyone, and trudge my way through the house, across the yard and finally to my car, where I melt into the seat, suddenly exhausted. *I need some sleep. After I tend to Jack, I have a date with my bathtub.* I can hardly wait to sink into some bubbles, read enough stanzas from my poetry book to thoroughly relax me and then slip under my covers to allow sleep to find me. *And find me you will...you elusive bastard.*

****

I sleep throughout the entire night, which is rare for me. Since Trevor's death, I've experienced awful nightmares, reliving our fateful kiss and the mayhem that ensued afterward. Unfortunately, they come so often I doubt they will ever go away. Each new nightmare is slightly different than the last, yet they are all undeniably the same. They usually entail me, a handsome man, which I assume is Trevor, and our first, yet definitely last kiss.

Most I can't recall by morning, but one continues to haunt me. Just after Trevor pulls away after a delightfully sweet kiss, he looks down at me, smiles, then starts coughing up buckets of bright red blood. It covers him, and me until I'm left screaming, staring at the palms of my blood-soaked hands. I don't need a shrink to tell me what that means. I have Trevor's blood on my hands. I took his life, just as I took Tony's.

I stretch my well-rested muscles and look down the length of myself. I'm surprised to find that I awoke in the same position I was in when I drifted to sleep. I didn't even stir. *That's a first.* And even more surprising still, it only took me reading the first line of a poem titled, *Bliss,* to succumb to complete exhaustion.

I glimpse the clock and am startled at the time. 10:28 a.m. Wow. I never sleep that late, and my body reminds me of such by being sluggish. I eat a bowl of my favorite sugary cereal, hoping it will give me some much needed energy and then head to my closet to find something comfortable. As I'm rifling through the rack of shirts, a sliver of red fabric catches my eye. I push the hangers aside, and stare at the deep crimson tank top. I run my fingers along the neckline, lingering there, contemplating.

Should I? I continue to gaze at it, tempted to rip it from the hanger and slip it on. But of course, like always, I'm uncertain. I sigh, wishing I had never seen it. It's a reminder that even on the outside, I'm not normal. Inside and out, I'm a freak of nature. Aside from the few times I've worn it either around the house or to bed, the tank has remained shoved into the dark recesses of my closet. Too ashamed to wear it in public, the shirt has sadly taken up permanent residence amongst the other articles of clothing I no longer wish to wear.

I bite my lip, studying it. *Come on, you know you want to,* I chide myself. I toy with the fabric, rubbing the soft cotton between my fingertips. *Aw, what the hell.* I free it from the plastic hanger and stroll to the full-length mirror in the corner of the room. I hold it to my chest, and smile. It has a drawing of Edgar Allan Poe on the front, his hands covering his cheeks in a mock "oh my" expression, and there's a laughing raven perched on his shoulder. Beneath the image, it reads: *"There will always be more books, but nevermore time."*

I grin as I wiggle out of my nightshirt and pull on a pair of worn jeans. I snap a cotton bra into place and then reach for the tank top. I hesitate at first, but then I tell myself, *just go for it,* before quickly slipping it over my head before I lose the nerve. I smooth out the fabric, forcing myself to focus on the tank top only. I blink at Edgar, who only stares back at me with his look of astonishment. I almost laugh.

Then my eyes drift higher, and all at once, they're there, staring angrily back at me. *Mocking me.* The ugly blemishes that have taunted me my entire life. The marks that keep me from donning anything strapless or sleeveless. I turn slightly to see them better, though it sickens me. The tank top conceals most of them, but a few feathered scars peek over my right shoulder.

I close my eyes, easily envisioning the scars in their entirety. The coppery webbing spans across my entire back, reaching like tendrils from my left earlobe, across my shoulder, and running all the way down to my right hip. It can be best described as picturing my spine as a lightning rod, resulting in golden scars searing themselves, like fire-bolts into my flesh. The scars feather out at the tips like delicate lace. Perhaps on someone else, they would be exotic, beautiful even. But on me, they're hideous.

I frown as I brush my hair, but in a stroke of

defiance, I weave it into a thick braid that settles between my shoulder blades. I tilt my head, and instinctively touch the tender skin behind my ear, tracing the vine-like scar. *Today, I think I'm just going to be me. Who gives a damn who sees my scars? I'm tired of hiding them.* I resolve to ignore any stares I may receive, and finish getting ready. Just as I spray on some juniper body spray, my cellphone rings. I stroll to the coatrack in the living room and retrieve it from my bag. Glimpsing the screen, I see it's Lora. I punch the call button and bring the phone to my ear.

I greet my friend with a simple, "Hey" and stroll through the bedroom to lift my favorite poetry book from the nightstand.

"Hi," she says. "Did you get some sleep?"

"Yeah. How about you?"

"Some."

The line goes silent and I chew my lip while I wait for her to speak again. When the seconds stretch on, I finally say, "Lora? Is something wrong?"

I listen to her quiet breathing, my heart rate swiftly picking up its pace as I pace back and forth. "Lora? What is it?"

"The results of the autopsy are in."

Chapter 8

My knees give out from under me and I crumple to my bed, sinking into the plush comforter. *It hasn't been forty-eight hours. They must have found out it was me.* I clutch my chest, fear and anxiety lancing through me like a burning laser. *I'll be arrested.* Although I knew this day would come, looking down the barrel of my destiny is sobering. I'll be arrested, and thrown into jail for murder. *I should have been put there eight years ago...*

"And?"

"Cardiac arrest."

My stomach bottoms out. Just like Trevor. I stopped his heart. With *my* kiss, I stilled his heart. *Forever.*

She sniffles, and says. "They said the muscle walls of his heart were thicker than usual, which is called cardiomyo-something. Anyway, it weakened his heart and during the...uh..."

Say it. Say, during the assault. Say during the fight. Say during the fucking beating, Tony's fucking heart gave out. Despite what the medical examiners believe, Tony's condition had nothing do with his death, but it had everything to do with me. My kiss ended his life. And given the situation, I'd do it again. Anything to protect Lora and those kids.

"During the excitement..." Her voice grows soft,

barely a scraping whisper across her lips. "His heart just stopped."

During the excitement? This grates me like nails on a fucking chalkboard. "During the excitement? Lora, really, what the hell? It wasn't excitement, it was a fucking circus, and Tony was the ringleader. He beat the shit out of you, and Mason. He tried to *kill* me! Did you know that Lora? Did you know that your husband, who you're still desperately trying to protect tried to fucking *kill* me!"

I'm practically screaming into the receiver. My chest heaving as though I'd ran a marathon as my heart pounds recklessly against my ribs.

She gasps, but otherwise remains stone silent.

"You've seen his handprints on my throat Lora, don't sit there and act like you didn't know he tried to strangle me."

Again, empty air.

"Damn you! Say something!"

"What do you want me to say Abby!" she shrieks into my ear. "That I'm a stupid lovesick fool? That my choice in men sucks? That I've endangered my kids, and possibly scarred them for life, all because I was too damn weak to leave?"

I can hear the sobs collecting in her throat, straining her voice. I just sit there, dumbfounded as Lora continues. "Or maybe you want me to admit that I was the reason you almost died! Of course I saw the bruises on your neck, and it kills me each time I see them. Tony almost *killed* you, and if he had, your blood would have been on *my* hands. I should have never called you that night. I should have never involved you."

Now, she's hysterical. I can barely make out any more of her ramblings through her tortured weeping. I feel awful. I pinch the bridge of my nose and close my eyes. *What have I done?* I should have never provoked her. The guilt she's bearing must be stifling, and who the hell am I to force her to admit it out loud?

"I'm so sorry Lora." I flop backward on the bed, flinging my arm across my face. "I'm so so sorry. I guess I just don't know when to back off."

"No, don't be," she says quietly. "Every now and then I need someone to set my ass straight."

"Yeah, well, why does it always have to be me?" I groan.

"That's what best friends do. They set each other's asses straight. I'd do it to you, if you'd ever fuck up once in a while. Damn you for being perfect."

I can sense her smile through the phone, but I purse my lips into a frown. *Perfect? I'm far from perfect...*

I change the subject by asking, "Did you get things at work sorted out?"

"Yes. My boss is very understanding. He's allowing me to take a leave of absence for as long as I need."

"That's nice of him." I sit up, and my gaze falls upon the bedroom window. The curtain is still drawn, but I can tell from the muted glow behind the silk fabric that the sun is shining brightly in the sky. *Finally, a sunny day.* I push myself off the mattress, the bed squeaking as I do, and make my way across the floor. "Need me to stop by? I can be there in twenty minutes."

I draw the curtain back and squint against the blinding rays. Once my eyes adjust to the light, I peer through the glass. Fluffy cotton-like clouds tumble across a brilliant blue sky. I can feel the warmth of the sun through the pane, and I long to bask in it. I turn my head, my gaze shifting to the poetry book on my nightstand.

"Actually, I'm dropping the kids off at my mom's. I have to be at the police station in an hour to pick up Tony's belongings, and sign a consent for his..." Her voice cracks a bit. "For his body to be released to the funeral home."

"I can come with you," I offer, though I feel as if I'd be tempting fate by walking through a police station's doors. As though the stars would align, and they would realize that I was responsible for Tony's death. That it wasn't actually a heart condition, and overexertion. That it was actually me. It was indeed, my curse that ended his life.

"No," she says with an exasperated sigh. "I'm a big girl Abby. You don't have to babysit me, or hold my hand. I'll be fine, I promise. It's your day off. Have fun."

I gnaw at my lip as I consider it. *Have fun? Is she serious?*

"Abby." Her tone is resolute, and I know it would be futile to try to persuade her otherwise. "I need to do some things on my own." She pauses, then says, "This needs to be one of them."

I sigh deeply, and say, "Okay. But I'm just a phone call away if you need anything. Promise me you'll call the moment you need me."

"I promise."

"Hisses and kugs," I reply automatically.

Lora says it back and hangs up. I lift the poetry book from the nightstand and cradle it. Time alone usually means time to read, so I decide to take advantage of the solitude, and the beautiful weather by losing myself in my favorite book. Before I take that much needed, "me time," I tend to Jack, whistling at him as I rinse his bowl out in the sink, and refill it. He just gawks at me with his beady little eyes, and flaps his wings in excitement when I fill his dish with fresh birdseed.

"There you go buddy," I say closing the cage door.

I quickly step into my battered sneakers and head outside. As soon as I crack the front door open, warm sunlight spills across the floor. I step out into the muggy August air and inhale. *Ah. Just what I need.*

I stroll through the yard, and settle into the hammock that stretches between a blooming mimosa tree and a grand live oak. The ropes tighten, supporting my weight as I adjust myself into a comfortable position. I open the book to the marked page, and dive into the flowing poetry, losing myself in the words just as I had planned. The breeze carries the sweet scent of mimosa blossoms, and in no time, I am in my Zen-like state.

I smile to myself, feeling completely fulfilled, just as I always do while nestled in nature, and lost in a good book. The hammock sways slowly, rocking me into a gentle lull as I read. Pinpricks of sunlight filter through the leaves, and fall across the pages, like golden raindrops. *What a beautiful day.*

I get halfway through the book when I feel a niggle of awareness trickle through me. *Someone is watching me.* I lift my gaze from the book, and carefully scan my surroundings. The fence line around my property is chain-link, with trumpet vines twining the length of it.

A lone squirrel scurries across it, then leaps to a nearby tree. My neighbors' backyard is quiet. Their patio is deserted, and their neglected flowerbeds overrun with weeds and tall grass. As far as I can tell, I'm alone. I turn back to my book, but am unable to concentrate on the words.

The sense of being watched sends prickles of unease through me. I glance over my shoulder. Still nothing. I consider going back inside, but I feel silly just thinking it. *No one is watching you;* I scold myself, and settle back into the hammock. I read a few more lines, but the gentle ringing in my veins keeps me from relaxing. It surges through me, keeping me alert, insisting that I am not alone.

I turn my head, surveying the yard once more. My bicycle lies upside down, from where I tried to change the tire a few weeks ago. It sits lonely and forgotten, since I left it there. The wheel squeaks as it barely turns in the breeze. *You're just being paranoid.* I return to the book in my hands, determined to rid myself of the awful feeling and enjoy my time outside. I turn the page and attempt to read a poem titled, *Ode of the Befallen.*

The wind picks up, rustling the furry mimosa blossoms overhead. The breeze is warm, but pleasant as it drifts through the trees. Then I smell a familiar scent. Honeysuckle and rain. *Nik.* My head snaps upright as I search for him. Other than myself, the only life I see is a blue jay. I watch him as he lands gracefully on the mimosa limb. He cautiously preens himself for a moment before fluttering away again. There is no sign of Nik, and I feel foolish for thinking he had been there at all. *Why would he be here?*

I climb out of the hammock, tossing nervous

glances over my shoulder as I make my way back inside the house. *I'm going insane.* I shake my head, annoyed that I'm acting so irrationally. *Why would Nik be at my house? And why would he be watching me?* I drop my book back onto the nightstand, and pick up my phone from where I left it. I glance at the screen. One missed call. I scroll through the missed call log, noticing it was Lora. My chest tightens, and I waste no time quickly dialing her number. The phone rings three times before she answers.

"Hey," she answers.

"Hey," I mirror. "What's up? Everything okay?"

"Yeah. I just wanted to let you know that I talked to Judy today."

"How's she holding up?"

"She's a wreck. But planning the funeral seems to bring her a little bit of peace."

"You got to take your peace wherever or however you can get it."

"The funeral is tomorrow," she blurts out. "Will you go?" She clears her throat, but doesn't say anything else.

I don't hesitate. "I'll be there."

"You will?" She sounds hopeful, and a bit surprised.

"Of course," I say. "For you. I'll be there." And I mean it. Nothing could keep me away from Lora's side. She's my best friend, and I won't let her go through this alone.

"Thanks Abby. Remind me to hug the hell out of you next time I see you."

I laugh. "Will do."

"See you tomorrow Abs."

"Bye Lora."

We hang up, and I realize with a pang of sadness that we just bid each other a normal good-bye. I can feel a shift in Lora, and I tell myself she just needs time. I sit down on the edge of the bed, needing to take a moment to gather myself. Tomorrow is going to be dreadful, but I must remain strong for Lora. I close my eyes tight and concentrate on controlling my breathing. *Dear God, please help me get through the next twenty-four hours.*

****

The sky is slate gray, casting an ominous backdrop as the funeral procession drives slowly through town toward the cemetery. With the funeral over, the last hurdle of the day is Tony's burial, which will be Lora's final good-bye. The funeral ceremony was a debacle, almost laughable as the pastor raved on and on about Tony, and how wonderful a husband and father he was. Mo had a death-grip on my hand during the entire service, just to keep me from jumping to my feet and hollering, *"Liar!"*

I understand why Judy portrayed her son that way, but it just wasn't true. But then, what mother wouldn't want the final tribute to their child to be beautiful, and dignified? As the funeral home's black sedan slows to a stop, I gaze out the tinted window at the hole in the ground. Tony's final resting place. A white tent stationed over it flaps in the breeze, and several flowered markers sit around it.

I look over at Lora, who's dabbing at her eyes with a lacey handkerchief. I reach across the space between us, and take her slight hand.

"You ready?" I ask gently.

She nods woodenly, wiping her nose before unbuckling her seatbelt. We step out of the car and make our way to the tent, where the other guests have started to congregate. Lora's mother, Maureen, finds us in the crowd. I wonder what she thinks of all this. Lora kept most of Tony's shenanigans hidden from her family, but judging by the look on Maureen's face, she's starting to put two and two together. She's carrying Ella and leading Mason by the hand. I smile down at Mason, and tap little Ella on the nose as Lora takes her from Maureen. She settles the baby on her hip, raking her fingers through her soft blond curls.

Lora looks the part of a grieving widow. Her face is splotchy from crying, her mascara long washed away, leaving dark rings around her hazel eyes. Her long black skirt flows to the ground. The toes of her boots peeking out as she sways back and forth, cooing to the infant in her arms. The pastor rounds the group of standing people; all eyes follow his movement until he stops at the gravesite. He raises his arms to the sky, and addresses us with a strong voice.

"Friends and family. Let us now send Tony into his eternal slumber with a hymn selected by his mother. Let the words wash over your souls and cleanse you on this sad day."

A woman I do not recognize emerges from the crowd and stands beside the pastor. She's wearing a white choir robe with a gem-green sash. She starts by humming, then breaks into a haunting rendition of "How Great Thou Art". As she sings, the pallbearers amble past us. A wreath of white carnations lie atop the glossy wooden casket they carry, and I feel Lora tense beside me. I slide a glance at her, my heart tugging as she clings to Ella. She clamps her eyes shut, and buries her face in the baby's hair.

I glance at Mo, who thins his lips and frowns. He steps between us, and takes each of our hands, grounding us in the moment. Like a chain, we stand there as the final notes of the hymn are sung, and a hush settles among the crowd. We watch in collective silence as the casket is lowered, ever so slowly into the dark hole in the ground. Sobs, gasps, and low murmurs float through the assembly of guests, but I remain quiet, unfeeling, as I stare at the shiny lid of the coffin as it sinks lower and lower.

Good riddance, I think, nearly smirking as it finally disappears from view. For a moment I fret about my lack of compassion. *When did I become so comfortable with death?* Perhaps it's because I killed two men. My stomach sours at the thought. *I'm the angel of death. The grim reaper in a cardigan.*

Tony was a poor excuse for a human. A drunk, a wife beater, and child abuser. I *will not* mourn him. What I *will* mourn, is the innocence he stole from Mason. What I w*ill* mourn is the blind trust, and love that Lora poured into their relationship. Virtues that are now lost, and will be next to impossible for any new guy to earn in the future.

The pastor calls the funeral to an end, and slowly the crowd disperses. Some linger near the gravesite, watching as funeral workers shovel loads of soft dirt onto the casket. The steady thump of falling earth echoes from six feet down, as it rains down on the coffin lid. Lora continues to stand there, staring down the dark hole, dumbstruck, almost disbelieving as they bury Tony shovel-by-shovel, dirt load by dirt load.

Mo's fingers loosen from mine, and he steps up behind Lora, and wraps her in a hug, resting his chin on her shoulder.

His black slacks are rolled above his ankles and his loafers are impeccably shined. Lora clasps her hands around his arms, sinking into his embrace. Tears run over her all ready wet cheeks. It's annoying to see her mourn Tony. The monster who put those fading bruises on her face. No matter how much makeup she slathers over them, they are still there. I know they still ache, because my own bruises still smart whenever I touch them. How can she forget how they got there? How can she ignore *who* put them there?

Tony's mother openly weeps over the grave. A crocheted shawl hangs from her shoulders, and her black silk dress makes her pale skin look washed out, and sickly. I begrudgingly walk to her, and touch her arm.

"It was a beautiful memorial, Judy."

She lifts her head, her eyes nearly swollen shut with outward grief. "Thank you." She wipes her face, and casts her gaze back to the grave. It's nearly covered by now. "I hope I did him proud."

"You did. It was lovely."

She nods, and sobs uncontrollably into her wad of tissues. I feel awkward, not to mention, hypocritical, so I back away and take my place beside Mo. Lora is now with family, each murmuring words of comfort, and sympathy.

"Sweet Jesus, we made it," Mo whispers.

"Barely," I reply. "If it wasn't for you, I think I would have burned the church down."

He smiles. "I know. I should have let your crazy

ass do it." He adjusts his bowtie, and for the first time, I notice the yellow silk fabric is covered with red lips.

"Nice," I say, giving him a sly smile.

He grins. "You like?"

"It definitely screams Mo."

"So did the cute salesman who sold it to me." He winks and pats at his hair, which is swept into a slick pompadour.

I roll my eyes and groan.

"Girl. You should see the six-pack on him. I was like, 'can I get a taste of that?'"

"Please, Mo. We're at a freaking funeral for god's sake."

"So?" He lifts a brow. "Just 'cause we're in a cemetery full of dead folks, sure as hell don't mean I am. I'm alive and kinky."

"I think you mean, 'alive and kicking'."

He waggles his eyebrows, and his smile breaks into a devilish grin.

"Or maybe you don't…" I say laughing.

We make our way back to the funeral home's sedan, and let ourselves inside. We slide into the leather seats and wait for Lora. Slowly, the rest of the guests return to their vehicles.

Mo squints at me from across the car, and I can tell he's trying to gauge my mood.

"What?" I ask pointedly.

He touches his chin thoughtfully. "I think you ought to start dating."

My mouth pops open in surprise. "What?"

"You need some ass Abby." He examines his fingernails impassively, then slides his gaze to me, arching an eyebrow. "It's about time you find yourself a man. Unless of course, you dig chicks, which is fine too."

"I don't...dig chicks," I stammer, completely caught off guard by this topic.

"Well then let some testosterone into your life. What little I provide is not nearly enough." His lips curl into a smile, and he crosses his legs dramatically.

I gape at him. "Are you seriously talking about this now? Here?" I gesture around us, looking down at my own dark gray knit skirt, and my legs clad in black tights.

"Oh who the hell cares where we are," Mo says with a flick of his hand, waving me off like I'm an annoying fly. "The fact remains that you..." He points at me with feminine flair, "Abby, need to date. Hiding from whatever it is you're hiding from is not healthy." He leans forward, placing an elbow on his knee, his chin resting on his closed fist as he regards me closely. "Don't you ever get horny?"

I sigh in exasperation. "Mo, please...just shut up." I cover my ears. "I don't want to have this discussion."

"Honestly, Abby. Come on, you're a grown woman. You have to have urges. Needs..."

"La la la la la," I sing.

"Oh grow up," he snaps, crossing his arms over his cashmere cardigan. "You should probably listen when I tell you I've set you up on a blind date." He fusses with the pearl buttons on his sweater as he waits for his words to finally sink in.

I slowly lower my hands, my eyes wide as I stare at him. "You what?"

"I said, I set you up on a blind date. It's a guy who works in the warehouse. He's really cute, and seems really sweet."

I glare at him, anger seeping through my veins. Mo knows how adamant I am against dating. Though he doesn't believe me when I say, I'm cursed with a deathly kiss; he still *knows* I refuse to date, out of fear that I will accidently kill someone. *Again.*

Thunder rumbles in the distance, and I grind out, "Fuck you Mo." I ball my fists in my lap, furious that he would intrude on my life this way. "You know I don't want a relationship. Not now. Not ever."

He sucks his teeth. "You might as well check yourself into a convent then." His head wobbles with attitude, reminding me of a bobble head.

"How dare you stick your nose in my life?"

"Oh please Abby. You know me well enough to know I like to stick lots of things where they don't belong." His mouth curves into a smirk, and then he licks his fingertip, running it along each of his eyebrows, smoothing them.

"This crosses the line, even for you." My tone rises with every word, and I'm trembling with mounting rage. He doesn't know what he's done. He's put an innocent man in danger. What if I like him? What if he likes me? What if he tries to kiss me? What if I let him…?

He ignores me entirely and says, "Any-who, your date is set for tomorrow night. Wear something nice 'cause he's taking you to Leu Bordos, and then to see *Pinckney.*"

Pinckney? I moan in frustration, and toss my head back on the headrest. Pinckney happens to be the play I've been dying to see since it hit the marquee last month. I close my eyes and count to ten, concentrating on breathing and keeping myself from hurling myself at Mo. I want to strangle him for this. *Pinckney? Why did it have to be Pinckney?*

"Girl, just go and have a good time," Mo says. "It ain't like you got to sleep with the dude or anything. But should it happen… I'm sure it would do your tense ass some good. Might take some of the edge off your bitchiness."

I roll my head to the side, open one eye, and peer at him.

"What?" He raises his hands in question. "It's the damn truth and you know it."

I open the other eye and scowl. Sure, I've thought about sex. In fact, I think about it all the time. But hell, let's be frank, with a kiss like mine, I'm destined to remain a virgin forever.

Before I could argue any more about it, the car door opens and Lora sinks inside. We slide over, giving her room, the leather seats squeaking as we move. Her nose is pink, and her eyelids are puffy.

Dark sunglasses sit nestled on top of her head, and her fist is clenched tight around a handkerchief. She gives us a flimsy smile, and lowers her sunglasses, hiding her bloodshot eyes.

"You hanging in there?" Mo tucks a strand of hair behind her ear.

Lora looks out the window, setting her mouth into a stern line before nodding. Mo casts me a fleeting look, before turning back to her.

"Honey, we are right here if you need a shoulder to cry on, or a hand to hold." He takes her fingers and cups her tiny hand with his.

She looks over her shoulder at him and gives

another weak smile. "I know."

"Are the kids back with your mom?" Mo asks.

"They're staying the rest of the week with her while I get some things in order."

"Like what?' I question.

She swallows. "Like going through Tony's things. Selling what I can't afford…"

Oh. I hadn't thought about that. How could Lora possibly afford all of Tony's toys now that she relies on just her paycheck alone to take care of herself and the kids? His motorcycle, jon boat, and the '66 on blocks will all have to be sold.

"Need any help?" Mo asks.

She shrugs. "Maybe. I don't know yet. I'll let you know if I do."

He pats her arms consolingly and they both turn to gaze out the window. I shift in my seat and peer out of my own window, watching the passing tree line and houses go by as we drive. The sky is still a murky collection of dark clouds on a stone gray background. The cab feels stuffy, so I crack the window open. The crisp air filters in, and it smells of impending rain. I eye the encroaching storm that is slowly churning overhead, and a memory surfaces.

It's of Nik, and the odd thing he said. *"Funny how the weather seems to match your mood."* I think about that, realizing I feel grumpy and just downright glum, which seems to mimic the weather above me. *That's ridiculous.* Then I recall the previous day. How happy I felt, how carefree. My stomach knots as I make another comparison. The sun was shining yesterday. A complete opposite of this dreary day. I cast my eyes upward again.

Connecting the dots further, I think about the terrible storm that knocked the electricity out during my altercation with Tony. And further still, the desperation, the rage that ensued afterward. The tornado. *No. That's absolutely ludicrous, not to mention entirely implausible.* Nik was just making a silly observation. There is no truth behind it.

I daydream about his eyes, the pools of crystal clear waters whose depths I could only wish to explore. And that smile, with those plunging dimples that begged to be touched.

"Thank goodness the sun is coming out," Mo says, interrupting my thoughts. "We all could use a little sunshine today."

Astonished, I gape out the window. The sun's rays are sifting through the rolling clouds. Golden bars of light shine down, illuminating everything it touches. *Did I do this?* The sky seems to break apart like puzzle pieces, revealing brilliant blue patches beneath the bleak storm clouds. *No fucking way...*

Thoughts of Nik continue to tumble forth. The warmth of his hand on mine, and the sweet smell that encompasses him. I realize then how much he affects me. How my stomach tickles with excitement whenever I think of him, or the way my skin warms pleasantly in very tender places each time he smiles that delicious smile of his.

"Well, well, well." Mo says. "Mother nature must be bi-polar." He chuckles. "Cause that bitch just turned on a dime. Will you look at that?" He jabs his thumb toward the window.

I gaze across the span of the cab, and out window beside him. There, in the open field of wheat that lines the back roads of Chion is a breath-taking rainbow. Its arc of colors emerge out of the clouds, and stretches across the sky, like a pathway leading straight to heaven's doors. Something in me rattles my blood, echoing in my veins with the solid understanding that my thoughts of Nik did this. *I* did this…

Chapter 9

I run a brush through my hair, staring at my reflection in the mirror, as I silently curse Mo for setting me up on this stupid blind date. With each snarl of knotted hair I find, I yank angrily at them, grumbling low in frustration. I finally toss my brush down, watching it slide across the dresser and knock over a perfume bottle. I leave it. *Damn you Mo.* I stomp to my closet. The first item I put my hands on, I snatch from the hanger, and trudge back to the full-length mirror with it balled in my fists. *Fuck Mo. And fuck this god-damn date.*

I pull the dress over my head, and shove my arms through the sleeves. I glare at myself in the mirror, crossly smoothing the pleats of the purple fabric. *This is as good as it's gonna get.* I slip a headband through my hair, and grab my patchwork messenger bag. Mo arranged for my date to meet me at Leu Bordos, thank God. This means that, if necessary I can hightail it out of there. I step into a pair of sparkly black flats and head darkly out of the house.

The drive to the restaurant goes by too quickly, not giving me enough time to prepare myself for the hours ahead. I park my car beneath the neon sign of Leu Bordos and am forced to take a moment, right there in the parking lot. I breathe deeply, and lean back against the headrest. *It's just one evening. I can do this.* With a sigh of resignation, I drag myself out of my car and up the sidewalk. Leu Bordos' lobby is full of people waiting to be seated. I push through the throng of bodies, toward the hostess at the podium. She wears the typical Leu Bordos uniform. Starched white shirt, and black slacks.

She greets me with a smile. "How many in your party?"

"Uh. Two, but I'm waiting on someone."

"Name?"

"Abby Cox," I say, looking around the candle-lit restaurant. Couples murmur softly over steaming plates of pasta, and flutes of red wine.

"Abby?" a voice says.

I turn around to find an attractive man with neatly combed hair approaching me. He's dressed nicely, khaki pants paired with a pale blue shirt. He looks a little apprehensive, but overall, he's quite cute. *Mo sure can pick them.*

"Morrison's cousin, right?"

I nod. "That's right." I fumble with the zipper on my messenger bag. I can feel my cheeks warming, though I'm not sure why.

"I'm David." He reaches out to shake my hand, and like a fool, I glance down at it, hesitating as I remember the surge of electricity that passed through me during my last handshake with Nik. Finally, I stick my hand out, clasping his in a weak shake. Nothing. I swallow and take my hand back with a jerk, sliding it along the fabric of my skirt. *What is wrong with you?*

His brows pinch a little, then he says, "I've already reserved us a table." He looks at the hostess, and tells her, "David Glick."

She scratches his name off her clipboard and says with a smile, "Right this way."

We follow her through the restaurant to a small round table. It's relatively secluded tucked away in the corner of the room, which makes me want to cringe. He pulls my seat out, which is very unexpected, but welcome. I settle into the plush cushion, and allow him to help me in. The table is draped with a red tablecloth. The silverware wrapped fancily within a golden napkin.

David sits across from me and opens the leather bound menu, his dark eyes dart back and forth, as he scans the page. I do the same, but instead of perusing the options, I steal glances at him from over the menu. He looks to be in his mid-twenties, and seems well mannered. A few buttons of his polo are undone, revealing some curly chest hair in the exposed wedge of skin. As usual, I sit there, cowering in my own pit of self-doubt, too petrified to break the silence, so instead, I wait for him to speak first. I bite at my lower lip, my stomach twisting in painful, anxious knots as the seconds turn into minutes.

"Ever been here before?" he asks.

"Once," I answer. "You?"

"First time. Got any suggestions?" He scrubs at his chin thoughtfully as he continues to scrutinize the menu.

"The rolls are good." I grimace. *The rolls are good? Really?*

His eyes raise and land on mine. I force a strained smile, though it feels awkward and out of place. Finally he chuckles.

"The rolls huh? Is there a plate of those on the menu?"

I cast my gaze to the table and place my palms over my cheeks, feeling them flare with embarrassment. I want to crawl under the table and disappear.

He lays the menu down, and leans forward on his forearms. His mouth quirks into a sympathetic smile. "Don't be nervous."

I stare at the crimson tablecloth, and mumble, "I'm not good at blind dates."

"So are you better at regular dates?"

I lift my eyes. He's regarding me with what could only be described as pity. And I loathe pity. All my life, I've been dealt a steady dose of it. *Aw. Your mom's dead? You have no friends? Oh, how sad…*

"Not really." I pick at the non-existent lint on my sleeve. "In fact, I hate to break it to you, but you've been suckered."

"Suckered?" He sits back, interested in where this is going. "How so?"

"Mo probably told you I was this…terrific catch. An outgoing, funny, beautiful girl." I breathe out an amused laugh, then look squarely at him when I say, "I'm sorry to be the bearer of bad news, David, but as you can plainly see…you've been duped."

His smile broadens. "Well actually…he did say you were funny, and beautiful, but he didn't once call you outgoing. His actual words were, 'she's a bit of a killjoy, but once you look past that…she's really cool.'"

I arch an eyebrow, easily hearing Mo say just that. *Asshole.*

The tension surrounding me like a shawl lightens. Though, I still want this night to be over as fast as possible. As long as he's with me, David is in imminent danger. I pray he's having an unpleasant time, if only to keep him safe. *Not to mention alive and breathing.*

Dinner passes with polite conversation, and delicious food. David is a nice guy, and giving him the brush off is going to be harder than I imagined. If only he was a jerk, then I'd have no problem breaking into bitch-mode and seeing to it that he thoroughly despises me, and Mo for arranging the entire thing.

****

The curtains close, and the cast lines up to take their final bow. *It's over, and so is this date. Thank God.* The audience files out of the auditorium, following the velvet ropes, and ushers obediently, like sophisticated cattle.

We filter into the mass of bodies, which eventually spills out into the plaza. It's busy with people walking to and fro. Families with strollers, couples holding hands, and professionals in business suits chatting on cellphones. David and I stand for a moment near the ticket booth, watching the collection of bodies, all illuminated beneath the blinking marquee sign.

Horns blare and some individuals try to shout above the noise. I swallow, and toy with the strap of my messenger bag. There's so many people all around. Too many. I feel breathless, and begin to panic. *I've got to get out of here.* The hubbub and din starts to suffocate me…and in all my introverted glory, I say, "I'm going to puke." I dart across the sidewalk, and duck into a quiet alley. Long shadows stretch across the pavement, and it smells of piss but compared to the chaos in the street, I'd rather take my chances with the rats and the axe murderer who may or may not be lurking in the darkness. I lean against the brickwork, dragging ragged breaths through my teeth as I fight to regain control over my body.

David steps up beside me. "Are you okay?"

"Where did all those people come from?"

"It's Friday night, and it's downtown Chion. It's always like this. Have you never been out on a Friday night?"

I look at him sheepishly.

He nods knowingly. "I take that as a no."

"Remember to punch Mo when you see him." I gaze down the length of the alley. Battered trashcans sit beneath a flickering security light. A raccoon must have pilfered its dinner from one, because the metal can is tipped over, litter spilling out everywhere.

David laughs, but it's a little forced. I turn my eyes to him, and he seems a little uncomfortable. *I made him that way.* I know I did. I always do. With my edginess and overall poor social skills, I tend to sap the energy and interest out people.

"You can go on home David." I straighten, and rest my hands on my messenger bag. I hold it in front of me like a barrier, though I have no reason to feel threatened by David. I suppose it's just a common reflex to keep people at a safe distance. "I'm sorry for wasting your time tonight." I pivot around him, and start walking out of the alley, my shoes scuff quietly across the pavement as I move. "Good night."

David catches up with me, walking at a steady clip beside me. "Let me at least walk you to your car."

"No thank you." I weave into the mass of people, realizing some are tourists, taking in the sights, while others are young clubbers, barhopping along the neon lit strip. I move at a hurried pace, desperate to get away from the bustle of downtown Chion, not to mention put distance between David and me. Sure, the date went better than I imagined, but I'm only here out of obligation to Mo. I have no interest in David. And David has zero interest in me.

"Come on Abby. Mo will bitch slap me if he finds out I let you walk through town alone. I'm sure he knows your phobia."

Phobia? I abruptly stop walking, and a plump man with an ice cream cone bumps into me. A glob of cold ice cream smears across the back of my neck. My shoulders shoot up at the sudden chill that ripples through me. I gasp, and whip around to face the man.

"You owe me a cone," he exclaims. His face is ruddy against his pale skin tone and his nose is bulbous, hanging from his face like a squash on a vine. His lame attempt at a comb-over only draws more attention to his shiny, round head.

I gape at him. *Is he serious?* He sticks the empty cone in my face, and something snaps in me. I slap his hand, sending the cone sailing to the ground. I stomp on it furiously, taking my bitterness toward Mo, and this sham of a date out on the cone, smashing it into a gooey mess on the sidewalk before stomping away. *I'm going to kill my cousin!*

I weave through the mass of people, keeping my head down and shoulders squared as though I'm a linebacker barreling my way toward a final goal. People do not part for me, in fact they're all elbows as they shove past me. Cool air-conditioned air spills out of the opened doors of local dives, and tourists meander through late-night souvenir shops. I keep moving, ignoring the peddlers on the sidewalk, and even covering my ears against the thumping music that rattles against the glass panes of taverns and bars.

Finally, I find my way back to Leu Bordos, hurrying through the now packed parking lot. As I pull open the door, I hear footsteps rapidly approaching. I turn in time to see David jogging up to me. He's breathless when he stops in front of me. His cheeks are flushed pink, and he takes a moment to catch his breath.

"What the hell are you doing?" I ask, irritated.

"I…I thought we had a good time tonight?" His words come out in pants.

"Are you fucking serious? It was a disaster and you know it." I narrow my eyes at him, suspicious. *Did Mo pay him?* I know it's a delusional thought and a bit paranoid, but I can't help but consider it. "You have no interest in seeing me again."

He runs a hand through his hair. "Maybe not, but I intend to end the date properly."

I glare at him now. "What are you talking about?"

"Mo is good guy, and I don't want him to think I didn't give this date an honest try."

I ball my fists at my sides. "Did he *pay* you to take me out?"

David's eyes widen a fraction. "Pay me? No, he didn't pay me. I'm not a damn gigolo." His eyes squint, and his gaze flickers away for a split second.

He's lying.

"You're a sweet girl Abby. I had a good time, honest I did." He closes the gap between us, forcing me to retreat a few steps. My back presses against the car, and I can feel a bubble of panic churning in my gut. *What is he doing?*

"You just said you have no interest in seeing me again," I blurt out.

"Why don't you change my mind," he whispers, reaching out and tracing my cheek with a finger. I cringe at his touch. It's too intimate, too close. Alarms sound off in my head, sending adrenaline through my bloodstream. *No, this is not happening.*

Before I can shove him away, he swoops in, and clutches my arms, pulling me into his chest. His lips press against the corner of my mouth, and I seize up. *Oh God, no!*

His kiss is warm on my skin, but all I can imagine is Trevor's look of agony in those last few, still hauntingly fresh, moments. *I will not take another life,* I think. Rousing myself out of my stupor, I flatten both palms against David's chest and push him with all the muscle I can muster. He stumbles backward, his arms flailing around him.

His dark brows pinch over his glaring eyes, and his nostrils flare as he says, "Forget it. The bet's off. I'm out of here." He stalks away, through the maze of parked cars and says over his shoulder, "Good luck finding a man with your hang-ups. Freak."

I stare after him, my chest heaving as I try frantically to draw in air, but my throat just won't allow it. *Bet? Mo fucking bet him to kiss me?* Red blankets my sight, and I slam my fist against my car, denting it. *Damn it.* My hand aches but I ignore it, fully pissed off that Mo would bet someone to kiss me. *What a fucking asshole!* I want—I *need*—to punch something, but my limbs feel heavy, rooting me to the pavement as I attempt to corral and dam my anger. *Save if for Mo,* I think.

I don't notice the storm clouds rolling overhead until a heavy rain lets loose above me. It's continual, raining down like sharp daggers, pelting me relentlessly until I take cover inside my car. I hastily shut the door behind me. The rain beats against the windshield and hood, echoing in the small cab. My clothes are saturated, sticking to my skin as I look out the window blindly, not really seeing the wash of rain around me, as I'm far too engulfed in my resentment to think about anything else. *How could Mo do that to me? He knows that I'm not interested in dating, let alone kissing anyone.* Thunder erupts, rumbling around me like knocked pins in a bowling alley.

I sit, drenched, and pissed off like a wet cat in a cage. I beat my fists against the steering wheel and let out a scream. Lightning brands the sky, casting a golden light across the parking lot. The wind picks up, rocking my car slightly, but I continue to screech, letting my frustration loose, and not giving a damn who can hear me. I am fucking livid, and without Mo around to tear into, this is my only way of releasing some of the pent-up fury. I close my eyes and let another roar rip through me. It rattles my vocal cords, but it's exhilarating to expel my rage this way. When I'm through, I'm left feeling spent, my throat vibrating and achy as I open my weary eyes.

I'm shocked to find the rain has slackened, but amidst the storm clouds is a swirling mass of ferocious wind. *A tornado.* My heart rate surges, ratcheting a few heated notches, as yet again, I'm staring into the heart of a dangerous tornado.

The funnel touches down in the parking lot, sending a car soaring through the air, and crashing into the back of Leu Bordos. The sound is deafening, as the buildings' cement walls crumble around the crushed vehicle. The kitchen of Leu Bordos is exposed, from the silver SUV laying in a pile of rubble. Restaurant employees dart frantically all around, like frenzied ants in a disturbed mound. *Oh no. No, no, no. Please be a dream. Please be a dream.* I shake my head back and forth, but I do not rouse from this nightmare.

I stare at the tornado, watching with sickening realization that, this time, it just may kill me. It pulsates with rage. As much as I hate to admit it, I know deep in my gut, that my anger bred this. So how do I control it? How do I tame this beast of my creation? *Happy thoughts?* Although if feels silly, I force myself to picture, kittens, puppies, rainbows, and everything else that may calm the raging storm.

It continues to tread the space between us like a stealthy warrior, hell-bent on destroying the enemy. *Me.*

Chapter 10

I do something incredibly stupid. I open the door, and step outside. My feet imbed in the asphalt as I stare, unmoving into the gaping mouth of the monster. It's dark, and menacing, like I'm looking down the barrel of a loaded gun. It hovers closer, wind sweeping at dangerous speeds around me, and the streetlights flicker a few times before the lamp bursts, sending shattered glass pinging across the pavement.

I drop to the ground and cover my head. *Dear God, make it stop!* The tornado begins to howl like a wounded dog. The sound grates across my bones, and shakes me to the core. I'm literally quaking with fear, and my knees refuse to cooperate. The asphalt chews into my skin as I huddle close to the ground, and cover my ears, though it's futile against the horrific cries of the storm. It merely muffles the angry shrieks, as it screams like a banshee above me.

A strong hand grips my wrist, and yanks me to my feet, sending my heart lurching into my throat.

"You really ought to look into anger management," a man says.

I whip my head around to face him, too stunned to respond. *Nik.*

I watch in amazement as he tucks me behind him, shielding me with his body. He lifts his right arm toward the tornado, and braces himself by spreading his legs apart. His hand trembles, and he groans as though he feels the weight of the storm in his palm. The tornado bays like a wolf as the mouth of the funnel breaks apart, like a shattering jawbone. I scream, and cling to Nik from behind, burying my face between his shoulder blades. The muscles in his back are corded like thick wire, taut and ready to spring into action. I close my eyes tight, pressing my face deeper into his damp T-shirt. I become engulfed in his sweet scent of honeysuckle and rain, and it soothes me like a comforting balm.

The wind dies down to a gentle breeze, sending small bits of debris and dirt scattering across the cars like sprinkled dust motes in the air. Hesitantly, I lift my face and peer over his shoulder, fisting his shirt in my hand. He's murmuring softly, but I can't make out what he's saying. The tornado eventually dissipates entirely. The only trace of its existence is the damage to Leu Bordos, as well as my own severely wind-chapped cheeks.

My breath comes in labored pants, and I reluctantly loosen my grip on Nik. I let my arms dangle at my sides, as I survey the eerie silence surrounding us. The storm is gone. My gaze shifts around the parking lot. It is ravaged with fallen debris. The storm left a trail of broken asphalt from where it touched down, but most of the damage is isolated to Leu Bordos. I'm racked with guilt. I know it's *my* fault. *I* created the monster, and it took Nik to tame it. *But how is that possible?*

He slowly turns to face me. His hair is flattened against his scalp, long strands sweep across his forehead. His eyelashes are wet from the rain, and he lowers them fleetingly. They are so thick, and long that

I'm envious. He wears a black T-shirt beneath a sleeveless, hooded vest. His jeans are sodden, just as my own clothes are, and I wonder briefly what I look like. I touch my hair, which is hanging in matted clumps, so I attempt to smooth it out.

I want to ask Nik about the tornado, and how he conquered it, but just the thought of saying it out loud seems crazy. Instead, I busy myself with wringing out the heavy pleats of my skirt, watching him from the corner of my eye. His lips purse tightly, practically disappearing as he wrestles with something internally. I wait him out, eager for him to explain what just happened. I stare at him incredulously, swept away by the clarity of his gem-like eyes. Like fine jewels, they sparkle even in the absence of light, and their genuine beauty is breath taking.

Finally he breaks the silence. "Do you have any idea of what you are?"

I give a faint shake of my head; snaring him with a desperate gaze, imploring him to *please*, enlighten me. "I've always known in my heart I wasn't normal, that something within me is *different*, otherworldly even." I stare at him, waiting for an explanation, my wet clothes casting a chill upon my skin. I hug myself to keep from shivering, my lips quivering as I fight back the impending tears. "Please. If you know what any of this means. I need to know," I plead. "Please. Tell me what I am."

The muscles in his jaw flex as he ponders this.

Please, I think. *Please. Just tell me.*

Regarding me with eyes as sharp as a hawk's, he says, "You're a Sky Sorcerer."

Sky Sorcerer? I waver on my feet, vertigo

threatening to pull me under at any moment. Before I can register his movement, Nik steadies me by holding firm to my shoulders. His scent floats through the air, enveloping me in its sweetness. "Nik," I start, studying his handsome face intently. "Did you really, just stop that tornado?"

He inhales deeply, and his mouth curves into a terse frown. "Yes," he answers plainly. "I dissipated the storm you created. And it took a lot of strength to do so."

My knees give out, and I collapse into his arms. "This isn't real," I say into his broad chest. "It can't be. You said yourself no one can control the weather."

"That was before I knew what you were," he replies with a tone that is almost tender.

I can feel his voice rumble through his chest as he speaks, his shirt is cool against my flushed cheek. His damp skin does nothing to douse the enchanting scent that surrounds him, and I find myself drawing in deep breaths of it. *Of him...*

"I had my suspicions," he continues, "but it's clear now that you are not merely a mortal. Tell me Abby, do you possess a Mark?"

"A Mark?" I swallow, somehow knowing without a shred of doubt he's speaking of the odd collection of amber scars that stretch across my back. Slowly I straighten my spine, and incline my head to the side.

With my eyes set on his, I smooth away the rain-soaked hair that conceals the feathery tendril of scars that mark the area just behind my ear. His eyes quickly light on the Mark, and his lips part as he sucks in a surprised gasp.

"So it's true," he murmurs. "You are a Bearer."

"A Bearer? I don't understand."

Before Nik can explain anything, the scream of police sirens roar past us. An ambulance is close on its heels, speeding through the parking lot behind the marked car with its lights flashing furiously.

My chest feels heavy with guilt. *I could have killed somebody...*

"Come." Nik extends a hand toward me. "Let me see you home."

I eye him as I consider it, recalling the last time our palms touched. The sizzle of heat, and spellbinding charge that ran beneath my skin as though my insides were lit up with electricity. *I want—no—I need to feel that again.* I take his hand eagerly, expelling a soft gasp as we touch. Again, I feel the spark as it simmers at the point of contact, then it flares through the rest of me, arrowing straight to my core.

"What about my car?"

"You can get it later. You are in no condition to drive."

He stands before me, and clasps my other hand. He gazes at me, unblinking, holding me firmly in place with just the weight of his stare. His chest rises and falls with deep and even breaths. The din from the emergency vehicles fades in the distance, as all I hear...is *him.* All I see...is *him.*

"What are you—"

"Silence," he commands, gripping my hands tighter. "Tonight, we travel by wind." He continues to stare directly into my eyes, like a laser on point. The air around us crackles with an invisible charge, sending a trickle of alarm through me. *Travel by wind? What does that even mean?* Something catches my eye, and I shift my gaze over his shoulder. I squint at it, and realize with a gasp that the air surround us is warping, wavering like a cloud of smoke caught in a windstorm.

A strong breeze whips around us, lifting my hair off of my back. I flinch against it, as it blows across my face. It's virtually silent, though you'd expect to hear the wind whistling past. The gust rushes on, like raging water over rapids, and then I feel weightless. I don't see the street moving beneath me, or even notice the change in location until I'm back firmly upon my feet.

With a startled gasp, I notice we're standing in my backyard. I gape, wonderstruck, at the length of grass that stretches from fence end to fence end. My modest brick home sits to our left. The back light is glowing, from where I left it on. *Oh my god.*

We're beside my rope hammock. It swings gently from the trees. The scent of mimosa flowers fills my senses, rooting me to the jarring reality that just seconds ago, I stood in Leu Bordos parking lot. Now I'm standing in my own backyard. *How in the hell?*

I look at Nik, where he's watching me with cool, impassive eyes. My gaze travels down his muscular chest, and follows along his arms to where our hands are still tightly locked. My heart is knocking wildly within my chest, and I'm tempted to rip myself from his grip, but I don't. I *can't.*

"What the hell was that?"

"Elemental Travel," he explains. "The wind carried us."

His fingers flex, and I reluctantly pull away before he does. My hands feel empty when I do, and the air between us no longer carries the charge, or the eerie stillness. The neighbor's dog across the street barks a few times, and a car with a thumping bass rolls past.

I try to pluck a coherent thought from my rampant brain. "How can any of this be possible? It doesn't make any sense." I sink into the hammock, the ropes twist and tighten beneath my weight. I twine my fingers through the rope loops, watching my feet as they drag across the ground as I rock.

"Reality doesn't need to make sense. It is what it is, and you have no choice but to live with it."

I look up, scowling, not liking his response. He's watching me from above, like a mighty king in a tower overlooking his kingdom.

I grunt. "Are you saying I should just accept things, without understanding them?" I give him a defiant stare. "If so, then you're shit out of luck on that one, Nik. I don't just *take* whatever's handed to me. I just *created* a tornado. Damn it, I *deserve* a fucking explanation." My tone grows more hysterical by the second, and I bite back saying any more until I can compose myself.

Nik crosses his thick arms over his chest, and stares back at me with an aloofness that makes me want to pound my fists against his rock-hard torso. We glower at each other for a long time, but I lose the battle of wills, and look away.

My fingers tighten on the hammock's ropes, my knuckles turning white beneath my skin. I glare at them as I say through gritted teeth, "I just want answers Nik." I lift my face, my eyes casting upward, landing on his unapologetic stare. "And by the looks of things…you're the only one who can provide them."

He sits down beside me. The shift of weight on the hammock sends me pitching sideways, and I slam into the length of him.

"Oh," I exclaim. My hands flounder as the hammock swings, and I brace myself by grabbing ahold of his strong thigh. My face flares with heat, as I look down at my fingers, digging deep into his denim-clad leg. I yank my hand away as if he were a scalding pot.

"I...I'm sorry," I stammer, clumsily adjusting myself on the hammock. I try to put space between us, but with him easily outweighing me by close to a hundred pounds, my body keeps dipping toward him. My muscles burn with exertion, as I struggle to hold myself at a safe distance.

Nik rests his elbows on his knees, and stares out into the darkness. He scrubs his hands back and forth as if trying to warm them. I take the opportunity to study him. The moonlight plays beautifully against his blond hair. Silver upon gold. Like expensive treasure, I gaze, transfixed by the stunning beauty of it. My eyes travel across his handsome face and down the lean muscles of his biceps.

He swings his icy glare on me, startling me. My ears warm with embarrassment for being caught staring. His mouth is set in a serious line, and he turns back to gaze out to the space before him.

"You possess the Mark of Light, which means one of your ancestors was struck by lightning." He sits up, twisting his torso to look me straight in the face. "Those hit by a fire bolt are branded with Marks...like the ones you bear." His eyes shift to my neck, and I can almost feel the scar come alive upon my skin, tingling with warmth. "The Mark is seeped within bloodlines, passing through generations of kin, until finally revealing itself again." He slowly lifts his hand toward me, hesitating, as though silently asking for permission. I close my eyes for a beat, then suck in a gasp as he traces the length of the scar, following its curves as it wraps around my earlobe and down the column of my neck. His touch is as light as a feather; stoking a want so primal within me, I have noticeable difficulty ignoring it. Especially when he is sitting so close.

My mouth slacks, and my heart pounds against my breast like a moth caught in a net. I lean closer, and the intoxicating scent of him engulfs me, impeding on my good judgment. For a foolish second, I lose myself in him, gazing at his full lips, longing to feel the plush warmth of them against my own.

But that can never be…

The feeling in my stomach flutters, like an awakened butterfly from a cocoon. *I cannot feel like this. It's too dangerous. For him and for me.* The poem that haunts me surfaces. *I know nothing of love, so why do I pretend, to agree tis a powerful drug, Deadly enough to seal my lover's end. If our hearts were meant, If our lives to be laced; Then shall I regret this kiss, That puts a frown upon my lover's face.*

This want, this need, must be smothered. I shiver from his tender touch, and shrink away, terrified of the stirring need within me. Sensing my apprehensiveness, his brow creases, but thankfully he doesn't request an explanation. He just lets his hand fall to his side, and he regards me with a thoughtful air. I open my mouth to ask him of my curse, my kiss of death, but the words do not come. It's then that I realize my sanity is tottering precariously on a blade's edge, and worry more insight on my strange abilities, will officially do me in. I tighten my jaw to remain quiet, though my mind is reeling from not only this harrowing ordeal, but also my newfound knowledge.

"Sky Sorcerers can manipulate the weather," Nik explains. "You have not been shown how to rein in your power, thus making you very volatile."

"Are you a Sky Sorcerer?"

He gives a slight shake of his head. "No."

My shoulders sink, as disappointment pierces through me. I thought I found someone like me, but clearly I am alone. I glance at his hands. They're strong, and his nails are trimmed short. They seem ordinary enough, but those hands just dispelled a raging tornado. Nik is supernatural, there's no denying that. The question is, what exactly is he? If only to mollify my own selfish curiousness, I say, "You're not human."

His jawline tenses, and he replies evenly, "No. I am not."

"So, then…what exactly are you?"

"I'm a Storm Thief." He juts his strong chin out proudly. "Son of Perun and Diva-Dodola." I detect a hint of falter in his voice, but he quickly regains his confidence, and says flatly, "Have I given you enough answers for tonight?"

"Almost," I reply. There is one more question that remains to be asked. "Were you watching me the other day?"

His blue eyes hold firmly to mine, but he doesn't offer a response.

"I was right here, in my backyard, in this hammock." I swallow, unsure if I should continue. "I…I smelled you…" I feel myself blush, and I fleetingly look away, intimidated by his level stare.

His lips curve into a ghost of a smile. "If I say

yes?"

My eyes move to his. "Then that'd make you a stalker."

His mouth spreads into a smile, and he gives a little laugh. Like notes lifted from the strings of a harp, it's beautiful and enchanting.

"So is that a confession?" I ask.

Though a sweet smile stays upon his full lips, his eyes turn icy. "I'm everywhere Abby. I'm in the sky above you, in the earth below you, and in the air all around you."

He stands, lurching the hammock into motion. I'm tossed back against the ropes, and I twine my fingers through the loops to steady myself. As I rock back and forth, I watch his eyes narrow with concentration. The space around him distorts and shimmers with a magical charge.

"You *will* sense me again Abby. Count on that."

His body bursts into tiny fragments, and is carried away by a gust of chilly air. Like snowflakes on a breeze, all traces of Nik disappear as the wind disintegrates into the night.

I inhale, feeling the boulder of contempt lift from my chest. I have answers. Even if they only create more questions...I *finally* have answers. I cross my arms in front of me, carrying the vindication like a shield. I am a Sky Sorcerer. I can create storms...

Chapter 11

I awaken to a rush of cool air ghosting across my face. I blink my eyes open sleepily, startling when I notice Nik standing at the foot of my bed. *Oh!* I bolt upright.

"What the hell are you doing here?" I question sharply.

"You need to retrieve your car...remember?" His eyes flicker to my chest, concealed only by a sheer camisole. A silk strap dangles off my shoulder. I quickly slip it back in place, and hastily draw my comforter to my chin.

How could I forget? Last night's events are forever burned to my memory. The tornado. The Elemental Travel. Learning of Sky Sorcerers and Storm Thieves...all permanently seared into the very grain of my being. "You can't just whisk yourself into my room whenever you feel like it."

He grunts, and crosses his arms in front of him. "I started at your front door, but you failed to answer."

"Did you knock?" I ask with a tone of irritation.

"Yes."

And I didn't hear it? I grapple with this, retracing the entire night, starting from the moment I finally fell into bed. I slept all night. No nightmares. I don't have time to make sense of it because Nik suddenly unfolds his arms, and is on the move. I watch him with round eyes, intimidated by the way he prowls, like a seasoned hunter stalking prey. He travels unhurriedly along the edge of my bed until he's standing beside my nightstand. At his impressive height, he towers over me like a looming shadow. My heart begins to hammer against my ribs.

"You are stricken with nightmares." It's not a question, but a cold-hard fact. I don't say anything—I can't.

"But they have recently subsided." He holds me in a hard stare, with eyes as icy as massive glaciers.

"How do you know that?"

"Sorcerers unfortunately suffer from ailments until finding their Polar Mate."

"Polar Mate?" I sit up higher, intrigued. "What's that?"

"The elements travel in polar opposites. Earth…wind. Fire…water. Sky Sorcerers require the same to function properly, and to rein in their power. They are dangerous beings without their Mate."

My mind muddles with questions. *What kind of ailments? Do I have a Polar Mate?* My curiosity is piqued to the point of giddiness. *Does this mean…?* I forget about my attire, fold my fluffy comforter away from my chest, and roll onto my knees. "Does that mean, I have a soul mate somewhere?"

"You have a Polar Mate somewhere," he corrects.

I don't miss his eyes skating across my bare shoulders, and I cast my own gaze down at my naked thighs. My cotton boy shorts are riding like a second skin, clinging tightly to my ass like underwear. Heat fills my cheeks as I try to adjust them, but they only cover the creases along my upper thighs. I give up, and yank my blanket back over me with a frustrated grunt.

His mouth quirks, and it's obvious he's finding amusement in my discomfort.

I huff in annoyance, and just as I'm about to say something smart, there's a knock at my front door. I recognize it immediately, which means that in two seconds, Mo is going to lift the welcome mat and remove the spare key to my house. In five seconds he'll be turning the door knob and letting himself in. In three seconds he'll—

"Abby!" Mo calls from the living room.

"Oh shit!" I leap from the bed, but my foot tangles in the folds of the sheets, sending me lurching through the air like a ballerina with two left feet. Nik reaches out with reflexes quick as lightning, and catches me by the waist. His warm hands brand my bare flesh, and my breath snags in my throat.

"Abby?" Mo is getting closer, I can hear his footsteps coming down the hall. "Are you decent? Even if you're not, I'm still coming in."

"It's my cousin," I explain.

Nik releases me, his eyes shift to the bedroom door.

"If he sees you in my room, he'll assume...uh...well, you know." I turn around and scurry to my door, placing a hand on the knob. "I'll never hear the end of it. So please, you got to—" I look over my shoulder to plead with Nik to leave, but the room is empty. "Go..." My eyes dart furiously around my bedroom. *No way...* I don't see a trace of him anywhere, then, by some sort of automatic urge, I take in a deep breath. Just a scant scent of rain and honeysuckle linger in the air, and somehow, I just *know* he's still here. *Somewhere.*

The doorknob jingles beneath my fingers, and I yelp, forgetting all about Mo. He pushes the door ajar and enters, his dark eyes quickly falling on me, and my flustered appearance.

"What's with you? Didn't you hear me?"

I glower at him, crossing my arms over my chest. "I should kick you in the balls right now."

He laughs. "Please don't. I'm quite fond of Coco and her handbags." He covers his crotch with both hands, shielding them protectively.

"Coco?" I gape at him. "*It's* a female?" I feel my face twist with disgust.

"You got a problem with that?" He gives me a snarky look. "It's sensitive as hell, and is afraid of being alone. So yeah, I figure, it's got to be a woman."

I roll my eyes at him.

"Enough talk about me, I want to hear about your date." He wriggles his manicured brows at me. "What did you think of David?"

My blood warms, and I glare at him, furious and hurt all at once.

"Well?" he urges, his eyebrows arching expectedly.

"You god damn asshole," I say through tight lips.

He pokes his bottom lip out, pouting like a child. "I take it you didn't like him?" He strolls to my bed and plunks down, bouncing lightly on the mattress. He folds his arms behind his head, and regards me with keen interest. "He's cute. He has a job. What's the problem?"

"Nothing, besides the simple fact that the entire date was a sham."

He screws his eyes tight and mutters, "Fuck."

"Yeah. I found out about the damn bet you had going on. What the hell Mo?" I stomp angrily across the floor. "Why would you do that to me?"

"It was a silly bet Abby. Don't get your panties in a twist."

"A silly bet?" My voice rises a few notches. "Mo, you sold me out."

He rolls over onto his stomach, and splays his fingers on the bed. "Oh don't be so damn dragmatic." He examines the clear coat of polish on his nails, and swings his long legs back and forth like a schoolgirl. "Speaking of drags, Jizzy's Jazz Quartet is playing tonight at The Bouffant. Want to go?"

I grit my teeth, and shake my fists with impatience.

He glances over his shoulder at me. "What?"

I throw my hands in the air. "You have got to be the biggest jackass in the world."

His brows pinch, and his mouth curves into a frown. "Why?"

"You have the balls to sit there and ask me to go see Jazzy Jizz—"

He snickers. "Jizzy's Jazz Quartet," he corrects.

"Same difference. It's still a distasteful play on words." *We're getting off track*, I tell myself. Which is common when you're riding the crazy train with Mo as the conductor. "How can you act like you didn't do anything wrong? You bet David to date me."

"Date you? Honey, I didn't bet him to *date* you. I bet him to *kiss* you."

My blood runs cold, and I feel as though there's a giant hand wrapped around my ribcage, squeezing like a vise. "You what?" I hold my head in my hands, an ache quickly spreading through my skull, and down my neck.

"He agreed to the date 'cause he thought you were cute. I just tossed in a bet that he couldn't kiss you on the first date. It was stupid, but innocent enough."

"Mo. It's far from innocent. You of all people should know that."

"I thought it would prove your little…" He lifts his fingers and marks quotations in the air. "Theory about kissing is foolish." The bedsprings squeak as he hoists himself off the mattress. He smooths his fuchsia tank top over his stonewashed jeans and inspects the fringed sash around his waist. His boredom with this discussion is evident, but we are far from done.

"I told you what my kiss does," I continue.

"Child, please." He hangs his hands low on his hips. "Let go of that lame excuse, and just admit you're asexual already."

"Asexual?" I repeat with revulsion. "I'm not asexual."

He takes several long strides to my full-length mirror, and cocks his head to the side, admiring his reflection. He fluffs his spiky ebony locks, which looks a lot like a prickly porcupine hide sitting atop his head, and says, "It has to be the only explanation on why you refuse to date, or even kiss a dude."

I slap a hand over my eyes, and drag it down my face. "I *can't* Mo. I *literally* cannot kiss anyone. I'll kill them." I begin to pace the floor. My bare feet slapping against the hardwood with each step.

Mo clucks his tongue, and rolls his eyes so hard I swear they will roll right out of his head.

"You're being about as ridiculous as anklets on a pair of cankles."

I stop in my tracks, glaring at him with all the intensity I can muster, but it's all for naught. He's gazing at himself in the mirror, totally oblivious to the daggers being tossed at him.

He licks a finger and runs it over his eyebrows. "When you decide to check out of La La Land…call me." He twirls around, and sashays out of the room. Jack squawks from his cage as the front door opens and clicks shut.

A gush of ice-cold air whips across the back of my neck, sending goose bumps across my skin.

"What did you mean, when you said your kiss will kill?"

I shriek, and whip around to stand face to face with Nik. His eyes latch onto mine with a ferociousness that almost physically reaches out and grasps me.

"Don't do that!" I stamp my foot, and although I know it's childish, it's the only reaction that feels fitting at the moment. I glance down at the length of me. Twin peaks poke out from my chemise camisole, and I blush instantly. I cover my chest with splayed fingers and hurry to my closet. *Oh my god!* I tear a pale blue sweater from a hanger and shrug it on. *He saw my nipples!* Humiliated, I quickly wiggle into a snug pair of black jeans and slip on a pair of ballet slippers.

"Again," he growls from behind me. "What did you mean, when you said your kiss will kill?"

I look up at him, and release a sigh of reluctant resignation. "Okay. Geez." I snag my messenger bag from the hook and cross the floor. I take a moment to frame my next words, taking a deep breath as I sit down on the bed, laying the bag across my lap and twining my fingers through the strap. "Eight years ago, I had my first kiss." I lift my eyes to him. "It was also my boyfriend's last."

He arches an eyebrow, interested in hearing more.

I clear my throat, and continue, though it breaks my heart to do so. The memory is so real, so vivid, that I can still feel the crackle of power coursing through my blood. "As we kissed, I felt something stir inside me, as if awakening from being dormant. Like a dragon rousing from its lair."

His brows pinch, and his expression hardens.

"Sorry. I went into metaphor mode…it's a book nerd thing." I look back at my hands and realize they are starting to tremble. "Anyway, I felt something come alive, and it traveled through my body, out my lips and straight into—" *Trevor.* I can't say it; his name hangs at the back of my throat like a lead weight. "Straight into my boyfriend. He…ah…well, he died right there." My nose tickles, and my eyelids feel heavy from the imminent tears collecting behind them. "I…" A sob breaks loose, but I force myself to say it aloud. "I killed him." I weep into my palms, the hot tears working their way through my fingers and trickling across the back of my hands.

The bed dips beside me, and a warm body presses along mine. Like a balm over a stinging wound, his presence soothes me, patiently comforting me until the tears concede. I sniff, and finally lift my head, meeting those striking blue eyes. It's like looking into still waters, my reflection shines clearly within them.

"I'm sorry," he says softly. "I know what it's like to be a danger to others."

I study him, trying to read his features, but they're flat, and expressionless. "What do you mean?"

"I too have poison within my blood."

His lips set into a firm line, and his eyes darken to pits of hard ice. The room around us warps and then, we are floating on a frigid breeze…

Chapter 12

After Nik delivers me to my car, he leaves me alone without so much as a parting word. I sink inside the car and start the engine. *What was that all about?* I roll past Leu Bordos slowly, assessing the damage I caused. The building is roped off with bright yellow caution tape, and a barrel-chested security guard stationed beside the rubble, wards off looters.

So much destruction...

I swallow on a dry throat, and continue on. I'm not due at the library for another half hour, but I go there anyway, needing the distraction. I park, and jog through the double glass doors. I don't bother clocking in yet, because if I do, Barb will ensure that I'm kept busy and there are some things I need to do first. I hurry through the aisles, setting my sights on the mythology section.

The library is virtually silent, aside from the soft scuff of my shoes across the carpeted floor as I round the towering shelves. I scan the titles, then pluck a thick book from the shelf. It's wrapped in a plastic protective cover, and the spine is well worn. The once golden words etched into the leather are long since rubbed away to mere flecks, but I can still make out the title. *Gods of Yore.*

I flip to the index, running my finger down the page as I scan the names. Pandora. Pelops. Perse, Perun. *Perun. That's him.* I slide my fingertip to the right. *Pages 214 and pages 347 through 352.*

I scour through the pages, until finding my destination, page 347. My eyes quickly light upon a picture of a tower of a man, carrying a mighty axe. His copper beard sways in the wind, and his eyes are as stark as white-hot coal. I pour over the text, devouring each and every detail.

Also known as the God of Thunder, Perun reigns the sky with his wife, Diva-Dodola. My eyes dart across the page as I read. After about ten minutes, I turn and lean my back against the shelves, needing to take a moment to reflect. From what I gather, Perun is temperamental, but overall a fair, and noble ruler.

I feel as if the oxygen in the room is depleting, and my head swims with this information, but I read on. Diva-Dodola was captured by Veles, the ruler of Earth and Magic. When she was finally rescued, she was with child and her mental state fragile. Perun cared for her, healing her external wounds, but her mind was nearly lost. Delirious with anger, and fed countless lies and betrayal from Veles, Diva-Dodola was a mere shell of her former self, unfit to raise a child. So, Perun raised the infant alone. Perun did the best he could, but vowed his revenge against Veles.

I close the book with a soft thud. *Nik.* He's the infant, raised by Perun, while his mother wanders the sky, lost in her own body. My chest feels as though someone has taken a crowbar to my heart. *Poor, poor Nik.* Though his mother is physically alive, she's all but dead to the world. Given my own experience growing up without a mother, I can't help but think; *perhaps it would have been better if Veles had killed her.* I quickly dash that thought. *Then that would mean that Nik would not exist.* I can't even imagine a world without Nik anymore. Nor would I want to. With a sigh, I slide the book back into place.

"Holding up the book shelves is not part of your job duties." Barb is peering at me from atop her glasses, her fists resting on each hip. With her sharp nose, and beady eyes, she reminds me of an ancient vulture sizing up long forgotten carrion.

"I…uh." My head is brimming with thoughts, clouding even my most innate functions, such as speaking, walking, and sarcasm. *No smart-ass comeback? Damn, what's wrong with me?*

She arches a brow, and gives me a severe look.

"Work," I eke out. "Now." I turn on my heel, and channel all my brainwaves to moving one foot in front of the other. *How can I work like this?* I somehow make it to the employee workroom, relieved to have done so without looking like a robot in the process. I fumble with my time card and attempt to clock in. It takes me three tries to correctly line up the card beneath the sensor so it prints out the date and time. With Nik at the forefront of my mind, I shove my messenger bag back into my locker and slam the door shut. *Get him out of your head!* I nearly laugh at myself. *Yeah right, like that's ever going to happen.* I re-strategize, and think, *Okay, new plan. Forget about him just long enough to get through the day.* I close my eyes, and draw in a deep intake of air before I set out to make it through the next eight hours…

****

And by some small miracle, I do, but it wasn't without its hitches. Barb was breathing down my neck the entire day, and a particularly unruly group of teenagers kept giggling over the book, *The Idiots Guide to SEX.* Needless to say, I am ready to part the exit doors, and get the hell out of here.

As I stroll across the small parking lot, I fish my cellphone out of the side pocket of my bag, and dial Lora's number before lifting the phone to my ear. It rings twice.

"Hello?" Her voice is low, but doesn't hold the same trace of sadness it has the past week.

"Hey. Just calling to check on ya."

"I'm okay." There's a pause, and I can't help but wonder if she's gauging the truth behind her words. "What are you doing?"

"Just getting off work." I stick the key into the car door and turn, hearing the *whisk* as the car unlocks. I toss my bag inside, then settle myself into the worn bucket seat. I consider telling her about Nik, but I decide against it. What would I say? I met a handsome guy who has rescued me twice from a tornado, which happens to be my own rage manifesting into storms. Oh, and he happens to be a Storm Thief. Whatever *that* is…

"Sold Tony's bike today," she says.

"I'm sorry," I reply, though I'm not sure an apology is really necessary. Perhaps she found it liberating to rid a piece of Tony from her life.

I can hear her soft breath blowing across the receiver, and again, there is silence. I start the engine as I wait for her to speak again. I back out of the slot, maneuver the car through the parking lot, and out onto Linwood Drive.

"I'm sorry," she offers. "I'm not really good company right now."

"It's all right. There's no need to act a certain way for me. You know that. I just want to make sure you're okay."

"Every day is a struggle, but I'm making it through." She must sense my eye roll, because she adds, "Look, Abby, I know you hated Tony. And there's no reason you shouldn't. He was not a good guy. Heck, he wasn't even a decent one. But I did love him, and he was the father of my kids."

"But he was awful to you," I counter. "I don't get how you can mourn someone who treated you like dirt."

"The heart knows nothing except what it feels. It doesn't give a damn about the side effects."

"Well, your side effects should have come with warning labels." I scowl into the phone. I should just let her be. Let her mourn the man who beat her, and kept her under his thumb, but I just *can't.*

A deep sigh crackles through the air. "Yeah. You're right," she admits. "What can I say? My heart is a selfish bastard who doesn't give two shits about me. Damn you heart. I would curse you, and wish you dead, but let's be honest. That would ultimately just screw me in the end."

I can feel her smile, and it makes my mouth respond likewise. *There she is*, I think. I'm slowly getting my best friend back. The funny, carefree girl is in there somewhere, and every now and then I see the ghost of her surface. I make a promise here and now to keep stoking that girl until she breaks loose and emerges again. Lora will return, just as the true Abby will finally find her footing in the world.

I ease my car into the driveway, kill the ignition,

and gather my messenger bag. I stroll across the lawn and suddenly catch a scent of honeysuckle and rain. *Nik.* I whirl around, searching the space around me. Nothing. The sky is taking on a silver sheen as the sun begins to sink behind the tree lines. Birds dart through the air, hurrying back to their warm nests before sunset. Their colors are muted and hard to make out in the waning light.

"I know you're there," I call into the emptiness.

The scent grows stronger, and Nik begins to slowly materialize beside me. I watch in fascination as his form takes on a watery appearance, like a mirage in the desert. The air around him warbles with a fine shimmer, like misting rain. When he finally solidifies, I can't help but notice his taut muscles rippling beneath the fabric of his clothes. My gaze travels across the length of his body. His feet are covered with tough leather boots and he's wearing worn jeans, and a fitted hooded shirt, the sleeves pushed over his elbows. His golden hair mussed to absolute perfection.

"You must learn to harness your emotions."

"Excuse me?"

"I've come to show you," he states. "But first, Elemental Travel."

I eye him for a moment. His thermal shirt is snug, molding to his firm biceps like caramel on candy. The hood is pooled at the nape of his neck.

"Do you own any shirts that don't have a hood?" I ask.

His eyes are glaring for a moment, then he blatantly ignores my question by saying, "We begin now."

"Are you always like this?" I brush past him,

taking care to not touch shoulders, and march to the front door.

"Like what?" He quickly falls into stride with me.

"Straight to the point. No preliminaries, no frills…" I single out my house key and stand poised at the door, ready to unlock it.

"I definitely don't do *frills*," he says.

I give him a sideways glance.

"However, there is *one* thing I do that almost always requires very singular, lavish attention beforehand…"

I choke and drop my keys, which jingle as they connect with the cement slab beneath our feet. I chance a quick look at him, and wish I hadn't. He's smirking at me, and I know without a doubt he's finding humor at my expense. At my own *prudish* expense. He cocks a daring eyebrow, and his mouth twitches further. I tighten my lips into a scowl and bend to retrieve my keys, just as he kneels down. Our foreheads collide and the impact has me swearing under my breath.

"Ow!" My hand shoots up to touch the tender spot, and I probe it tenderly. This is far from the usual rush of desire that ensues after I make physical contact with Nik. Instead it smarts to the point tears prick the corners of my eyes. I lift my gaze to him, and he's rubbing a faint red spot between his eyes, his face twisted into a grimace.

Laughter rumbles deep within my belly, and before long I'm chuckling uncontrollably.

He looks at me through his splayed fingers, still massaging his forehead. "What's so funny?"

I hold my ribs as I say through my laughter, "I actually hurt a big bad *Storm Thief,* just by knocking heads?"

"You have a remarkably solid head." He winces, then drops his hand to his side.

My giggles fade and I glare at him through narrow slits. "Why are you here again?"

"To train you."

"To train me?" I rise and start fumbling for my house key. "Train me for what exactly?"

He straightens to his full height. "Elemental Travel. But first, you'll need to control your emotions. In turn, you will learn to manipulate the elements at your will."

I ponder this, staring blankly at the slab of wood before me. *Manipulate the elements. At will?* My keys feel like anchors in my hands, and my head fills with dozens of questions. *Why me?* seems to be the most reoccurring.

"Abby," he says gently. "I know all of this is…overwhelming." He pauses, possibly waiting for me to agree, but I continue to stare ahead. "And I am sure you have even thought of this to be implausible. This…*other* world hidden amongst your own. But I encourage you to embrace it. You belong in that world, Abby. Just as I do."

I turn to him, and realize a sliver of air is the only boundary between us. My breathing comes out in shallow pants, and I can't help but sweep my eyes across his full lips. They're voluptuous, and they look hungry. The carnal part of me wants to feed them unhurried kisses, and I squirm with longing. The corner of his mouth lifts, drawing me from my salacious daze. My cheeks heat and I have an embarrassingly difficult time putting the key in the lock. Finally, I get it, and push the door open and scoot inside.

Nik follows me in, taking a quick assessment of my living room. I look around myself, checking to make sure it isn't overly messy, or that I'd left out a bra or something. *What does that matter?* I think. *He's already seen me without one.*

The room is tidy, as usual. The sandy colored walls make the room warm and inviting, and the laminate floors are covered with a giant area rug. Jack's cage sits between the double windows. He chirps at us a few times from his swing. An antique desk is tucked into the far corner. A small lamp, which I always keep on, illuminates the pages of a notebook. I feel a pang of guilt, realizing that I haven't sat down and written in days.

I usually write a few lines of poetry every day, but lately my head has been too mixed up to concentrate on much of anything that doesn't consist of Nik, Storm Sorcery, or Lora. I notice dozens of scattered books littering all the available spaces. The desk, the coffee table, the end table, the armrest of the couch and even the seat of the rocking chair are covered with books. It's then that I realize, *Wow. I really am a book nerd.*

I loop the strap of my bag over the coat rack hook, leaving it to dangle as I make my way out of the foyer and farther into the room. I look over my shoulder at Nik, wondering what he's thinking. His eyes quickly settle on me. I know he's about to tell me.

"We should begin now."

I cross my arms and lift an eyebrow at him, silently saying, *See! Straight and to the point.*

His mouth spreads into a smile, casting his handsome features into an even lovelier light. My stomach flutters with delight, and when those twin dimples surface, the flutter accelerates to a frenzy. This charade of indifference is unraveling with each reveal of those damn dimples, and it terrifies me. I quickly work to cinch myself together, grappling for any shred of cool detachment though every fiber within me screams for him. *Yearns* for him. Even just the *smell* of him attracts me like a butterfly to nectar.

I automatically take two paces back, needing space, needing to step out of the bubble of *Nik* scent that sends my pulse roaring.

He scrubs his hands together eagerly. "Ready?"

"Now? Here?" My eyes flick to the wall clock. "It's seven-thirty."

"So? Do you have an eight o'clock bedtime?"

I breathe forcefully through my nose, and stare at him. There's no dissuading him, I don't know why I'm even trying. I massage the inner corners of my eyes, and say, "All right. All right." I look back up at him. "What do we do?"

"First of all, you must be aware of your body." He walks toward me with a purpose, and my heart picks up. His eyes are dead set upon me, like crosshairs on a target. My chest heaves. He looks as though he's about to plow right into me. He sidesteps around me at the last second, nimbly moving behind me.

He bends slightly to speak against my ear. "Be aware of each and every sensation, Abby. The race of your heartbeat. The pull of air as it fills your lungs. Feel the gentle skate of air across your skin. The chill or warmth of it. *Feel* it." His fingers graze my hip. "Inside you, there is a power. It will spark, and when it does, cling to it and will it to heel. It is then, you will be able to call upon the elements."

I nod woodenly, all too aware of his hand on my waist.

"Shall—" My voice cracks, and my cheeks burn with embarrassment. I tuck a piece of hair behind my ear, and try again. "Shall I try it now?"

Nik's hand slips away, but the weight of his touch still lingers hotly upon my skin. He takes a few graceful strides away, then turns back to face me.

"No," he answers, giving his head a little shake. "Elemental Travel will come later. First you will need to govern your emotions. Heed your power."

I wrinkle my nose. "Sounds difficult, and a little frightening."

His lips press into a stern line, and he's on the move before I can even process it. His hands lie heavily upon my shoulders, and he peers into my face. "You can do this Abby. You are a remarkably strong woman."

I'm taken aback, so I stand there dumbfounded as he continues to talk.

"Don't allow your emotions to control you," he says. "That's when your abilities are at the most dangerous, most unpredictable. You *must* learn to yoke the anger, the sadness, the desperation, and swallow it whole."

And how the hell am I supposed to do that?

"I can show you how to locate the power inside you, so when you feel it rising, you can either smother it, or stoke it." His eyes flash, hard as steel and irrefutably intimidating.

I lick my dry lips, and remain quiet.

"When your emotions begin to overtake you, the elements around you respond. It is then, you should feel something deep within you come alive. Many have described it, but not everyone feels it the same way. Some say it's painful, like a fist to the gut. Others say it's euphoric, even...orgasmic." His lips curve into a fraction of a smile, not enough to reveal a dimple, but enough to make me wish it had.

Curiosity eats at me, so I ask, "What does it feel like for you?"

His smile falls into a terse frown, and it's a long, silent moment before replies. "Like poison has charred my insides, and all that remains is tainted power that cuts like razors."

A shudder wracks through me, and he makes no attempt to comfort me. He doesn't offer an explanation, nor does he assure me that that won't happen to me. It's almost as if he wants me to be scared, and if that's true, well, mission accomplished.

"The only way to rein in your emotions is to first allow them to consume you. The pain will be raw, and unyielding, but once you finally allow yourself to immerse in it, it is then you can stand tall amongst your fears and stare them down until they cower at your feet." A gentle waft of Nik's heavenly scent surrounds me, and like a shield, it ensconces me. For a moment, I feel safe. He places a hand on my shoulder, and the now familiar zap of desire surges through me.

"You must relive your pain."

My gut turns, and I know what he's referring to. *Trevor.* I don't meet his flat stare. I can't. Just the thought of reliving that day sends my body into a full-blown panic attack. My head grows heavy, and the room tilts. I cover his hand with mine, clutching it to steady myself.

"Abby?" He digs his fingers deeper into my skin.

I close my eyes and force calming breaths through my nose and out my mouth, counting silently to ten as I do.

"Abby," he repeats with urgency. "Are you all right?"

"Dizzy," I manage to say through the haze of anxiety that is raging upon me like a tidal wave, threatening to swallow me whole.

"Sit," he orders, guiding me to the sofa.

I sink into the cushion and hold my temples. *I can't do this. I can't!*

He crouches before me, our faces becoming level. "Work through it. Do not shut it out."

"I can't do this Nik." I shake my head back and forth, expressing the thoughts that keep repeating like a mantra in my brain. "I can't."

"You can," he insists. "I told you this would be hard, but you *will* overcome it."

"No!" I cover my face with my hands in a desperate attempt to block him out. Block everything out, even for just a moment.

He tugs my hands away. "Damn it Abby." His grip is like iron shackles, strong and unmoving against my wrists. "I didn't lie when I said it would be the worst pain in your life…just as I didn't lie when I said it will pass."

I want to push him away, and cast him from my house. I need to be alone. Whenever the memory of Trevor surfaces, that's how I chose to be. Alone. I begin to sob, but Nik holds firm to me, and his face is grim. The shadows of my poorly lit living room dims the usual brightness of his eyes, and his mouth is twisted into an angry scowl.

"Do you trust me?" he asks, his voice so sharp it feels as though it's cutting right through me.

I blink, which is the undoing for the fragile puddle of tears that is pooling around my eyes. A stream flows, uncaring, down my cheeks and drips from my chin.

He jerks my wrists roughly. "Do. You. Trust. Me?" Each word is hissed through clenched teeth, and for a fleeting beat of a second, I'm tempted to scream *Hell no!* But I know it's a lie. No matter how strange, or how intimidating Nik is, I honestly trust him. I trust him with my very life.

I wet my dry lips, tasting the salt of my tears before I choke out, "Yes."

I feel him relax, his grasp loosens marginally, but his strong hands remain on me. The contact, though not romantic, still ignites me like a firebomb.

"Submerse yourself in the memory…in the grief. Allow yourself to wallow in it. To nearly drown in it." The weight of his stare draws me from my weeping, and I look up to meet him in the eye. "I will be here to pull you out."

"How?"

"Focus on my touch. Use it as a beacon…follow it out of the despair. I will be your anchor."

My breath catches. His words are lovely, and I wish to scribe them to my journal, but somehow I know they are forever seared into my memory. Just as this very moment will be.

"Close your eyes and concentrate on the memories that bring you the most pain, and the most joy. When you feel as though you cannot bear another second, reach for me, Abby."

A pulsating warmth blooms below my waistline, and I stare straight into his glistening blue eyes. The lack of light in the room makes them look steely, much harsher than normal.

I close my eyes, plunging myself into darkness and seek out the horrible images that haunt me every day. Then, I see him. His curly locks bouncing as he lightly jogs toward me, and his smile stretched wide across his youthful face. The knot in my stomach pulls tighter, nearly doubling me over. *Oh Trevor.* It's as though I am right back to that fateful day over eight years ago, standing alone on the outskirts of the soccer field. I can smell the fresh cut grass, and even the tinge of perspiration that clung to Trevor that day.

A strangled sob escapes me, and I'm rapidly spinning out of control. My breathing becomes a laboring task. I feel as though a giant hand has clamped its mighty fingers around my windpipe, sealing off my air supply. Trevor is now in front of me. His eyes are soft, and gazing at me with a fondness that makes my heart ache. He leans in to kiss me, and before I can get away, he seizes me with hands as quick as a striking serpent.

He claims my mouth with a fervor that is unlike him. I fight against it, feeling a fastening upon my arm that makes me cry out.

The memory is now warping into a nightmarish vision, and I feel as though I'm suffocating. I gasp for air, thrashing beneath the crushing grip until my skin burns from it.

Trevor suddenly pulls away from me, his mouth replaced with a gaping maw. I shrink away from the black, endless hole, but it grows wider and wider until

I'm almost sucked inside it. I scream, letting my vocal cords rattle until they are raw.

Chapter 13

"Abby," says a gentle voice.

I whimper. My eyes screwed shut so tightly my cheeks hurt.

"Reach for me," the voice coos. "Listen to my voice. I am right here."

My lips part and I'm panting. "Am I done? Can I stop now?"

"You haven't reached the threshold yet. Continue."

Continue? How can I continue when I can barely escape the grotesque version of Trevor? The image of him glows angrily against the back of my eyelids.

"Again," he urges with authority, snapping me to attention.

Again I picture Trevor as I remember him. Kind. Carefree. Alive. My heart tumbles into my stomach, which is churning anxiously as I relive our relationship. The simplicity of it. The sweetness of it. I let myself feel happiness, recalling those fun, flirty months we dated. A smile forms on my lips, and then I see Lora. She's laughing and we're in her childhood bedroom, giggling, and exchanging silly secrets.

There's a tap at her window, and when she draws the curtain aside, Tony is standing there wielding an axe. He snarls and bursts through the window, shattering the glass into tiny daggers. I shield my face, but they stab into me like needles, tearing my skin into bloody shreds. The pain quickly ebbs as a flood of white-hot anger flows through me.

I leap onto Tony and crush my lips against his, smothering his breath and absorbing his groans. I fist his shirt in my hands until my fingers go numb, and he's flailing like mad but I do not let go. My hate and rage clash, making a deadly combination and I see nothing except the sheet of red that blankets my vision. I refuse to release him until I feel his body go limp in my arms, and when I finally do, I let him drop to the ground.

That's when I notice my rounded belly. My hands automatically fold across it, and I'm taken completely by surprise at this turn of events. *This isn't a memory. What is this?*

In an instant, my pregnant belly disappears and is replaced by a newborn infant. I'm cradling him close, my nose skimming across his sweet smelling skin. I place a kiss upon the sleeping baby's pouty lips, and it's then that I realize my fatal mistake. I watch in horror as the child struggles for air, his skin taking on an ashen hue and his lips turning blue. My heart feels swollen, too enlarged for my chest to comfortably contain it and I want to rip it out. Hot tears stream relentlessly down my face, and it feels as though fire pokers are jabbed into my eye sockets. Bile stings my tongue, and I swear I'm about to vomit when a soothing presence begins weaving its way through me.

It flows like a balm, tamping the mounting panic, and mending the fraying filaments of my broken heart. *Nik.* I reach for him, and his strong hands rest upon my skin, and I cling to them as though they are my lifeline. The crashing waves of sorrow lap at my feet, but I trudge on, following the beacon of light calling for me to come back home. I focus on his touch, relishing it, and depending on it to get me through this hellish ordeal.

"Abby," Nik says softly.

I blink my eyes open to find him tenderly stroking my arm. I follow the steady movement of his fingers as he trails them across my skin. Chills zip through me and I shiver.

"You did well," he says with a small smile. I think I catch a hint of pride in his voice, but I'm not sure. He hooks a strand of hair behind my ear, his finger lingering at the scar behind my ear. I feel it pulse beneath his touch, and it triggers a heat that blossoms deep within my belly. I swallow and push myself back against the couch cushion. *Oh boy. I need space from him.*

I take a weary inventory of the living room. Everything seems to be intact. Jack is even napping on his perch. "What happened?"

"You faced your demons…and you persevered."

I don't say it is because of him, and his unwavering strength that pulled me through. That it was him that kept me grounded, that called me back into reality just before I fell into the abyss of no return. Instead I ask, "Is that it? Is that all I have to do?"

"You will need to learn how to tap into your abilities, but your power can no longer control you. You braved your darkest fears, and that is the hardest lesson of all."

I hug myself, recalling the series of images that rose before me like shadows upon a wall. I can reason almost all of them, knowing that I carry the burden of

Trevor's senseless death like a noose around my neck. My hatred of Tony is a no-brainer, although my lack of humanity as I relish his death is frightening. I'm not sure what to make of it, and actually, it makes me uncomfortable to even dwell on what it could mean. The image that wrenches me into a useless shell is that of the infant. The future me, embracing my first child, just minutes after being born. Rooted deep within my self-consciousness, I suddenly realize my ultimate fear. Killing my child with my kiss. The thought twists like a knife in my heart. This valid concern supersedes the guilt I carry, and it eclipses any happiness I've ever experienced.

"Want to tell me about it?"

I slide my gaze to Nik. His face has softened, his golden brows arched high above his watery blue eyes.

I open my mouth, but close it again. Where do I start? There was so *much*. So much rage. So much anguish. Though fleeting, there was so much happiness, but it was quickly doused and replaced with tremendous fear.

"Just start at the beginning. What did you see?"

"Trevor," I breathe, taking a moment to let his name hang in the air. I haven't said his name out loud in years. It saws across my vocal cords like the first drag of air you take after holding your breath underwater. Hearing it should have sent me over the edge, but instead I feel...content. Peaceful. My heart even feels lighter, and my throat doesn't constrict.

Nik throws his arm across the back of the couch, and slants his head just slightly as through he's examining me with keen interest. "What else?"

I inhale deeply, then say, "We kissed." My eyes

flick to him. I'm not sure what kind of reaction I am hoping for, but when he merely blinks, disappointment runs through me. I bite my lip to keep from scowling. "And when we were done, he wasn't the same. He was...scary." I shudder as I envision his monster-like mouth hovering over me. His eerie silent scream and the gaping abyss that replaced his mouth. My stomach turns. I wish to forget all about that, so I keep talking to distract me from the horrid image. "Then I saw my best friend, Lora. We were happy. Laughing and having fun. But her husband shows up and breaks through the bedroom window. Glass flies everywhere."

Nik frowns.

"Then..." I pause to lick my lips. "Then...I kiss him. With the sole purpose of killing him." I pick at a hangnail and struggle to keep my breathing steady. I may have faced my demons, but my anger for Tony remains raw, like a week old wound that refuses to heal.

The cushions move as Nik shifts into a close lean. His eyes hold firm to mine and he brings his hand to my cheek. His palm is warm and I resist the urge to nuzzle it. I don't miss the acceleration of my heartbeat, nor can I ignore the roaring of my pulse in my ears. This close, Nik reminds me of beautiful artwork, skillfully created with a mastery that is beyond human perfection.

"And that frightens you?" he asks. "The propensity of killing?"

"Of course," I reply. "It means I'm a monster."

"You're not a monster Abby."

"I killed him, Nik." I stare, unblinking at him. "I *killed* him. And I know that makes me a horrible, despicable human being, but I am certain that if I had it to do all over again...the result would be the same. I'd *kill* him again, for what he did to my best friend."

"What did he do?" He gives me a questioning look, his hand dropping into his lap.

"He was an abusive drunk," I say with a shrug. "And that's just a couple of his useless qualities. Let's just say, he'd never be nominated for husband of the year."

Nik's frown deepens. "From the sound of it, the scum got what he deserved."

"Did he really?" I search his eyes. "Did he really deserve to die? I've asked myself that question a million times, and I can't answer it."

"Abby," he starts, sliding closer to me. "Justice had to be served, and you dispensed it."

"It wasn't my place," I say. "But I didn't have a choice. He would have killed me." I touch my fingertips to my neck. A reflex I've developed whenever I relive that night.

Nik's eyes flash something dangerous. "What are you talking about?"

"He had me pinned beneath him, and he was choking me." I can still feel it, and my throat begins to ache from the phantom fingers digging into my flesh. "I had no choice Nik." My voice cracks. "I *had* to."

For a moment he appears conflicted, but ultimately his anger wins out. His mouth cranks tightly into a grimace, and he's practically seething when he finally grinds out, "He is lucky to have died by your lips, rather than by my hands." His hands curl into fists; his knuckles bulging white beneath his skin.

My breath catches at his words. *What?* I search his face, desperate to decipher his meaning. *Does he ... care for me?* I'm split. Part of me wishes it were true. To know Nik felt even a fraction of what I feel for him would be a dream come true. But the other, more realistic part of me knows that can never be. I feel a stab of sadness lance through me, because I know that part of me is right.

His eyes roam across my face as though he's memorizing every inch of it. When his gaze finally settles upon mine, he says, "You are a noble woman Abby. You were put in a position in which you were given no option. No way out. There is no fault in what you did."

I find some solace in his reassurance, his confident aura creeping in like a fog. I find myself giving him a small smile, and he sweeps my hair from my face and cups the back of my neck. His fingertips nearly touch my scar, which has it tingling with anticipation. He tilts forward, and now we are sharing the same sliver of space. The air feels charged, like a downed power line, its energy wild and dangerous. I'm rendered speechless as I gaze, transfixed by the gem-like gleam of his eyes. His scent is all around me, filling me, engaging me, overwhelming me. I want his lips on me. I want to feel them, taste them, devour them.

I lean closer. The tips of our noses touch and I inhale the very breath he just expelled. It's intimate, and provokes feral desire to trickle through me. One hand is still rooted to my neck, holding me in place as the other skims across my knee. Even through the fabric of my pants, I feel the heat of his touch. I want him. I *need* him. A whimper escapes my lips, and my chest rises and falls with rampant anticipation. If I cock my head just slightly, our lips will surely meet. I follow that train of thought blindly, until my mouth brushes across his bottom lip. It isn't a kiss exactly, but more like an exchange of breath.

Nik tunnels his fingers through my hair, and pulls me into him. Just before he brings his mouth to mine, I'm hit with sudden clarity. *No!*

"Stop!" I exclaim, startling Jack off his perch with a squawk. I flatten both palms against Nik's chest and give him a stern push. His muscles are like a slab of stone but he allows me to shove him away.

His eyes are wide, confusion coloring his handsome features and I notice his cheeks are flushed with color.

"What's wrong?"

I leap to my feet and begin to pace. I clutch my hair with my fists. "Oh my god. Oh my god. Oh my god."

He watches me cross the floor several times before standing up and taking me by the shoulders. "Abby. What is it?"

"We...I..." My stomach churns like sour milk in a blender. "I almost..." Disgust claws at my throat, and I can barely speak.

His eyebrows raise expectedly.

"We almost kissed." I snap my mouth shut, guilt stinging me as I realize how repulsed I sound. Nik looks hurt, but doesn't say anything. I want to kiss him so badly it hurts, and because of my lack of will, I almost did. My heart wrenches with sickening realization. "I almost killed you," I whisper.

I wriggle out of his grip and dash down the hallway and into my bedroom. I slam the door shut and lock it. *As if that will keep him out*, I think. If Nik really wants to come in, there is nothing that can stop him. I press my forehead against the door and close my eyes. *I can't believe I almost kissed him! What the hell is wrong with me? I could have killed him!*

There's a soft knock at my door.

"Abby?"

"Go away," I shout, clamping my eyes tighter.

"Abby, please."

The doorknob jingles, and I jerk my head to watch it twist and open. It doesn't. "I said go away!" I back away until my legs collide with my bed. I sit, grasping two handfuls of blanket to keep me steady. I stare at the door through a blur of tears. *Please. Just go away...*

I hate myself for allowing all self-control to evaporate whenever Nik is near. I have carefully crafted myself into an unaffectionate robot, whose sole function is to merely exist. But Nik has unearthed the deepest, darkest part of me that I painstakingly buried many years ago. The part that yearns to love, and to be loved. Tears slip down my cheeks and I realize there is silence in the hallway. *Did he leave?*

I rise and cross the room. I wipe my face with the back of my hand and press my ear to the door, straining to hear through it. All is quiet. I reach for the knob and twist it slowly. For a fraction of a second, I find myself hoping to find Nik standing there, but the doorway is empty. I sweep my gaze down the hallway and see no trace of Nik. Unthinking, I take a deep breath, searching the air for his particular scent of honeysuckle and rain. There is none. *He's gone.*

I close the door again and press my back against it. My brain is a fog, clouded with guilt and a dozen other emotions. I drag myself down the length of the wooden door, sinking lower and lower until I am huddled into a pathetic lump on the floor. I hold my head in my hands and sob into my fingers, slowly rebuilding the walls that Nik had scaled with one graceful jump. This time I must make them higher. Stronger. But I can't help but question myself. *Am I capable of building something that can withstand the mighty storm that is Nik?*

Chapter 14

It's been four days and I still haven't seen Nik. I find myself inhaling deeply whenever I walk into a room, trying to track his scent like a hound, but I always come up empty. I begin to wonder if I scared him off. *I wouldn't be surprised if I did.* It's not the first time I screamed at him, or told him to leave. I think of the first time we met. He had just saved me from a tornado, but still I yelled at him and ordered him away. Nik is an attractive, sexy guy, why would he stick around? What would make a man like that, stay with a head case like me? I frown a little as I resign myself to the fact that I finally pushed him away. *But, isn't that exactly what I wanted?*

It's my day off and I consider stopping by Lora's. We talk almost daily, but it's been awhile since I've seen her. She keeps insisting that she wants to be alone, and out of respect for our friendship, I've obeyed her wishes and kept my distance.

After finishing off my plate of macaroni and cheese, the doorbell rings. For a cruel second, I actually think it may be Nik. I dash down the hall and through the living room. When I reach the door, I smooth my hair behind my ears and pinch my cheeks for color before yanking the door open with a frantic air that isn't lost on Mo, who looks at me with wide eyes.

"Damn girl, who you expecting?" He pushes past

me and lets himself into my living room. He flops onto the couch, and kicks his lean legs out across the cushions. "Well?" He lifts a brow in question.

I push the door closed and carry myself through the living room, my nose lifted in the air as I waltz past him and head straight into the kitchen. I start washing my dish, allowing the running water to drown out Mo's yapping mouth. He finally realizes I'm not listening, and comes into the kitchen.

"Uh oh. I do believe I'm getting the silent treatment." His hands rise and cover his cheeks. "Whatever shall I do?"

I scowl and continue to scrub furiously at a non-existent spot on the dish.

"Come on Abs," he says, poking me in the ribs. "You can't stay mad forever." He jabs at my side again, making me jump.

"Stop that," I bark.

"Well, stop acting so bitchy and get over it already." He leans against the counter, watching me as I rinse the plate and set it on the drying rack.

"You're an ass," I say as I pat my hands dry with a towel. I breeze past him and head to my bedroom.

His thick-heeled loafers clip across the hardwood floor as he scurries behind me, but I ignore him and go to the closet.

"You going somewhere?" he asks.

I sort through the rack until I settle on a sheer, off the shoulder blouse. I sling it across my arm, then select a black T-shirt to wear beneath it as well as a pair of charcoal gray jeans.

"Let me guess." He surveys the outfit piled in my arms and says, "Lora's?"

I skirt around him and dump the clothes onto the bed.

"Abbyyyy," he whines. "Please. Don't be mad at me. It was stupid. *I*...was stupid. It won't happen again."

I give him a long sideways glance.

"Please. Come on. How can you be mad at this face?" He smiles sweetly and folds his hands under his chin as though he's posing for a tight-framed picture.

My lips twitch.

His mouth spreads into a cheesy grin and he bats his eyelashes.

I break, chuckling at his goofiness and toss a wadded up scarf at him.

He catches it and whisks it around his neck, smoothing the tasseled edges. "This is fabulous." I laugh at him as he sashays over and kisses me on the cheek. "Mo is gonna make this mo' betta."

"Oh yeah?" I arch a dubious brow at him.

"I'm going to stay out of your love life." He covers his mouth as though whispering to an invisible person. "If you can call it that."

I punch his shoulder. "It isn't funny."

"Ow." He touches his arm. "Who's laughing?" He walks over to my bed and sits down, crossing his leg over his knee. "Honey, I sure ain't. It's depressing." He toys with the scarf tassels. "But if being a nun is what you want, then girl... I say go for it."

My shoulders sag as I let out a disgusted sigh. "I don't want to be a nun."

"Well you sure uphold their celibacy policy."

I shoot him a pointed look and walk into the adjoining bathroom. I hear the bed squeak as he stands, and I know he's about to follow me. Mo has zero shame, and he gladly invades everyone's personal space. I lean over, and turn the shower on, running my hands beneath the steady stream of water until the temperature is just right. I stand, finding Mo behind me, peering into the illuminated mirror above the sink. He looks to be scrutinizing his upper lip, though I'm not sure why. He's never been able to produce any semblance of a moustache, so checking for a five o'clock shadow is out of the question.

"What are you doing?" I ask.

"Thinking about getting injections," he says flippantly. "I want full, voluptuous lips that will make a man want to slap his mama and goose his grandma for."

I can't help but giggle and shake my head "You are something else," I tell him as I usher him out of the bathroom. "Now get out of here. I need to take a shower."

He raises both hands. "Okay okay. I'm going. You don't have to tell me twice. I sure don't want to see any lady parts." He shudders and starts to leave, but thinks better of it and turns around. I watch him curiously as he bounds back to me. He wraps me in a hug, pulling me close. "Sorry Abby. I do love you, you know that right?"

"Of course I do." I return the strong embrace, then can no longer take the pungent cologne that he seems to have bathed in this morning. I playfully shove him away. "Now get out of here will you? You're being mushy and I'm liable to stick you with a fork if you continue with all that lovey dovey crap."

He laughs, and tussles my hair like I'm a child. "Oh you."

He saunters away, grinning. I hear him using the spare key to turn the lock in the front door on his way out.

By the time I step into the bathtub, the room is steamy from the warm water flowing from the showerhead. The glass doors are clouded and I touch my fingertip to it, dragging it down, cutting a clear path through the fog. I let the water run over me as I idly write out a few words. When I'm through, I take a step back, the spray of water splashing across my shoulders as I read the glass panel. *Abby. Cherish The Day. Seize Your Power. Nik.*

I smile to myself, watching the words mist with condensation before I duck under the showerhead, letting the water cascade over my head, and down my back. I lather my hair with my favorite coconut shampoo and rinse it away, watching the foam collect and disappear down the drain. I shave a little too quickly, nicking myself with the razor.

I curse under my breath as a tiny stream of blood runs down my leg, mixing with the bathwater. It stings as I finish bathing, and I take extra care around the cut as I pat myself dry. Steamy air ghosts around me, suffocating me with its humidity. I wrap my towel around myself, ready to escape the warm bathroom. I open the door to find a tall figure standing in the far corner.

I startle at the sight and my heart pounds painfully against my chest. "Oh my fucking god! You need to learn boundaries!"

He grunts, but there is a smirk hinting at his lips as his gaze lazily rakes across my body.

I grip the towel tighter. "What are you doing

here?"

"You're bleeding." He gestures to my knee.

I look down and notice a small bead of blood. "I cut myself," I say. "It's fine."

He crosses the floor with a few brisk strides. I watch in wonder as he kneels before me and examines it. *What is he doing?*

"Do you have bandages?"

I can't help but laugh. "For a nick?"

He glares up at me; the view of him below me, hovering so close to my bare thighs it makes my insides quiver.

I point behind me to the mirrored medicine cabinet.

His eyes follow my direction. "Stay." He rises and goes to the cabinet, pulling the door aside and searching the shelves. He removes a small box and lifts it to me. "This?"

I nod, slightly shocked that he's never seen a Band-Aid before. *I guess Storm Thieves are too macho for such things.*

He closes the door softly, takes a washcloth from the towel rack, and returns to where he left me standing like a dumbstruck fool. He selects a bandage from the box and squats before me. Ever so gently, he pats the cut with the washcloth. I watch him work, his fingers moving deftly as they peel back the wrapper and tears the tabs from the bandage. He carefully arranges it across my skin, and swipes his thumb across it to seal it.

"There," he says.

I'm aware I'm biting my lip, but I can't help but stare at him wide-eyed, stunned by how tender he can be.

He brings himself up to his full height, and now I'm forced to look up should I want to keep gazing at him like a silly, lovesick fool. I do, of course. My eyes sweep up his chest, across his creamy throat, past his sensuous lips and settle on his beautiful eyes.

He seems bemused for a moment, as if what he'd done was totally natural and that I shouldn't be surprised at all. But it's Nik. Honest to the point of hurtful, fly by the breeze, Nik. Aside from saving a perfect stranger, I have only seen this side of him once, and it was nearly disastrous. I think back to our almost kiss. *Snap out of it Abby.* I clear my throat, wrenching the wad of towel in my hands tighter.

"I need to go change," I say, circling a wide arc around him before I head for my closet. *There you go again,* I scold myself. *You let those eyes draw you in again...*

Those eyes. Yes, those damn, shockingly blue eyes that put the purest of gems to shame. The way they pierce into me, as if daring my demons to come out of hiding so he may slay them one by one. I expel a breath, collecting myself alone, standing in the threshold of my walk-in closet. *Forget about Nik. Forget about him. Forget about Nik.* Reciting the mantra only makes my insides ache further.

I snatch a sweater and a pair of dark jeans free from their hangers and dash across the floor, back to the bathroom. I start to shut the door, but his stare intercepts me from across the room and for a moment I stand there. Nik cocks his head to the side just enough to make his golden hair fall across his forehead and partly into his eyes. He gives me a devilish smile that makes my insides turn to liquid. I swallow against the dryness that has suddenly caked my throat and I push the door closed with a definitive *click.*

"Damn it," I mutter, turning and pressing both hands against either side of the sink to brace myself. I hang my head, staring into the ceramic bowl, wishing I could fit myself down the drain and disappear into its darkness. Staying away from Nik is becoming increasingly difficult. Somehow in just a few short days, he's managed to imbed himself within the very recesses of my soul, and I *want* him. I know it's an invalid feeling, something that will never come to fruition. But I also know it's just a matter of time before I lose the last shred of willpower I have left. And then…all hell will break loose.

I take my time dressing, needing the distance from Nik to rein in my raging hormones. *If I care for him, then I must forget about him.* I tell myself this as a sick feeling gnaws hungrily away at my gut. Just *thinking* about never seeing his handsome face again sends a sadness through me like a sinking stone in a riverbed. My footsteps feel weighted as I emerge from the bathroom. He's sitting on my bed, gazing meditatively out the window. I study his profile. His strong features prominent against the wash of waning daylight that filters through the glass.

"You mustn't be afraid of me Abby," he says flatly. He doesn't move, nor does he take his eyes from the window. He continues to stare ahead with a look of quiet pondering and contentment.

I walk to him. "I don't fear you Nik." I barely recognize my own voice. It's throaty and borderline sensual. Nik finally turns to look at me. His blond hair is tousled, framing his head like splaying bars of sunlight. He's absolutely stunning.

His eyes tighten, scrutinizing me to the point of being imposing as he watches me draw closer. "Then why do you hesitate?"

"It's complicated," I answer.

"Your body reacts to me. I sense it."

I shiver at his frankness, and it's not the first time I feel as though he has a direct portal to my soul. He seems to know me better than I know myself.

"Why deny yourself what your body wants?" he asks.

I'm beside him now, though I refuse to sit down. My eyes scan briefly across the bed sheet, imagining our slick, naked bodies twisted amongst them. I quickly shake that thought away and force myself to focus on something—anything—else. But I can't. It's impossible when a beautiful man is taking up so much space before you, sitting on your bed like a king upon a throne. His legs are spread wide, and his hands are resting on his thighs.

"How do you know what my body wants?" It was meant to come out scornful, but instead it came out exactly how I felt. Unsure and curious.

His eyes trail over me lazily, starting at my hips then linger at my ear, just where my scars begin. *Not scars*, I think. *Marks.* They tingle, sending a sharp shiver down my spine.

The corner of his mouth quirks, and he lifts a finger to point to my neck. "*That's* how I know." He pulls me by my waist, eliciting a startled gasp from me, and I grab onto his broad shoulders out of instinct. "Your Marks are practically purring, begging to be petted."

I'm speechless because it's true. Every time Nik is

near, not only does my body react, but my Marks come alive. They usually pulsate with a soothing warmth, but right now, they are coiling, like they are shrinking. His movement causes the air to stir, and with each draw of his heavenly aroma, the intoxicating scent pulverizes my willpower. *How can I possibly stay away from this amazing creature?*

"Abby." Although his tone is low, it's hardly a whisper. It's more like a raspy scrape against his throat. "Your body is mine for the taking. You just don't know it yet."

He guides my hands away from his shoulders and up to his face. He places a kiss on each of my palms and liquid heat darts straight to my middle. He casts his eyes up at me. They are darker in the dim lighting, like tempered steel. I lay my hands across his cheeks, and I notice how small they look against him.

"God, Abby," he growls. "Don't you see what you do to me? I'm completely torn apart because of you. Every part of you drives me half-crazy with lust." He cups my hips and lowers me into his lap. "May I kiss you?"

Any other time the question would have deserved an eye roll for an answer, but coming from Nik, it ignites my want into an explosive hunger that is truly insatiable. I should push him away. I should pry myself from his embrace and walk away, but I can't. I want him. I need him. Can I have him without *kissing* him? I am willing to try.

I guide him backward until he's lying flat against the bedspread. I'm straddling his muscular waist, well aware of the heat that is spreading through my core. Never have I had a handsome man lying beneath me. I feel empowered, I feel sexy, and I feel...*so turned on*. His hands find my back, and he caresses me gently at first, but when I bend and place a light kiss on the edge of his chin, his touch becomes rougher, soon traveling up to fist my hair. His golden skin is as smooth as honey, and I am almost certain just as sweet. Temptation proves too great, and I must taste him. I trace my tongue along the creamy column of his neck.

He growls, blowing a hot breath across my ear, and my Marks flare with desire. I moan, and arch, allowing him better access to them. He presses tender kisses across my Marks, and my skin suddenly feels too tight for my body. He encircles me with his arms, and rolls us over so he's lying atop me, his weight sinking me further into the mattress.

He runs a finger lightly across my skin, tracing the Marks that are stamped behind my ear. "You're so beautiful."

I gaze up at him, lost in his own rugged beauty, almost oblivious to the cellphone ringing beside me on the nightstand. Nik's eyes track the sound, but I quickly reach over and silence the phone without even checking the caller ID. His brows raise, and a sneaky smile pulls at his luscious lips. *God, how I want them on me.*

Nik carefully slips his fingers beneath the hem of my sweater, and all my muscles bind, drawn firmly like the strings on a harp. They long to be plucked, to be released of all tension, played into a frenzy of bliss by his exquisite hands. He rears back a little, to watch me as he ventures further, the pads of his fingertips leaving warm trails along my skin.

If he continues to tease me this way, I'm going to implode. But who cares? To be loved by Nik, and left as nothing more than a singed pile of a wanton woman would be an honor. This handsome creature has a hold of my heart, and I never want it back. It's his. I know it, and he knows it. Hell, even my Marks know it.

Even before the thought is complete, my Marks warm with confirmation, and it takes me aback. My breathing hitches, and I finally understand. *Polar Mates.* I stare into his eyes, my heart filling with the overwhelming notion. *Nik is my Polar Mate.*

Chapter 15

I am about to ask him if it's true, but just as I open my mouth, the phone rings again. Nik groans and buries his face into my shoulder, but reaches a long arm out and retrieves the phone from the nightstand. I take it from him, glancing at the screen to check the caller ID. *Dad.* My chest squeezes and I quickly answer it.

"Dad?"

"Honey," he drawls in his thick southern accent. "Where you been hiding sug? I haven't heard hide nor hair from you in weeks. Everything aiight?"

Relief runs through me and I touch my forehead. "Yes Dad. Sorry. I've been a crappy daughter lately." And I have. I'm usually close with my father, but the situation with Lora, and not to mention my own paranormal drama, I've been a bit too preoccupied to call and check in with Dad.

"I know things have been testy lately sugar."

"No," I say adamantly.

Nik lifts off me and sits back on his heels, studying me as though he's gauging the severity of my conversation. I give him a small smile, ensuring him everything is okay.

I sit up and lean against the stack of pillows behind me. "That's not a good enough excuse for not calling you." Dad has always gone too easy on me. Being his only child, and having to raise me alone, as he mourned the loss of my mother turned him into a spineless pile of mush when it came to me. I often took advantage of it as a kid. I remember pitching a full-blown fit in the toy aisle when he refused to buy me a doll I wanted. After a few shed tears, I left the store toting the beloved doll in my arms. As I grew older, I learned why he treated me the way he did. Why he gave me everything I wanted, and why he rarely scolded me. Aunt Blair once said, *"You have your mama's smile, and that's what makes your daddy's knees go weak."*

So that was it. I reminded him of her. *Her.* The woman who's always been an unknown presence in my life. She wasn't there physically but she was all around me in spirit. My father kept her clothes just as she left them in the closet. As a little girl, I'd go into her closet and sit on the floor, letting her dresses sweep across the top of my head. I'd imagine it was her hands running through my hair.

"Well now. Don't be too hard on yourself sug. I know life gets in the way sometimes. Plus, the whole hoopla with Lora. How's she doing by the way?"

"She still struggles with it, though I'll never understand why."

"It's not for you to understand. The heart wants what it wants."

I lean my head back and look at the ceiling. "I know. But why did it have to be *him?* I get that love is blind or whatever, but for god's sake it can't be that stupid. Love isn't supposed to hurt."

I feel the bed shift, and Nik is adjusting his position so that he's sitting at my feet. His eyes are firmly set on me, no waver in them at all as he clenches his jaw.

I want to look away, but I can't. It's as if we are

mirrored, our gazes matching stare for stare and I'm unsure why. *What did I say to make him look at me this way?*

"Dad," I say. "I'll call you back in a little bit, okay?"

"Call me tonight sug. I'm heading to the bowling alley with the fellers. Got my lucky rabbit foot with me, plus my last game was one-forty. I'm about to make them pansy pants weep into their bowling shoes." He chuckles.

I try to smile, but Nik's unrelenting stare is rendering me fear-stricken. Prickles of unease creep along my scalp, and I draw myself taller and look down my nose at him. "Okay Daddy. You have fun and I'll call you tonight."

"Will do. Bye-bye dumpling. Your old man loves you."

"I love you too. Bye."

I end the call and calmly lay the phone on the bed. "Why are you looking at me like that?"

"Do you honestly believe that?" He's blunt, though his tone is razor sharp, like a dagger. Hard and deadly.

I blink, puzzled by the question. "Believe what?"

"That love isn't supposed to hurt."

"Yes," I answer with a frown, reliving my words. "I do believe that. Love is supposed to be simple, and full of…of…" I pause, the words not coming as easily as they should. *What should love be? Do I even know?*

"Full of what?" he snaps. "Hearts and flowers?"

My frown sinks deeper. "Well, no." I cross my arms in front of me. "It shouldn't be a teenage girl's diary entry for crying out loud, but it should be full of laughter, sweet kisses, comfortable silences, and deep conversations." *Yes, that,* I think. *Love should be exactly that.*

"Is *that* your definition of love?"

I notice his hands are curled into fists, and his muscles are strapped tightly beneath the thin layer of cotton tee. *What is with him?*

"What's yours?" I counter, setting my chin stubbornly.

He grunts and stands from the bed. "It is surely not full of the pettiness you have described." He stalks to the window, and places one hand on the pane. He's glowering, flexing the muscles in his jaw over and over before he grounds out, "You know nothing of love."

My blood burns through my veins, and I'm instantly furious. "Who the hell do you think you are?" I swing my legs over the edge of the bed. "You don't know me well enough to speak to me this way. How dare you?" I rise and stomp over to him, not sure what I'll do once I get there, but I stomp with determination anyway. "How can you say something so cruel?"

He whips his head sharply to look at me, and his eyes flash something dangerous. "Cruel? You think I'm being cruel?" His hand balls into a tight fist, and I am certain if he slams it into the wall, he'd leave a jagged hole in his wake. "I am nothing but honest, when it comes to you." Hard, probing eyes sear into me, unforgiving and unashamed.

"Yeah," I reply, my voice dripping with sarcasm. "*Brutally* honest."

His eyes squint, and he's studying me like a petri-dish beneath a microscope. "Honesty equates protection."

"Which then equates to what," I ask. "Love?"

"To protect is to put someone else's life above all else. That to me, is love."

I think about the night my rage manifested into a terrible storm. The screaming winds and the fury that swirled around me like a dark, menacing cloud. Nik rescued me from the tornado. He *protected* me. My heart swells a bit, and my breath catches at the back of my throat. *Does he…love me?* I eye him closely, trying to glean any hint of emotion that would confirm it, but his mouth is set firm, and veins bulge from his clenched fists. My stomach drops, and a chill cuts though me. *No, of course not. And I'm a fool for even thinking it.*

I square my shoulders and say, "Basically, you described love as a seat-belt. There to protect, and serve no other purpose." I let my eyes graze across his rigid arms and then move pointedly to his clamped fists. "Hm." I tap my chin thoughtfully. "I wonder why that is?"

He pushes himself away from the window, and drops his hands to his side, though they remain tense. "Careful Abby. It's not wise to rile me."

I glare at him challengingly. "I would say you're the same as a seat-belt. Stiff, and only here to keep me from killing myself, but that's not even true. At least seat-belts embrace you while they are protecting you."

His eyes flash, and it takes all my willpower not to react. He looks lethal standing there. Like a delicious drug that will poison your bloodstream and corrupt your heart. Perhaps I'm stupid, or brave, or confident enough to believe that he would never hurt me, but the eerie shadow of his hard stance that lays stretching across the floor before me says otherwise.

"You're a foolish woman."

"And you're a callous brute," I respond hotly.

His lip curls into a snarl and he breathes out a huff of laughter. "For someone who has never experienced the love of a man, you surely pride yourself on being an expert."

I scoff, but the statement cuts right through me. *He's right. I have never experienced true love. Trevor was puppy love. Far from the real thing.*

The space around Nik begins to warp and shimmer. Something comes over me, and I reach out and touch his wrist. There's a charge in the air, and it raises the hairs on my arm like static electricity on a winter day.

He looks down at my hand, and I think I see disappointment in his face, which sends a blow straight to my heart.

He says, "I thought you were strong enough to handle me." His eyes lift and meet mine. "I guess I was wrong."

A chilly breeze whisks past me, blowing my hair wildly around my face, and it takes Nik with it, leaving me standing alone in my bedroom. I hug myself, trying to rid the goose bumps that have cropped up along my skin. I look around, feeling lost and wooden. The room seems so empty, the air stagnant, as though it had been drained of all oxygen.

My footsteps thump loudly against the hardwood floor as I meander to the edge of my bed and sit down. I fold into myself and stare unblinking at my knees. I want to be angry. I want to hate Nik for saying such hurtful things, but instead, the moment his scent fades, I miss him. And what's worse is the unshakeable feeling that I will never see him again. A stab of cold runs through my Marks, jarring me upright. *No. Oh god, please, no.* Did my Marks just validate my worst fear? Was this the last time I'll ever lay eyes on the beautiful Storm Thief?

Chapter 16

The days turn into weeks, and the town of Mepelo is knee deep in a record rainfall. I'm to blame. I admit, I feel a twinge of guilt each time the weatherman announces another day full of the unseasonal rain, but I cannot shake this gloom. I miss Nik. I work through my shifts at the library absently, like a wind-up toy that goes through the movements without an ounce of emotion.

I think about him constantly, clinging tightly to his memory until it leaves my heart aching like an exposed nerve. Even my nights are haunted by him. My nightmares have returned and they've returned with a vengeance. Not only do Trevor and Tony's faces plague me, but now Nik's beautiful smile lingers just out of reach. In each dream he's just as handsome as I remember, standing amid a stretch of fluffy clouds, beckoning to me. Just when our fingers touch, the clouds give way, plunging me into a freefall. I scream and catch a glimpse of Nik shaking his head with disgust before I'm sent streaking through the air. The rush of wind snatches my breath away. My lungs burn. Then just before asphyxiation sets in, I slam into the ground.

Tonight I'm especially distraught. After completing my shift at work, I drive home in a daze and when I climb into my bed fully dressed, I automatically bury myself in a mound of blankets and somehow fall into a fitful sleep. A few hours later, I awake with a start, sweaty and panting from another horrific nightmare. I slide my blurry gaze to the clock on the nightstand. It's just past midnight. I squint against the darkness of my room and untangle the sheets from my legs.

I feel as though I'm confined in a box, the air warm and stuffy around me. I kick the blankets off the bed and sit in the middle of the mattress. *You have to get over this,* I tell myself.

My heart hurts, literally aches, like nothing I've ever felt before. I cover it with my hands and allow the collecting tears to fall unapologetically. I weep until I'm left a clump of shivering bones.

The rain picks up outside my window, beating against the glass relentlessly as if it's trying to break through. I stare at it unseeing, knowing deep in the pit of my soul that I am causing it. I should try to control it, the way Nik instructed me to, but I'm too exhausted to try. Instead I let the rain come down in angry sheets, and I honestly do not wish to tamp it. I say, let it pour.

I climb clumsily out of the bed and stalk to the bathroom. When I come out, fear pricks along my scalp and I *know* I am not alone. *Nik?* I search the darkness, wishing I had left the lamp on. Shadows fill the room, obscuring everything in a sheet of blackness. I do the only thing I can do. I close my eyes and inhale a generous pull of air. The stench of burnt flesh fills my senses and I jerk my eyes open wide.

"Who's here?"

The lamp turns on but no one is near it. A man materializes a few feet away, and my chest ratchets tighter. I am rooted into place out of pure fright. He appears human, but since he used Elemental Travel, I know he isn't. Or at least he isn't completely human. His skin is pale, almost ghostly and his hair is a brilliant orange, like a campfire. His head is cocked to the side, examining me with a look of disinterest.

"You don't look like much," he says, his voice holding a trace of an accent I can't place. "Hard to believe you're capable of all of this."

"All of what?" I ask.

He leisurely strolls a tight circle around me. His arms are bare, and I notice a network of tangled Marks running along the length of them that resemble my own. *A Sky Sorcerer.*

"Who are you?" I demand.

"My name is not relevant." He stops in front of me and takes on a stance that I can only describe as serpent-like. He reminds me of a cobra, ready to strike at any moment. I am careful to stand stock-still, not wanting to provoke him. I swallow, and only move my eyes to watch him as he surveys the entire length of me.

His mouth constricts and he looks thoroughly unimpressed.

"What do you want?"

"I've been sent to collect you."

Dread flows through my bones. "What do you mean...collect me?" I begin to back away, sick to my stomach. He grins like a crazed man. He must thrive on the game of chase, and I am about to give it to him. My eyes dart to the hallway, and I gauge the distance to the front door. *Can I outrun him?*

His eyes track my direction and he laughs like a cackling crow. "Please do it. I love it when they run."

I break into a sprint and make it half way down the hallway before he's filling up the entire space in front of me. I hear Jack screeching like mad in the living room, as though he senses the danger I'm in.

The Sky Sorcerer is smirking, with an obvious thirst for blood. Both hands are braced wide apart on the walls, blocking my path to the front door. He looks like he's about to lunge at me, so I turn and dash back into my bedroom and slam the door shut, quickly turning the lock.

There's a mock laughter at my elbow, and I whirl around to find him standing behind me. His lips are pulled into a warped smile. The kind you find plastered among the faces of patients in a psych ward.

The temperature in the room drops dramatically, and my teeth begin to chatter as I hold him in an anxious stare. My heart is pounding in my ears, and my fingertips go numb.

The man assesses the room around him. "Frozen in fear," he says with satisfaction. A cloud of icy air puffs out of his mouth and it carries across the air as he speaks. "Just like I like 'em."

Frozen in fear. This resonates with me like a bellowing chime from a church bell. It awakens my fighter's instinct, and I scramble to form a plan. *I am doing this,* I think. *Which means I can use it to my advantage.* I center my focus and mentally will the elements to follow my instruction. At first nothing happens, but then a whistle of strong wind echoes off the walls. I give it a sharp mental command, and the stranger is sent sailing through the air. The gush of wind throws him backward. The room shakes as his back crashes into the wall with a loud bang. I flinch, but

I do not take my eyes off him. He easily regains his footing, and shakes out his hands. He smiles, and looks completely unaffected, even though his body left a patchwork of flaking drywall behind him.

"Things are about to get interesting," he says, narrowing his eyes. He breaks out in a full-blown lope toward me, and I channel my thoughts on intercepting him with a wall of rushing wind. He staggers back, but charges through it without so much as a moment's hesitation.

This is not working! I consider my kiss, but instantly rule it out. There is no way this guy is going to let me close enough. *Not without being unconscious or dead maybe...* I flounder for a minute, racking my brain for another plan. My thoughts are all over the place, like panicked fish in a draining puddle, then finally...I settle on something. I know I have electricity surging through me, I often feel the crackle of it just below the surface of my skin. I command all of the heat, and anger within me to flow to my fingertips. My hands tremble with the power and I'm a little scared. I stare at them as they start to glow like the embers of an extinguished fire.

With a roar, the man charges me again. I stretch out my arms and hold my hands in front of me, steeling myself for his attack. He crashes into me and we fall together to the floor. I plant my hands firmly against his chest. The charge rises through me and his body starts convulsing on top of me. His shirt singes under my touch, and his skin sizzles and peels away from the lethal energy coursing from my fingertips.

His face is twisted with pain, but he's relishing it, grinning at me like a lunatic. The stench of charred skin hangs in the air and I gag, still I refuse to let him go. Finally he howls, and spittle sprays from his teeth. His eyes bulge, the whites of them now blood-red. *I'm bursting his blood vessels.*

He wrenches himself off me and stands, wavering slightly on his feet. I scramble to my feet, holding my hands in front of me like weapons. He swipes his mouth with the back of his hand. "Well played." He examines his shirt, carefully touching the raw, gaping wounds on his chest. He lets out an amused, but sinister chuckle. His eyes lift and he says, "My turn."

I brace myself, but he just stands there staring at me. My heartbeat pounds painfully in my ears. The air around him warps and I know exactly what's happening. The wind whips by and carries him away, but I remain standing with my feet spread apart, half-expecting him to attack again.

The minutes stretch on and on until finally I let my hands fall to my sides. My gaze slides to the hole he left in the wall. *What did he mean, "My turn"?*

Before I can mull it over a second further, the air across the room warbles like a mirage. I stumble backward, putting space between me and the undulating sphere. *Dear god, he's back...*

I smell him before I see him. The scent of day old cinders and charred skin weaves its way throughout the room. I bite back the bile that stings my tongue. His form takes shape, and he's just as menacing as before. He glares at me with blood-red eyes. As badly as I'd like to cower in a corner, I stand my ground, squaring my shoulders and leveling my stare.

"Check mate," he says, and his lip curls into a vicious snarl.

Then I notice it. There's a small figure in his arms. A set of wide, fearful eyes meet mine and my mouth drops. *Lora!* Her back is flat against his chest, his arm wrapped fiercely around her delicate throat. The intricate webbing of his Marks burn brightly against his fair skin and I wonder if he carries the same charge in his flesh that I do. If so, that means he's hurting her. Without thinking, I run to Lora, but the man seizes her tighter, causing her to choke and gasp beneath his grip.

I stop abruptly in my tracks, holding my hands out in surrender. "Please," I beg. "Don't hurt her. Just let her go. It's me you want."

The man's eyebrow arches, and his mouth quirks into a satisfied smirk.

"Your vulnerability means an easy victory for me." He slides his gaze to Lora and begins petting the length of her hair. She closes her eyes, and begins to whisper a low prayer.

My heart squeezes painfully. If I could take Lora's place, I would.

"She's pretty," he says. "Such a shame to have to end her life." Lora breaks into a sob and it wrenches my chest like a girdle.

"Let her go!" I'm trembling with anger, and on the verge of losing all self-control. I desperately wish to use my elemental power, but with Lora in the way, I'm hesitant because I cannot guarantee her safety. "Damn you, I said let her go!"

"Can't," he answers coldly. "My orders were direct. I'm to collect you, and guarantee your submission." He places a hand against Lora's forehead and turns her ever so slightly, illustrating how easy it will be to break her neck. I feel as though my heart is trying to leap through my throat as I watch the tears streak down her red face. She's openly wailing now.

"Please. I'll go with you. Willingly. Just let her go."

He looks thoughtful. "Fine. *She* is free to go, but someone will have to take her place."

I step forward, my chin set sternly as I offer myself.

His grin turns ghastly and he summons the Elemental Travel faster than I can register the atmospheric change. He returns just that quickly, now with my father held possessively in the cage of his Mark ridden arms.

I choke back a gasp. "Daddy!"

My father opens his mouth to speak, but the Sorcerer cocks a crimson brow at me, grabs my father's chin and twists. *No!* The loud snap renders me speechless as I stare at my father's body, hanging lifelessly from the Sorcerer's arms. I cover my pounding heart with my hand and fall to my knees. *Oh Daddy.* My vision blurs with tears, and I choke out a ragged sob.

The Sorcerer tosses my father away like a rag doll. I feel his eyes burning into me like lasers. Daring me, taunting me…but I am centered on my father. He can strike me down right here. I simply do not care. *Why? Why is this happening?*

My eyes are fixed on my father. He's lying in a heap at the man's feet, his hazel eyes lifeless as they stare out at nothing. *He's gone,* I think. *He's really gone.* I am distantly aware that the Sorcerer is now prowling me. Stalking me like the weak prey I am. Out of the corner of my eye I see him snicker. That's when I see red. A blaring, blinding, wall of red. *He killed my father. He must pay!*

"You son of a bitch!" I shout as I hurl myself at him, the fire and fury within me scorching me from the inside out, but I don't care. He killed my father, Goddamn it! I want revenge, and I want it to *hurt*. When I get within arm's reach of the Sorcerer, he snatches me with an iron grip and holds me at bay. I rile against him, thrashing like a rabid dog caught in a net.

A great wind stirs, cutting across my skin like a blade.

"No!" I scream. "You can't take me now!" I struggle against his strong grasp, but it's like shackles on my wrists. I catch a glimpse of my father. He's stone still, and my chest splits open with heartache. The wind whips sharply, stinging my eyes. I'm weightless as I'm carried away on a gust of cold air. Carried away from my father, who lies dead on my bedroom floor...

Chapter 17

My feet stumble as we touch down in an unfamiliar land. The trees are draped with curling vines filled with broad, waxy leaves. Flourishing plants sprout around the bases of thick trunked trees, and bizarre flowers with lavish petals dot the ground as far as I can see. *Where am I?* This place looks magical. It even smells magical with the traces of strange, exotic flowers.

My legs shake and threaten to give out on me at any moment, but still I snatch my hands away from the Sky Sorcerer. I'm surprised that he releases me so easily. I rub my wrists and look around. The sky is a strange shade of burnt orange, and it reminds me of a smudge of watercolor across a canvas. A sprawling castle sits nestled among the abundant foliage. Its aged stones are almost completely covered with fuzzy green moss, and creeping vines cling to window ledges as well as the dual towers.

The evil Sky Sorcerer shoves me hard, and I'm thrust toward the castle's expansive courtyard. My shoes crunch on scattered rocks and twigs that litter the once well-crafted cobblestone floor. There are holes in places where the stones are missing and thick roots channel their way across the plaza. This place was beautiful at one time, but neglect and time have taken their toll. Now it's spooky and desolate, an ominous air shrouding it like a dark shadow.

I'm pushed from behind again, and I bite my lip to keep from swearing.

"Move," demands the Sorcerer.

"Where are you taking me?" I question. "Where the hell are we?"

He ignores me. I'm led through the castle's foyer and into a vast stateroom. As we move deeper into the castle, the pungent odor of manure and sodden dirt grows stronger. I take note that there is no extravagant furniture, no expensive paintings hanging from the walls, nor are there any chandeliers or candles lighting the way. What little light there is seems to merely exist. Illuminating our path from unknown sources. My shoes scuff against the worn stone floor as I walk, each footstep muffled by the collection of white-gray lichen that clings to the damp floor.

There's a grand throne sitting upon an elevated platform. A shallow row of cobblestone steps lead up to it. Willowy weeds push up from every dark crevice, and clumps of wet dirt fill every corner.

"Sire," my capturer greets. His voice rings off the rock walls. "I have brought you the Sorceress."

It's then I realize there is someone—or some*thing*—resting in the impressive chair. My chest constricts with every step I take, bringing me closer and closer to the unknown presence that is taking up residence in the throne. It's as though an invisible python lays coiled around my ribcage, squeezing tighter and tighter with each exhalation of breath.

The flame-haired man stops at the bottom step of the dais, and drops to the ground to kneel. My capturer bows his head respectfully as he waits for either acknowledgement, or instruction, I'm not sure which.

The man on the throne remains silent. I can feel his eyes scrutinizing me head to toe. His hand is clasped tightly around a blunt club, though it rests lightly across his lap. It looks mean, and is well worn, which sends a sick twist to my gut.

"This is the one responsible for all the discord on mortal soil?" he finally says. His voice is cutting and deep, tapping into my marrow like a chisel.

"Aye Sire. I watched her for days to be sure."

The man grunts. Thick metal cuffs encircle his wrists and the sparse light sparks off them as he adjusts the weapon that lay sprawled across his knees. His skin is almost translucent, like the glossy underside of an oyster shell.

"What's your name?" he demands.

Fear grips me so severely that I can't speak. The words simply won't come.

"Name!" he exclaims. His eyes grow wide as they flash unnaturally, like twin flames set deep in his skull.

I wince and eke out, "Abby."

He tastes my name saying it slowly before narrowing his eyes into slits. "The final piece of the puzzle is unexpected, though it fits with precision." He trails his fingers across the wooden club as though he's stroking the skin of a lover. "I am Veles."

Understanding slams into me like a wrecking ball. *Veles.* The passage I read in the library surfaces. *Veles is the ruler of Earth and Magic.* I study him. His features are sharp and angular. His cheekbones like dual blades piercing his thinly stretched skin. *This is Nik's father.* There is no resemblance between the two, save for the towering height. *And intimidating demeanor...*

Gnarled roots and winding branches reach across his torso like a wooden sash. They twine up his shoulders and neck, then wrap around the back of his skull, like a crown resting upon his head. A set of nasty, pointed branches lift from the rest, forking outward like sharpened stakes. I try to swallow the dry lump that has formed in my throat when I realize they look like great horns impaled within his forehead.

He stands and my gaze moves up, and up as he is a massive wall of power. He lowers the club, but he keeps a firm grip on it. His black hair flows past his shoulders, and he is a strong presence, both visually and spiritually. I can almost *feel* him in the air, and it's highly unnerving. He nods curtly to the cruel Sky Sorcerer, and I feel a weight press upon my head. My hands shoot up out of instinct.

"Leave it," the man behind me orders.

"What is it?"

He wrenches my hands away, but not before I feel the woven vines and roots that circle the crown of my head. *What the hell?*

Veles cocks his head. He lifts the club toward me, and I tense, staring down the blunt weapon as it comes to rest lightly on my chin. Veles runs the club along my jawline, stroking me. I jerk away, glaring hotly at the smug expression on his face. "You are quite the distraction for my pathetic excuse of an heir."

My heart squeezes. *Nik.* Hearing this fierce, warrior-like creature speak of Nik's fondness of me is disarming. Too intimate and too invasive. *How does he even know about us?*

"I know all," he states, no inflection in his tone, just flat and confident. I panic, my heartbeat accelerating several, fevered notches. *Can he read my mind?*

Veles' eyes flick to the crown of twisted root work atop my head, and I'm hit with clarity. *The crown. It's allowing him to read my thoughts.*

The corner of his mouth inches upward. I *know* he heard me.

I tear the crown from my head and fling it across the floor, watching it slide several feet before landing in a shallow puddle of mud.

"I know all I need," gloats Veles. "My advice to you is to tame those emotions of yours. You're drawing senseless attention to yourself. If you have caught my notice, then surely the mighty Perun has as well. Even mere mortals are questioning everything they have come to understand about their environment. Their so-called *science*." His tone drips with disgust.

I pinch my eyes tight, studying him with careful restraint. He draws himself straighter. "Allow me to state this in simpler terms, so that your partial-human brain may follow. You're affecting the natural ebb and flow of humanity's earthly climate. Sooner or later, you'll dampen their fragile egos, and then chaos will ensue. Perun may even smite you himself." With that, he smiles, his teeth like a shark, serrated and lethal.

Something's not right, I think. *What am I missing?* Irritation rings through my blood. "So, you brought me here to warn me? Out of the goodness of your heart? Somehow I really doubt that."

His mouth morphs into a wide, wolfish grin. "Ah…my lovely. So fair, and so wise. You don't need the Diadem of Truth to see right through me." His steps rattle the walls as he leisurely moves down the dais until he is standing before me. His immense size reminds me of a slab of granite, resilient and unmoving.

He gives me a measured look and says venomously, "Stay away from Nikolas."

My breath snags at the back of my throat, and my hands shoot to my chest, covering the dull ache that pulsates from my heart. *Nik.* I had never heard him called Nikolas before. It's a beautiful name, for an equally beautiful man. As much as I want to be defiant and say something biting like: *"stop me"*, or *"you can't keep us apart"* the queasy turn in my stomach keeps my lips tightly sealed. *Nik and I aren't together, we never were.*

Veles glances at the other man. "Take her away." He turns his back to me and slowly climbs the stairs leading back to his throne. I have been dismissed. I'm grabbed roughly by my forearm and the now familiar gust of chilled air slices through the fabric of my clothes just before it whisks me away.

I'm deposited back into my bedroom. Just before my capturer materializes back into thin air, I say, "Wait."

He slides a bored look my way, his form blinking in and out as if lit by a strobe light.

I frantically search my room, dashing back and forth like a crazed bee buzzing flower to flower. "Where is he?" My voice comes out panicked, and several octaves higher than usual. My floor is bare, not a trace of my father's fallen body, or the damaged wall for that matter.

His brows lift marginally and he vanishes.

"No!" Tears blur my vision as I run to him, but I'm too late. He's gone. And so is my father. I look over my shoulder to the very spot he died before my eyes. It's as if nothing ever happened. The floor is clean, and the wall where I blasted the terrible Sky Sorcerer looks untouched. *What the hell?*

The emptiness in my chest swells, threatening to swallow me whole. I lost Nik, and now my father. *How am I supposed to go on?* I sweep my gaze bleakly around the room. It's quiet and undisturbed. *Surely I didn't imagine that?* I shake my head fiercely. *No.* I can still clearly see my father's sightless eyes as they stared out into nothingness. A dull ache blooms behind my eye sockets, and I hook my fingers behind my neck, and squeeze. I slowly pace the floor. *What happened?* My feet drag to a stop and I slide my hand across the wall. It's smooth, the pale lavender paint still intact. *Am I going mad?* I let my hand drop as if it were weighed down with an anchor.

"His body has been incinerated and returned to the cosmos."

I scream, and turn around to find a woman standing a few feet away. She observes me quietly, her steely eyes searing into me like twin branding irons.

"Wha…what did you say?"

"The man," she says. "I assume your father. His body was incinerated. The remains blessed and offered to the cosmos."

I sag into the wall, sliding down the length of it until I'm huddled into a ball on the floor. I hug my knees. *Oh Daddy.* All at once, tears prick around my eyes, and wet my cheeks as though I were standing amidst a furious downpour. I press my forehead to my knees and just let them come. I stay this way so long I almost forget about the mysterious woman standing in my bedroom. It isn't until she speaks again that I lift my head.

Her gown, though once lush and beautiful is now a tattered frock that hangs plainly from her frail body. The velvet hem is fraying from constant pacing, and her feet are bare.

"Do you know what happened to my friend?" I question. "Did he...did he hurt her?"

"She was returned home safely. I wiped her mind clear of the memory."

For a fleeting moment, I am relieved. I exhale a trembling breath and fold my hands in prayer. *Thank god Lora is okay.* But as quickly as the relief washed in, it is quickly doused and again I find myself distraught, and fumbling for a shred of hope.

I set my gaze on the woman. "Who are you?"

Her eyes are quick as she openly appraises me. She clasps her hands in an attempt to be dignified, but her once intricately braided blond tresses lie in a disheveled clump of tangles. A tarnished tiara sits amid the cluster of dirty mats. The tempered gold weaves through her hair, a single teardrop-shaped ruby dangles from the delicate crown, resting against her forehead.

"I am Diva-Dodola."

I gasp at the name. *Nik's mother.* She is not exactly what I pictured. Somehow I envisioned a beautiful woman, full of grace and nobility. *This woman.* I gaze at her weathered face. It's plain, save for the faint lines fanning out around her eyes and lips, revealing years of sadness. *This woman is a ghost of that image.* Her shoulders had been trained to hold an air of superiority in them, but now she stands hunched, almost as if she wishes to hide within herself from the world.

"What are you doing here?"

"Isn't it obvious?" She turns her face, and I see the similarity of Nik's profile in hers. The strong nose and harsh collection of angled bones. "I've tended to Veles' mess."

My heart lurches in protest as a mixture of anger and agony seeps through me. "And by mess you mean my dead father?"

Her eyes are cast down as she slowly turns back to me. Her lips are practically non-existent as she purses them so tightly.

"How did you know he was here? Have you been spying on me?" I climb to my feet, relying on the wall to support me. "Did you *watch* him murder my father?" My hands tremble with building rage.

"No," she says simply.

I huff out an unamused chuckle, though there is absolutely nothing funny about this conversation, or the situation. I cannot seem to wrap my head around the fact that Diva-Dodola is standing in my bedroom, admitting to me that she…*burned* my father's body and delivered the ashes to the cosmos.

"Want to know what I think," I ask mockingly. "I think…*stalking* runs in the family. You, and your son like to *poof* yourselves anywhere you damn well please. I don't know what it's called in your world, but on earth it's called stalking, and it's a criminal offense."

Diva-Dodola's eyes blaze. "Do not waste my time with your senseless rambling."

"Then how did you know?" I demand through gritted teeth.

Her small hands clench into fists. "Do you think that I do not know my enemy?" she shouts hotly. "That

I have not studied each wretched intake of air he takes? That I do not know the gait of his walk, the weight of his blows, the tone of his sadistic laugh?" Her lips quiver with vehemence. "I've been hiding among the shadows, waiting to take my revenge."

"So why now? Why are you here?"

"Veles is tampering with my son's happiness. I can no longer bide my time."

Even though she stands halfway across the room, I search her eyes, and her face, desperately needing clarification on those powerful words.

"My son loves you greatly," she says.

My heart nearly goes nuclear within my chest. *Nik loves me?* Before Cloud Nine can whisk me off my feet, Diva-Dodola continues to speak.

"But his acceptance of what he is overrules that love. He knows of the evil that poisons his veins, and has come to terms with it. Until you can love him in spite of his tainted blood, he will choose to stay away. To protect you."

"Protect me from what?"

"From being hurt." She pauses, her eyes fluttering closed for a moment. "As the son of Veles, Nikolas is bound by his father's blood. The connection keeps him submissive. The only way to break the bond is death, or with the strength one finds when connecting with their Polar Mate."

Like two magnets, her eyes pull me, and I unknowingly move across the floor. "What are you saying?"

"I do not need to confirm what you already know."

I'm breathless as I murmur, "I'm his Polar Mate?"

She straightens, and for a fleeting moment, she

looks like a regal queen upon a throne.

"Without his Polar Mate, Nikolas is volatile, and easily swayed to wickedness. But now that Nikolas has found you...Veles worries that he will undermine him, and the very foundation of his power will crumble."

"That will never happen," I admit. Remorse overcoming me like a slap to the face. *Nik has never said he loved me, and besides, with my kiss of death, we can never be...*

"It's already begun."

"How?" I ask disbelieving.

"He rescued you from yourself."

I recall the first time I laid eyes on Nik. His hooded shirt soaked to his skin, and those captivating eyes as he regarded me with the intensity only he can possess.

"You're wrong about Nik," I say. "He walked out on me weeks ago. I haven't seen him since." I close my eyes and quietly absorb my own words. I hear the soft padding of her bare feet as she walks toward me, and I blink them open again.

She stands before me. With her this close, I can make out the distinct scent of roses. Clearly not what I expect as I take in her tattered rags and neglected hygiene. Diva-Dodola is undeniably a tortured soul. Her body merely a shell and her heart simply beating out of obligation rather than drive.

"I am not wrong," she insists. "It may not look like it, but I *do* know about love."

I feel a pang of pity. She was robbed of the fairytale she deserved. Kidnapped, imprisoned, raped, and then left with the tormented memories of it all. And to make matters worse, she was impregnated by the foul Veles. When she finally bore his son, the child—Nik—

serves as a constant reminder of that harrowing ordeal. *How horrific that must be for her,* I think.

"Perun," I test cautiously.

She cuts me off with a brusque wave of her hand. "Perun loved me *before* I was defiled by that monster."

My brows pinch tight as I consider that. *No. He raised her child as his own...when she was too lost within her despair to do it herself. That...*I think. *That...is love.*

"Heed my advice," she says, her tone taking on an iciness that matches the steel in her eyes. "My son cares for you. He needs you to accept his dark side as readily as you do his good. As much as I'd like to stamp out Veles from the universe, it is nearly impossible given his place among the Underworld. You are the only one capable of diminishing the hold Veles has over Nikolas." She retreats several steps.

"Destiny is like the sun, Abby. It's constant and eternal. Hiding from it is always short-lived, as it continues to beckon with its promise of better tomorrows. As Polar Mates, you and Nikolas are fated to pair. Your differences will only draw you closer."

Her eyes rake unhurriedly over me. "And surely there is something *vile* about you that needs tamping?" She cocks a challenging brow and her mouth twists as if she's tempted to smirk. The air vibrates, and a rush of wind cuts past me. Diva-Dodola's fair hair blows wildly around her head, her simple gown flutters around her ankles, and then...she is gone.

Chapter 18

My body is weary and yearns for rest. I forgo a shower and fall into bed fully clothed. I worry that my mind is too befuddled to sleep, but as soon as I settle beneath the blankets, exhaustion overwhelms me, and I fall into a fast, but fitful sleep. Ever since Nik walked out of my life several long, lonely weeks ago, I am again plagued with nightmares.

Tonight I'm bombarded with images of my father. Forced to relive his final moments over and over, I stir the entire night. Constantly waking to find myself tangled in the sheets, or covered in sweat. I eventually give up, and stare at the ceiling for a while. I replay the night's events continuously, until I'm on the verge of madness. I sit up, realizing I ache all over. It's as though someone has taken a shovel to my chest, ruthlessly digging until there's a gaping hole in my heart. *How will I mend this broken heart?* I wonder.

My Marks tingle in response. It's so faint I barely register it, but as they warm, it affirms what I was thinking. *I need to find Nik.* Sadly, I cannot remedy the emptiness I feel from my father's loss. I will mourn him for the rest of my life. The gruesome image of him lying still on the floor will be forever imprinted on my memory. I can, however, attempt to mend things between me and Nik. No matter how hard I fight against it, there is undeniable attraction. It's impossible to deny it any longer. Not only do I *want* Nik, I *need* Nik.

I stand with shaky knees and move to the center of my bedroom. This will be the first time I have ever tried to conjure the elements for travel. I close my eyes, and Nik's voice resonates soundly within my head, "*You must be aware of your body. Be aware of each and every sensation, Abby. The race of your heartbeat. The pull of air as it fills your lungs. Feel the gentle skate of air across your skin. The chill or warmth of it. Feel it.*"

I close my eyes, directing all of my focus on the air around me. At first I feel nothing. How does one *feel* the air anyway? I center myself by concentrating on the rise and fall of my chest. Feeling the weight of my breath as it fills my lungs. The sting, whenever I inhale too deeply, and the pain whenever I forcefully exhale, expelling all my oxygen. Gradually the air takes on a definite shape, possessing a palpability I have never experienced before. I gaze in awe.

Dust motes sparkle as they dance through the air, and the temperature encases me like a warm shawl. Flecks of silver and gold shimmer beautifully all around me, reminding me of a gentle snow flurry. I giggle, turning myself around in child-like wonder, lost for a moment in the splendor.

Something flickers within my belly, and an uncomfortable heat spreads through my veins. Startled, I reel back. My fingertips go numb, and I must shake out my hands to urge the blood to flow back into them. A cold draft slices across my fingers. I flex them, and draw them to my chest. The wind follows my movement, whipping around my body as if tethered to my hands by an invisible leash. It's then that I realize the elements are responding to me. I stare at my hands, and pour all of my mental energy into willing the elements to obey my commands.

The wind races wildly around the room as I struggle to train my thoughts. Its reckless flight dizzying as it blows picture frames off the walls, sending glass shattering and skittering across the hardwood floor. I stand there wide-eyed, witnessing the destruction, absolutely terrified of my own power, but before I can attempt to restrain it, a gust of icy air circles around me and whisks me away.

****

I land face-first on a patch of dewy grass. My chest stings from the impact, and I look out across my outstretched arms. I am back in the Underworld. I squeeze my eyes shut, wincing as I lift onto my hands and knees. With a groan, I force myself upright, and dust off my knees. I'm back to the strange land where Veles rules. I can't help but feel a niggle of unease. Veles is powerful and incredibly dangerous. Stepping foot back in his realm is risky, but it's the only way to find Nik.

A stretch of clouds, like metal bars reach across the glistening copper sky. The pungent smell of sulfur mixed with the thick perfume of wildflowers fill the air. The distant howl of an unknown animal prods me to get on the move. I'm not sure which way to go, as the expansive landscape shows no indication of a path or definitive direction. I have no option but to trust my instincts, so I begin to weave my way through the thicket of peculiar bushes.

They cut across my legs, imbedding prickly burs into the fabric of my pants. Every shade of green fills my vision, the deeper I trek through the jungle-like foliage. I walk until my feet ache, and finally the trees open up. My throat closes at the sight. I stand for a moment, wiping a hand across my sweaty brow. I stare at the old, weathered castle looming in the distance. *There it is,* I think. *And here I go...*

With heavy, reluctant feet, I trudge onward, my chest tightening like a fist the closer I get. Panic builds and every warning alarm within my body shouts at me to turn around. To run like hell in the opposite direction, but I shove those thoughts away, and continue on until I'm standing in the center of the forgotten courtyard. Cracks in the stone layout mar the once beautifully crafted brickwork, giving it an eerie presence. Like an ancient tomb, long abandoned and left to the wiles of nature.

I gather what little courage I have and enter the seemingly always-open entry gate. The castle's dank odor fills my nostrils, and I choke back a gag. Black cobwebs, as thick as cotton threads hang from every dark corner. I study one as I pass. In the center, a bulging wrapping of webbing sits ensnared. It suddenly jumps and thrashes, and I startle with a jolt. *Jesus!* I pick up my pace, not wanting to meet the spider responsible for the strange web work, nor do I want to be here whenever it returns to feast on the poor creature trapped inside.

I move through the foyer, trying to keep my footsteps light as I do. I'm vulnerable here in Veles' castle, and I desperately need to find Nik, before Veles finds me. I hug the stone walls, creeping slowly through the hallways, keeping to the shadows as I carefully skirt the grand throne room. A winding staircase opens up before me. My eyes dart in every direction, but I see no one. I start to climb the stone steps. Rusty metal sconces line the wall, each burning plump candles. The stairwell reminds me of a cavern, with its damp air and trickling moisture that clings to the stones. The higher I ascend, the deeper the dread runs through my bones. I feel as if I'm walking straight into the heart of a lion's den with a loin of pork around my neck.

The last step brings me to a deteriorating archway. My shoes crunch on the fallen sheets of rock. As I tread my way through it, I accidently kick a few pebbles, sending them pinging across the floor. I flinch, and quickly scour the area around me. Still no one. I breathe a sigh of relief and that's when I catch it. The scent of honeysuckle and rain. *Nik's scent.* My heart lurches with excitement. *Surely it can't be this easy?*

I track it hungrily, hurrying through the sprawling hallways and savoring each deep pull of the heavenly scent until I'm standing at a thick wooden door. I *know* he is behind it. I can smell him. I can *sense* him. My Marks flare, sending a zap of pleasurable warmth through me as they confirm it.

My heart pounds anxiously against my ribcage anticipating his reaction when he sees me. Will he be happy? Angry? I take a deep breath and lift my hand to knock. Fingers cover my mouth, almost smothering me. I jerk and claw at them, but they dig deeper and I am yanked into a shadowed corner.

My back is pressed against a slab of muscle, and the putrid smell of burnt flesh rolls through the air. *The Sky Sorcerer.* I scream into his palm, but it comes out strained and muffled.

He smooths my hair like I'm a child.

"Shh."

I close my eyes and shiver. His tenderness is repulsive, and I can't help but think it's all part of his demented game of cat and mouse.

His lips brush against my ear as he says, "Miss me?"

I'm gripped with panic as he leads me down a flight of stairs. Our footsteps echo in the narrow corridor, and the sconces flicker in a maniacal frenzy, throwing off a splash of pale glow against the walls.

He takes his hand away from my mouth. Before I can summon a scream, he snatches a handful of my hair, and cranks a tight fist. I wince. It feels as if he's about to rip each strand from my scalp. He steers me in the direction of the throne room, and I can see Veles' silhouette draped across his massive chair. The tips of his horned crown cast a thin shadow across the dimly lit floor.

I dig my feet into the stones, trying desperately to slow our pace, but he thrusts me harder. A gasp escapes me, and I lift my hands to my head trying to relieve the pressure of his hold. We are at the bottom of the dais now, and I keep my eyes downcast, finding a crevice in the stonework to concentrate on.

"Well, well, well," Veles says. "Look what vermin we have found amongst our walls."

I press my lips together, forcing shallow breaths through my nose.

"Look at me when being addressed."

I refuse.

The Sky Sorcerer yanks my head, easily tearing out a clump of hair in the process. I cry out, and my eyes fall upon Veles. He's watching me with minimal interest. His club propped against his shoulder, and his knees spread wide.

He shakes his head in pity, and says, "Mortals are dreadfully uncouth." His face artificially brightens and he manufactures a faux smile. "Oh but wait. You are not merely a mortal. You possess the Mark of Light."

I struggle under the Sky Sorcerer's firm hand, but he only ratchets his grip tighter.

"How did you know?" I demand.

His smile collapses and his sharp face is carefully sheathed into neutrality. "The power within you is potent. The taste of it burns my tongue like acid."

I study him, thoroughly confused. *The taste of it?*

He smiles thinly. "Call it a gift," he explains. "Magic is something I can sense on many levels. Yours is highly toxic, which makes me wonder why a fragile thing like you was chosen to possess it."

I bite my lip as I try to keep my thoughts at bay, but they run unbridled around my head. *Ah, fuck it. Veles is going to kill me anyway, so why the hell not?*

"I was chosen," I start, giving him a level glare. "So that one day I may cross paths with your son."

Veles' mouth twitches into a scowl and his brows pinch over his dark eyes. "Indeed," he finally replies. "Allow me to enlighten you, young Sorceress, to a fact so steadfast it may as well be chiseled into stone."

I hold his stare defiantly, yet I stand on trembling legs.

"As of right now, Nikolas is loyal to me." He touches his fingers to his broad chest. "As long as you're alive, you will always be a direct threat to that." He removes his intense glare from me, and orders, "Kill her."

"No!" I buck and flail against the Sky Sorcerer. Adrenaline courses through me as every bit of instinct kicks into overdrive. *I must get away!*

He releases my hair, and before I can anticipate the movement, his hand comes up and backhands me. Pain shoots across my cheek, and my vision blurs around the edges. I blink and try to focus. He snares me by the arm and hauls me out of the throne room. I refuse to go easily. I drag my feet, and dig my heels into the stonework floor, railing against him until the last shred of energy and muscle is spent.

"No," I yell. "You can't do this!"

Amid the commotion, I happen to catch a glimpse of Veles' satisfied smile. This unleashes a fury within me that sends a piercing heat through my blood. I am about to shout something vulgar when the Sky Sorcerer whispers against my ear.

"You didn't get your fighter's spirit from your father. The old bastard didn't give me an ounce of resistance. It was pathetic."

He laughs sadistically, and my skin sizzles like burning coal. He thrusts me through the archway leading back into the castle's courtyard. It's raining now, and the chilly air cuts through my clothes. It's not long before I am completely drenched, my hair hanging like a weighted curtain down my back.

He's stalking me like a hungry wolf. My stomach twists so violently, it nearly doubles me over. There's cotton in my mouth, and it will not moisten no matter how much I swallow. I close my eyes for a beat. I know it's unwise to be vulnerable at a moment like this, but I can't help it. I *need* a moment to collect myself.

"Come now, Sorceress," he says. "Are you really

going to make this easy for me? What happened to the fire you had before?"

Fire? Anger stirs within me as I realize he's absolutely right. *Where is the fire I had before?* I open my eyes, and glower at him, wriggling my fingers, searching the depths of my body for it.

He crouches, ready to spring like a deadly predator, and the corner of his mouth quirks into a sinister smile. I retreat a few steps, keeping a watchful eye on him, as he reminds me of a tomcat playing with his prey right before he eats it.

"I'm going to leave your body to the vultures." He hurls himself forward, the momentum crashing into me like a freight train. The air is knocked out of me, and I wheeze and struggle to siphon in just a fraction of oxygen. His hands wrap around my neck and I'm catapulted back to Lora's living room. The squeeze of Tony's strong grip and the desperation to draw in a single gulp of air.

"Take your hands off her." His voice is frosted with carefully contained anger. My breath hitches, and it feels as though a thousand hands burst into applause within my chest. I shift my eyes to look upon the face I've been dreaming of for weeks. *Oh God. He's so beautiful.* A gray hood is pulled low over his eyes. Water glistens off his full lips, and raindrops pelt his shoulders and chest, making his shirt stick to him in a sinful manner.

The Sorcerer doesn't free me, in fact, he digs his fingers deeper. I wince, but bear through the blinding pain.

Nik lets out a throaty growl. "I said…take your god-forsaken hands off her." He slides the hood back from his head. His normally golden hair has turned nearly black from the rain, like tarnished brass. We lock eyes. Our electric exchange relays unspoken words in the matter of seconds. *I've missed you. I'm scared. I want to hold you. I love you.*

"Nik," he says, his tone condescending. "You musn't be serious?" He releases me, pushing me away with a hard shove.

Nik is carefully controlled, but I catch the muscles in his face strain a fraction, his eyes sweeping across me, ensuring I'm okay before his heated glare swings back on the Sorcerer. The contempt radiating from him is tangible, and practically crackles with energy.

"Touch her, and I will break your bones with my bare hands."

The man scoffs and glowers darkly at Nik. His lip curls into a snarl, and he says, "If I don't feast upon yours first." He breaks into an even lope, quickly making haste across the courtyard. Through the sheet of rain I see Nik charge forward. I hold my breath as the men clash like two rolling tides.

I remember my power; my fire. I blot out the disturbing activity around me, and will the spark of heat within me to ignite. It flickers softly. Then, I feel it licking at my veins, racing just below my skin like an electrical charge. I command it to my fingertips, and fix my eyes upon the Sky Sorcerer. He laughs maniacally as he shoots icicle darts from his palms. I watch in horror as they embed like needles in Nik's chest, and his body jolts with obvious pain.

"Nik!"

The Sky Sorcerer divides his attention between the both of us, but he looks far from worried. In fact, a giddy excitement colors his sharp features. *Killing is just a game to him,* I think. *But I refuse to crown him victor.*

"You were told to kill me," I taunt, though my voice is diluted with stark fear. "Not waste time playing in the rain."

He snickers, and his focus becomes singular as he studies me.

Just one touch, I think.

He charges, and I move to meet him halfway, thrusting my hands out like a shield before me. My fingers twitch with the underlying power, and just as I'm about to make contact with the wicked Sorcerer, he deflects, and casts a frosty wall of ice between us, blocking my touch. I reel back and ready myself again, but he bursts through his own barrier with a shoulder, roaring like a savage lion. His face is warped with bitter anger, and his eyes ricochet wildly within his skull. I fumble to align all my energy, but he is too quick, too strong, and too damn ferocious for me to compete with.

A deafening boom rings through the air. I watch in shock as a thunderbolt pierces the Sky Sorcerer's chest. The lightning bolt vibrates with crackling power, sending his body into violent convulsions. His body is jerked backward, falling heavily to the ground. My stomach heaves at the disturbing sound of bone and skull cracking against the stone floor. The stench of burnt flesh is overwhelming. I wrinkle my nose, swallowing back a lump of bile. *I don't care who, or what you are. You don't come back from a thunderbolt through the heart.* His eyes bulge from his sockets, and a wispy cloud of steam wafts off him, like fog across water.

I think I'm about to be sick, but my Marks ripple, grounding me back to reality. I turn to find Nik. He's still standing at the far end of the courtyard, his eyes staring intently, as though he's seeing directly through my skin, and right down to my very soul. He remains statue-still, making no effort to close the space between us. *Perhaps he doesn't care for me anymore.* My chest constricts a little at the thought.

The rain is now a light drizzle. The peculiar sky a shimmering stretch of rust. We stare at one another from across the courtyard, the space between us is unbearable for me, but he makes no effort to remedy that, so I stay rooted.

His shirt is plastered against his brawny chest, artfully revealing each breath he collects and expels. His skin glistens like diamonds from the misting raindrops. Slowly, his hard stare softens, and a smile replaces his rigid scowl. Then, the dimples surface. Those damn dimples. I find myself wanting to run my fingers down each valley. I smile back, and my heart spills over with love.

All at once, we both are on the move. Our paces picking up with each and every step until we collide into one another's arms. His embrace is strong, and comforting and it feels so right. *We* feel so right.

We cling tightly to one another, allowing the seconds to give way to minutes. His scent is potent, and I wonder if it's because of the rain, or from the adrenaline of the fight. Either way it's utterly enchanting. *Oh, how I missed his delicious smell.*

He releases me, then frames my face in his hands. I nestle further into his warm palms, relishing his tenderness. He gazes back at me with those strikingly beautiful eyes. The splash of blue is bold against his tarnished locks, and I want nothing more than to stare at them forever.

"Why are you here?" he asks. His voice is gentle, which is a welcomed contrast to his usual abrasive tone.

"I had to find you," I say.

He implores me to continue, his sparkling eyes desperately searching mine.

"Nik, you are my Polar Mate. I know this not only because my Marks have confirmed it but my heart has as well. It longs for you whenever you're away. It beats only for you when you are near. Irrefutably, I am hopelessly in love with you."

He lets out a huff of sweet laughter. "Oh Abby. You don't know what those words do to me. I have been torn apart since I left."

"Then why did you leave me?"

His thumbs knead comforting strokes across my cheeks.

"I was afraid you could never love me wholly. That you wouldn't be able to accept what I am." He sighs. "Though I consider Perun my father, I cannot ignore my bloodlines. The man who sired me is Veles. His wretched blood runs through my veins." His eyelids close, shuttering his crystalline eyes for a long moment. He finally opens them again, settling them on my face with a seriousness that hits me like a blow to the gut. "I have grown to accept it, but I understand if you can't."

I touch his wrists. "We both have shadows within us that we wish to keep away from the light."

"Abby," he murmurs. "I want to taste your sweet kisses. I want to have comfortable silences and deep conversations with you." The corners of his lips curl into a smile. "Tell me you still want the same."

My heart swells as he recites the very words I used to define love. *God, I love this man.*

"Only if you protect my heart, as I promise to protect yours." I smile up at him, knowing he recalls the conversation we shared all those weeks ago.

He grins and his dimples deepen in his cheeks. *He's going to kiss me. I just know it.* My body buzzes as sirens sound off in my head. I can't allow the kiss to happen, though I desperately want it to.

"Nik," I start, casting my eyes to the creamy column of his neck. I can see his pulse throb against the hollow of his throat. "We can't—"

He dips his head and crushes his lips to mine before I can finish. My eyes grow wide, and I grab his shoulders, trying desperately to push him away. His hands are still on my face, his long fingers reaching behind my ears, touching the vine of Marks that coil behind my ear. They respond eagerly to the touch, flaring with a warmth that arrows straight to my core.

I gasp beneath his expert lips, and his tongue slips past my teeth. He explores the depths of my mouth, and it sends a shiver down my spine. I lean my trembling body against him, relishing the way I fit perfectly against his firm frame. The kiss is desperate, passionate, tender, and absolutely all consuming.

His strong hands refuse to let me go, his palms hot on my already flushed skin. I synchronize my lips to his movement, and our kiss deepens until I feel as though I'm going to burst into a quivering pool of nerves. His body reacts to our kiss as well, sending me into a frenzy of wild, squirming desire. *God, this feels so good.*

My insides erupt into a lightning storm. Spangles

of rippling currents flow through my veins. *No!* I try to pull away before it reaches my lips. But I'm too late. It tingles as it passes through our kiss. Nik trembles from the raw power. *No! Please god no.*

Nik breaks our kiss, and when he lifts his face, his eyes blaze with something unnatural, and I know it's *my* electricity coursing through him. *I killed him…*

He stares, deadpan into my eyes and declares solemnly, "I've been struck."

Chapter 19

I seize Nik possessively into my arms, and bury my face into his chest. "I'm so sorry Nik." I weep into his shirt, my tears quickly merging with the misty rain. I'm chilled to the bone, and sick to my stomach. I'm ashamed of losing all control, and now Nik is dead because of a lustful whim.

Two strong hands fasten to my upper arms, carefully prying me away from Nik's body.

"No!" I clutch tighter, not ready to let go.

"Abby." His voice is like velvet, and I snatch my head up to look into his face.

Nik smiles kindly, his hands lifting to hook damp strands of hair behind my ears.

"You didn't let me finish," he says calmly. He peers into my face, his blue eyes shining even through the gentle mist of rain. "I've been struck, Abby. *Love* struck." Nik presses a tender kiss to my forehead, and whispers against my skin, "You feared your kiss would steal my life, but what it stole…was my heart."

My heart is full, and my body light, as if I'm ready to float on air. But, there is something I must know. I catch my lip with my teeth, and consider how to frame my question, quickly realizing there is no way, except to just *ask*. "How are you not…dead?"

His hands travel to my back and clasp between my shoulder blades. I am locked within the solid cage of his arms, and I feel safe. Protected. The epitome of Nik's definition of love.

"A love between Polar Mates is exceptionally strong," he explains. "Just their presence alone, is enough to oppress the other's demons." He brushes a feather-light kiss to my lips, then says against my mouth, "Looks like I'm the cure to your lethal kiss." I can feel his smile, and it triggers my own. If a person could literally burst with happiness, I undoubtedly will shatter into confetti right here in his arms.

I raise my head, and as my gaze settles upon him, my eyes grow wide, and my hand flies to my mouth, smothering a startled gasp. There, drifting through the strands of Nik's golden hair is a rainbow. An honest to goodness rainbow! It doesn't arc, like traditional rainbows you see stretching across the sky. Instead, the colors are watery and faint, like bars of waning sunlight. It glimmers like a halo around his head, and is absolutely breathtaking.

Nik grows rigid, and releases his hold around my shoulders. He casts his eyes downward, as if in shame and runs a hand through his hair. It's such an automatic and innocent gesture, but he looks so vulnerable, I feel the need to take him into my arms and comfort him.

"Nik," I begin. My eyes again shift to the top of his head. The wisps of watery color undulate like a pulse. I open my mouth to say more, but I can't find a way to express my thoughts. I stare, transfixed and breathless by his beauty, truly humbled by it. There are simply no words in the human language that can portray the awe he instills within me. Just the sight of him is enough to send me to my knees.

His eyes lift, and he regards me with a timidness

that I have never seen in him. As though my next words are capable of making him whole or breaking him into a thousand pieces.

I touch his cheek. "This is why you always wear a hood after it rains?"

He nods. "Mortals wouldn't react well to seeing me this way." He draws the hood over his head, extinguishing the rainbow.

"My cousin Mo would adore you," I say with a smile.

Nik snorts. I slide my hand up, tunneling my fingers through his surprisingly fine hair. I sweep the hood from his head, letting it pool at the back of his neck. I'm disappointed to find that the rainbow has dissipated slightly, its colors faint like a distant haze. Just like a regular rainbow, the beauty is impressive, but fleeting.

"It's beautiful," I say. "*You* are beautiful."

I lift onto my toes and press my lips against his, cherishing the feel of them. Every expert move of them. Even the taste of them.

Our kiss becomes urgent, and we pull eagerly at one another. *Needing* to be closer. *Needing* to be deeper. If I could share the same body as Nik, I would. To experience every part of him, to feel what he feels, and to share the very same breath.

His hands softly graze my hips, then slide along my lower back. I moan against his lips as his fingers slip under the folds of my shirt and skim across my skin. The heat of his touch sends a maddening rush of need coursing through me. He flattens his palms against my back, lovingly caressing my spine.

My hands seek out his shoulders, then slowly move

to the back of his neck. He groans, and catches my bottom lip with his teeth. The muscles in his arms tighten as he pulls me closer, my feet lifting from the ground from his strong embrace. I can feel his heartbeat quicken, as if pounding out Morse code against my breast.

A loud clash, like a cracking whip breaks through the air. I jump at the sound, while Nik reacts with a cool ease, tucking me protectively under his arm.

"Don't worry," he says calmly. "That was my father. He's summoning me."

My eyes round at the mention of Veles, and my stomach clenches into a complicated knot.

Another deafening boom explodes overhead, silencing me instantly. *Veles is pissed,* I think with a dart of terror traveling up my spine.

Nik collects my hand and leads me back to the castle. As I pass through the entryway, I walk with reluctance, my feet practically dragging across the ground. I'm being lead straight into a vicious lion's den. *At least this time, Nik is here to protect me.*

We enter the throne room, finding Veles standing a few feet away. His eyes burn like twin furnaces as he glares angrily at us. His deep, furious breaths are like controlled pants, each filling the crawling branch work that reaches across the breadth of his chest.

He points at me with his club, staring down the length of it with a look of dark resentment. "Why is she still alive?" he demands.

Nik steps in front of me, shielding me with his body. "You ordered her dead?" The tension in the air thickens as comprehension slams into Nik. I feel his whole body stiffen, the cords of muscles tightening, becoming battle-ready, like a suit of armor.

My eyes are wide with fright as I cautiously peer around him.

Veles snorts in response, but he looks far from amused. His features are like cut glass. One touch, and the sharp angles would surely rip you into shreds.

A rumbling growl works its way through Nik, the sound primal and threatening. He crouches slightly, like a jungle cat ready to pounce on unsuspecting prey.

Blood rushes to my ears, and I feel as though I'm underwater. I know Nik is strong, but Veles is the God of the Underworld. His magic is dark, and extremely dangerous. I touch Nik's lower back, reminding him I am here, silently urging him not to react too hastily.

He glances over his shoulder at me. His face is solemn, drawn into a quiet seriousness that causes the hairs on my arms to rise. He turns his attention back to his father, but not before his hand finds mine, and squeezes. I cling to him, allowing his soothing touch to bring me courage.

Veles settles his stare on Nik. "Your loyalty has been faltering, my son. I believe I have found the poison that has tainted your allegiance." His eyes darken, and flick to me.

I feel Nik stiffen, and his grip on me ratchets tighter. He seems to be barely breathing, his muscles strung taut like a set trap. I'm afraid to even touch him for fear it will spring him into motion.

"The decision you make within the next thirty seconds will determine your fate. Choose wisely Nikolas."

Nik stands glowering at his father. Their heated exchange reminds me of the standoff between two snarling dogs, each cautiously sizing the other up while baring their razor-sharp teeth. Nik finally says without a hint of indecision. "I will always choose her."

The sarcastic curve of Veles' lips shifts into an angry scowl. His eyes flash menacingly, as he lifts a heavy foot and slams it back down into the floor. The walls of the castle shake and the stone floor crumbles to dust beneath the weight of his boot. Packed earth shifts, and begins to rise from the cracks in the stone. Chunks of rock and centuries old dirt move like magnets, rapidly congealing into the shape of a massive creature. Veles grins mockingly as the figure draws itself to its full height.

A scream bubbles up inside me, but I gnash my teeth together to quell it. I stare up at the colossal beast. Made mostly of black soil, the creature reminds me of an ominous shadow. Jagged pieces of rock protrude like claws from his club-like hands.

Nik tucks me further behind him, his strong grip still fastened to me, and I have never been so grateful for his unwavering strength. My legs feel like water beneath me, and I fear that I will collapse at any moment.

"Kill them," Veles orders.

Nik retreats several steps, and says over his shoulder, "Abby, run!"

"No," I shout.

Nik shoots me a dark look. "Damn it, Abby. Get the hell out of here!"

"I won't leave you," I say, straining to be heard over the menacing, moan-like battle cry of the dirt monster. Nik's face pinches into a look of contempt before he yanks me by the hand. Together we turn from the creature and sprint through the corridors, our shoes slapping loudly against the ground. Each hurried step echoes off the constricted passages and carries straight to my eardrums. My head is ringing by the time we make it to the end of the hallway.

As we round the corner, I chance a peek over my shoulder. The creature is fast approaching; its root-tangled feet are swift as it closes in on us with just a few quick strides. Clumps of dirt tumble from its body as it moves, falling across the stone floor like rain. Though it's faceless, it still seems to have the ability to see, tracking our movement with precision. His willowy body bends like an ancient oak tree in a hurricane as he hunkers into a steady run.

His pounding footfalls rattle my teeth, so I grind them together to keep from going insane. With an explosive yell, he lunges for us. I feel the wind cut past me from his swing, as he narrowly misses my head. I run until my lungs scream for mercy.

He charges again, this time seizing me by the leg in mid-run. Before I even hit the ground, Nik summons a lightning bolt, which suddenly illuminates the shadowed room. Like a fissure in a sheet of ice, it stretches and breaks the space lying between the dirt creature and us.

I hear the creature screech, but I am already lying flat on my chest. Pain detonates like a time bomb through my body. My elbows are raw, and my face aches from connecting with the uneven cobblestone floor. My vision dims and the taste of salt and copper fills my mouth.

Nik drops to his knees beside me, touching my shoulder as he quickly assesses me. His eyes are wild, full of concern, and fear. I wince when his fingers move across my cheek. He pulls his hand away, his fingertips tinged with my blood. I hurt everywhere, my muscles, my bones, my skin. I bring my fingers to my face, cautiously probing the throbbing welt that covers my right cheek. I suck a surprised breath in through gritted teeth. My nose is sore, and I carefully touch the bridge. It smarts, but it doesn't feel broken.

The growl that comes from Nik is teeming with white-hot rage, and he wastes no time directing that anger into action.

With a grunt, I roll onto my back, blinking repeatedly to try to clear my swimming vision. I lift my head, which is challenging, as it feels as though it weighs a hundred pounds. I can barely make out Nik's shape as he races toward the creature. The monster runs to meet him head-on. The cry it emits sends a shiver of terror through me.

Another crack of lightning breaks loose, and the beast staggers momentarily.

I struggle to prop myself into a sitting position, steadying myself by planting both hands in front of me. I squint, and my heart lurches as it takes a few scary seconds to locate Nik. I find him, running full speed toward the creature. It takes all my concentration to track his movement. With a ferocious roar, he leaps into the air, and cocks back a fist. His face twisted in heated fury as he slams a fist into the center of the beast's chest. Electric bolts spangle from his clenched hand, bursting the creature from the inside out. Dirt and clumps of earth shower overhead, landing with soft thuds against the stonework. Nik lands gracefully into a low crouch, the volley of dirt raining over him like a hailstorm. His golden hair is now dark and his face streaked with soil.

He's panting heavily, but when his eyes land upon me, he easily makes haste, quickly covering the space between us. He draws to an abrupt halt beside me, and falls to his knees.

"Abby," he says hurriedly. "Abby. Are you all right?" He looks me over frantically, touching me everywhere, as if checking a porcelain doll over for chips or cracks.

I give him a small nod as he takes me into his arms. I sink against him, nestling into his chest as close as possible, savoring his sweet smell. I never want to let him go. *He could have been killed.* The thought sends my stomach into my toes. There is a wedge of exposed skin peeking out of the top of his shirt. I lay my cheek against it, his skin smooth and warm at the hollow base of his throat. I listen to the steady rhythm of his heartbeat, and close my eyes, relishing it. *Thank you God for protecting him.*

"Seems as though you have a plenitude of lives *Sorceress.*"

I gasp and turn. Veles stands framed in the stone entryway. The weight of his stare is enough to trigger body-numbing terror throughout my blood. He saunters forward, the muscles in his thighs flexing with each heavy step.

"No matter," he says with a smile. "I'm a patient man. I'll enjoy tearing through each and every life you have until I finally destroy you." He adjusts his grip on the club handle. The massive weapon is like an extension of himself as he slings it over his shoulder assuredly. Then, with determined clips, Veles moves swiftly across the room. I scramble back, ignoring the sting in my palms as I scrape them across the coarse stonework floor. Nik stands and steps in front of me, blocking my view of his fast-approaching father.

"I won't let you hurt her," he growls.

"Then I shall dispose of you as well," Veles counters without so much as a fraction of hesitation or remorse.

My heart is like a captured bird in a net. I have to do something—but what? I don't know how to command storms, or lightning. The elements react to my emotions, but right now the only thing I feel is *fear*. The fiery power that exists within me is stagnant, as if it's recessed into my blood. I'm weak against Veles, but I refuse to just sit idle while he sets his evil sights on Nik.

I climb to my feet and search for something to use against Veles. The castle furnishings are scant, and the vestibule is completely stark. There is not a single embellishment, aside from the torches that line the walls. I look back at Veles, my eyes drifting to the dried branch work that cages his chest. *That's it!* I turn back to the torches. They look out of reach, but I dash to one anyway. *I have to at least try...*

I crane my neck to look up at the torch. Bits of ash flutter through the air. Some land lightly, like snowflakes on my face. I stretch my arms as far as they can reach, spreading my fingers until they hurt. My fingertips barely brush the rusty metal sconce that holds the torch in place. I jump, madly trying my best to budge the enflamed torch.

Behind me, Nik commands a charge of lightning. The sound is thunderous, ringing through my bloodstream and piercing my eardrums like daggers. I wince as the fire bolts come in quick successions, branding the air with an electric charge that lifts my hair from my head. The strike barely slows Veles. He barrels through the assault without so much as a flinch. Smoke wafts from his body, so I know that he's been hit, but he appears unfazed. His eyes blaze through the smog. Like heat-seeking missiles, they never falter, easily staying fastened to me throughout the din and chaos surrounding him.

Nik stretches his arms outward, locking his elbows. He claps his hands together, and as soon as they connect, a sonic boom explodes through the castle. It rattles the walls as if hit with a bomb. I fall to the ground and scramble to plug my ears.

Nik stands firm, his feet planted solidly into the ground. He opens his arms, and again he blasts Veles with another thunderous wave. This time, Veles loses his footing. He stumbles slightly, recoiling a few steps as the vibration still clings to the air.

Stones shift from the walls, and tumble to the floor. I cover my head and flick my gaze upward. The sconce has slipped, and now hangs precariously above me. Filled with renewed hope, I slip my fingers into the cracks of the stonework walls, and heave myself upright. With all the effort I can muster, I leap again and wrap my fingers around the base of the torch, channeling all my strength to pull it out. With a grunt, I tug and am relieved when I finally free it from the metal sconce. *Yes!*

I land on my feet, gripping the torch in my hand. The heat from the crackling fire licks the side of my face. I glance over my shoulder, and catch sight of movement in the shadows. *What was that?* My eyes wildly search the dark corners for it, but whatever—or whoever—it was is gone.

I shift my gaze back to Nik. As if sensing me, he turns his head and our eyes meet. His face is drawn, but he is a source of keen skill and grit. His stance is controlled, and his shoulders sit broadly, like a warrior ready for battle. His eyes soften as he takes in the length of me, and my heart swells to aching proportions for him. *I would gladly risk my life for him.* For a sliver of time, it is just he and I, our exchange intimate and reassuring.

A shred of enflamed wick breaks loose from the torch and falls, landing lightly on the back of my hand. It burns as soon as it touches my skin, and I react with a startled yelp. The pain is quick, but relatively insignificant in light of what is happening. I do my best to ignore it, but Nik's brows are furrowed with concern. *Don't worry about me,* I think desperately. *Worry about—*

My thought is interrupted by a blast of invisible force ripping through the air. It sends Nik flying backward. I scream when his back connects with the rockwork, and he slides to the floor. His head rolls heavily to his chest, and his is still. Too still. My lungs burn and I realize I'm holding my breath as I run to him. *Please be all right. Please be okay. Please be all right.* This is my mantra as I pump my legs faster.

"Nik!" I shout.

I collapse beside him, taking his face into my palms. "Are you okay?" I slide my hands down to his neck, feeling his pulse kick under my fingertips. I expel a breath of relief. Nik lifts a hand to the back of his head, and slowly looks up. The dark scorn that flares within his eyes is absolutely terrifying. His handsome features are chiseled into something harsh, and unforgiving. His lips curl into a snarl, and he shifts forward, ready to hurl himself like a deadly blade.

"Nik," I say gently. He disentangles me from him, and climbs to his feet, staggering a little in the process. I try to reach for him, but he's already on the move. The two men stalk one another like vicious wolves. They circle a wide arc around each other, their gazes locked in a heated exchange.

It's a battle of wills, and neither is going to bow down. Veles growls, the sound sawing through his bared teeth. He quickly advances on his son, and though he is thick in stature, he is quite nimble on his feet.

Nik breaks into a stride, meeting Veles head on, like a horrific collision. My heart is in my throat, watching with rising panic as their movements blur into a series of hard jabs, blocks, and crushing blows. *This is personal*, I think as I watch the two men's fists fly without hesitation or mercy toward the other, despite the shared blood. *This is built up resentment, and flat out animosity.*

Veles sends a terrible uppercut to Nik's chin, snapping his head back. *Nik!* Without even a second thought, I launch myself toward him. All I can think about is protecting Nik. Now fiercely possessive, I will not allow Veles to take what's mine. My love. *My Polar Mate.*

Just before I reach him, I'm hit with a blast of icy air. I let out a strangled gasp, as it carries me clear across the room and slams me into the throne. My skull bashes against the heavy wooden headrest, igniting an incredible ache through my body. A heavy, pressing weight settles on me, and I'm trapped. I'm shackled to the chair, my efforts completely in vain as I struggle against the invisible force. *No!* I look wildly from Veles to Nik.

My hair whips around my head, as I frantically attempt to free myself from the throne. The pressure strengthens, and even my bones seem to cry out from the crushing force. I let out a scream. My vision dims, unconsciousness threatening to pull me into darkness. With the pain being so intense, I find myself welcoming it.

Distantly, I'm aware Nik is calling to me. His voice urges me to fight against the impending sleep, and I blink furiously, directing all of my energy into staying awake. *Come on Abby. Stay awake, damn it!*

The fuzziness surrounding my vision wears off, and I can finally make out the muscular figure of Nik. He's on his hands and knees. Veles plummets a hefty boot into his ribs. Nik collapses to the ground, his body writhing in pain. Veles is like a swooping vulture, patiently awaiting his prey to finally take his last breath.

"Nik," I scream.

Veles slowly turns to look at me. His eyes are harsh, piercing me like needles. I quell the shiver that pricks my spine, and instead, I glower at him.

"Leave him alone!" I shout, thrashing against the invisible chains holding me in place.

Veles give me a sinister smirk as he strolls over to Nik. He takes a clump of Nik's blond hair into his fist, and yanks him to his feet. Nik groans, his hands going to his head, and he winces beneath Veles' unrelenting grasp.

"I swear to all the Gods in this universe," I scream. "I will kill you."

He strikes a blow to Nik's ribcage, buckling him to his knees. With cobra-like reflexes, Veles wraps a thick arm around Nik's neck and squeezes. Nik claws at him, trying to free himself, but Veles tightens like a vise.

Nik chokes and sputters for air. His eyes are round, and bouncing wildly around his sockets. I feel dizzy, recalling the way Tony's hands felt around my own neck. Sealing off my air supply with his two bare hands. *Nik! No!* I can't—I won't—let him feel that pain, that desperation.

Anger boils and surges like molten lava through me. I strain against the unseen force, using every ounce of muscle I can, but it's unmovable. I watch wide-eyed as Veles constricts even tighter. Nik's eyes bulge, and in their frenzy they happen to land on mine. He holds firm to my stare, his mouth gaping open as he fights for each sip of air. Thick cords of veins lift from his neck, and forehead. His face reddening, and soon turning a sickly ashen.

My heart hammers away mercilessly against my ribs, and then...all the fight in Nik stops. Just *stops*. "No!" I shriek. "Stop it! Let him go!"

The corner of Veles' lip curls into a sneer. With slow and deliberate precision, he flexes the muscles in his arm, cutting off the last traces of oxygen to Nik's lungs.

Tears well, and run hot down my cheeks. "Please," I beg through my sobs. "Just let him go. He's your son for god's sake!"

"The moment he chose you over me, Nikolas

died." Veles' eyes cast downward, regarding Nik as he hangs from his arms. He lifts his stare back to me, and gives me a hard look. "He just didn't know it." And with that, he cinches his hold one final time.

My vocal cords rattle until they're raw against my throat as I let out a long scream.

Something emerges from the depths of the shadows. My breath hitches as a slight figure creeps up behind Veles. Materializing from the darkness like a ghost. It's Diva-Dodola. Her small frame is dwarfed by Veles' massive stature, but she does not falter. Her movements are steady and sure as she raises a short sword in the air. A flash of light sparks off the polished metal just as she drives it down into Veles' back. His eyes widen, and his jaw sags in unison. He releases his hold on Nik, and looks down at himself helplessly. His skin pales, and looks paper-thin as the blood spreads, like a blooming rose across his chest.

Nik crumples to his knees, gasping and sputtering as if he just emerged from the depths of the ocean.

Veles' hands clumsily reach for the blade, but as if made of tarnished bolts, his movements are mechanical. He stumbles forward, then sinks to one knee. His face is twisted in a tormented grimace, as his eyes dart madly around the room.

With folded hands, Diva-Dodola reveals herself. Her footsteps are silent as she steps before Veles. Her face is not the face of victory, but of quiet satisfaction. Veles looks stunned, and he grips his heart. His lips quiver, and his mouth hangs open, but only garbled sounds come from him.

"You gave him life," Diva-Dodola says hotly, her brows pinched tightly over her flashing eyes. "Hades will flow with rivers of gold before I let you take it away."

Veles swipes at the air, noticeably missing Diva-Dodola by several feet before he collapses onto his chest. I stare at his still body. The sword still stands brazenly tall from between his shoulder blades. *Is he dead?* As if answering my unspoken question, the weight holding me in place vanishes. *He is,* I think. *He's really dead.*

I am instantly on my feet and running.

"Nik!" I call as I pump my legs as hard as they will go. My lungs burn and my heart feels as though it's beating from inside my throat. Finally, I reach him. I drop to the floor in front of him, and rake my fingers through his hair.

He lifts his head wearily, and gingerly touches his neck. His blue eyes are now framed with a heart-wrenching bloodshot red. It does little to eclipse the beauty of them, and I'm thankful I am still able to gaze into his amazing eyes.

"Oh my god, Nik. I thought I lost you," I say, feeling my face flush, and my eyes prickle with collecting tears. I am a well of emotion, and I am about to overflow, right here, right now. I hurry to press my lips against his hair, hoping it will help quell the impending tears, but as soon as I make contact, I crash against him, weeping and utterly spent.

His arms circle me, scooping me into his lap. I melt into him, allowing his comforting embrace to warm me, to soothe over my frazzled nerves and make me whole again. We sit there, holding tight to one another for fear if either of us let go, we'd fade away. Perhaps I would. Now that Nik is mine, it's impossible to imagine a life without him in it. He is everything to me. I couldn't possibly fathom a smile that he didn't put upon my face, or a flutter in my heart that he didn't ignite. Nik is my everything. I nuzzle against him, drawing in deep, long pulls of his heavenly scent, savoring it as if it were a delicacy.

The gentle padding of bare feet slowly approaches. We rouse from our tender moment, and find Diva-Dodola standing nearby. She fiddles with the folds of her gown, but her eyes settle like bricks upon us.

"I hope," she starts, but her voice cracks and she's forced to clear her throat. "I hope you can someday forgive me for what I've done."

Nik untangles himself from my arms, and climbs to his feet, pulling me up with him. "How can I forgive you, when I've never even condemned you?"

Diva-Dodola's steel-blue eyes shine with renewed hope, and a fragile smile hints at her lips.

"Mother," Nik says. "All of my life, I've waited for some sign…some indication that you loved me…"

Diva-Dodola's mouth opens in shock.

"I thought you despised me," Nik whispers. His fingers tighten around mine, as if drawing strength from me. "Nothing more than a bastard child made of demon seed."

Diva-Dodola shakes her head. "No, Nikolas." Tears trail down her drawn face. "I've always loved you."

"Until today, you never showed it. You left me." He touches his chest. "You *left* me, but I forgave you."

She squares her shoulders, and defiantly wipes her face dry. "You don't understand, Nikolas. You couldn't possibly understand what I went through. You are the *only* reason I still exist."

Nik releases my hand and walks to his mother, his gait a little haggard, a little battle worn. He collects her hands into his and places a light kiss to her knuckles. "It's not for me to understand," he says. "All I needed then and all I need now, is to know that my mother loves me. Tonight, you proved that."

She smiles and breaks into a sob at the same time. They embrace, and even where I stand, I can tell it's been long overdue. Diva-Dodola hugs him as though she's holding her son for the first time. Maybe it is.

They finally break apart, and Diva-Dodola steps back, gathers the top layer of her gown, and dabs her eyes with the tattered fabric. Her eyes flicker to me, and she says, "I shall bow at your mother's feet tonight Abby. Her daughter has made my son whole, and for that, I must thank her."

My heart jumps at her words. *My mother?* I stare at her in disbelief. "My mother died just shortly after childbirth."

The corner of her mouth curves into a knowing smile. "Indeed," she declares simply.

Chapter 20

"I don't understand," I say.

Diva-Dodola crosses the space between us, practically gliding over the worn stone floor. She touches my arm gently, and I recoil slightly.

"Abby," she says calmly, as if talking to a frightened child. "Your power was potent even as an infant. Unfortunately your parents knew nothing of your bloodline, and when your mother placed a kiss to her newborn's lips—"

"No," I say vehemently, growing increasingly dizzy with each passing second. "No, I don't believe that. I did *not* kill my own mother."

"You didn't know any better, Abby. You were merely a baby, without a notion of what you were."

I clamp my eyes shut. "I did *not* kill my mother," I repeat.

Nik reaches for my hand, and I jerk away. I open my eyes and shift them to him. "Tell her to stop this. I didn't kill my mother. My father said her heart gave…" Clarity strikes like a lightning bolt. *I did. I killed her…* My stomach sours and I double over, cupping my knees for support.

I swallow on a dry throat. "Her heart stopped," I say to the floor, feeling the familiar twinge in my nose that comes just before I breakdown. "Just like Trevor's did, and Tony's. I did do it. I killed my mother." Tears flood my eyes, and streak down my face, leaving hot trails behind them.

Nik takes me into his arms, smoothing my hair with a gentleness that washes over me like a salve. I thank God for him. He's the comfort I have sought for so many years. Though I'm not sure even he can console me now. *I killed my own mother.*

"It's quite common Abby," he murmurs against my hair. "So called labor complications in the mortal world are in fact the result of a child Bearer accidently killing their purely human mother. It's not the fault of the child, Abby. They know nothing of their power. Just as you didn't."

I weep into his shoulder. "That doesn't change the fact that she is dead…because of *me.*"

"She is proud of you, Abby," Diva-Dodola says.

I lift my head, peering across Nik's shoulder at her. Her gaze is serene, almost motherly as she says, "She watches you from above, and know that she is at peace."

"How do you know this?" I shift out of Nik's arms, but twine my fingers through his, drawing comfort from his warm touch.

She smiles fondly. "I converse with her nightly."

I'm dubious, but intrigued. "You talk to my mother?"

"Those with the fire in their veins are returned to the cosmos, as is anyone who is wrongfully killed by a loved one who possesses it. They take their place among the stars." She paces a few steps. "While I wandered all those lonely years, the voices in the sky consoled me. Kept me company. Were a constant voice of reason, and kindness in my world of bleak despair."

She stops, and turns to me again. "Your father is now among the stars as well. He's reunited with your mother."

A series of conflicting emotions cut through me. Sadness, marked with uplifting gratification are the crests of the tidal wave of feelings. *At last, they are together,* I think. I am the reason my mother was taken from my father in the first place, and by some sick twist of fate, I am responsible for reuniting them. I find a speck of solace in all this overwhelming heartache by knowing they will exist eternally among the stars now. Somehow that notion is almost poetic.

My mind is a mess of thoughts, but somehow I grasp onto one, my eyes widening as I put the pieces of information together. "Wait. You said only those who possess fire in their blood, or those whose life were taken by a Bearing child. I didn't kill my father, so does that mean he was Marked as well? Was he a Sky Sorcerer?"

Diva-Dodola watches me with kind eyes as I work through that question myself.

"No, he couldn't have been. I never saw any Marks on him, and he wouldn't have been able to kiss my mother if he were a Sorcerer."

"The Mark of Light ran through his lineage," she explains. "One of his late ancestors was struck by lightning, thus carrying the Mark through the Cox family bloodlines. Which is why your kiss never affected him…"

I never even considered that. She was right. I recalled all the innocent pecks I planted on Dad when I was a kid. It wasn't until my kiss with Trevor did I discover the toxicity of my lips. Nik squeezes my hand, grounding me back to the present topic. My father gave me my power. My mother died because of that power. And I have found love in spite of that power. I look over at Nik. His eyes are soft, and full of compassion. A small smile forms at his lips, and he gives me an encouraging wink.

"Your parents will forever reside among the stars, Abby. Take solace in that, and know they are together again." The temperature drops several degrees and a breeze picks up, whisking frantically around the stone walls. From inside the whipping wind, Diva-Dodola looks wistfully at Nik. Her long hair blows, and like long tentacles they lie across her face. Her image warps and vibrates just as she mouths, "I love you, son." Then she is gone.

"Where do you think she went?" I ask as the wind dies down. It's once again stark within the walls of the castle.

Nik shrugs. "In time I hope she returns to Perun."

The memory of my first experience with Diva-Dodola surfaces, and I remember what she said, *Perun loved me before I was defiled by that monster*. My heart bleeds for her, but to endure everything she has and still be as strong as she is, is a testament of the woman's courage and resilience.

"Does Perun still love her?"

Nik's eyes tighten slightly. "Of course he does," he answers. "He has never stopped loving her. A love between Polar Mates is eternal, Abby. He continues to pray for the day she will return to him."

"Then he should go to *her*," I say. "She thinks he stopped loving her after Veles kidnapped her."

Nik's lips smooth into a terse line, and he nods

gravely. "I will talk to him." His eyes drift to Veles' lifeless body. "We should go."

"I truly thought he would be harder to kill," I blurt out. I realize what I said, and cover my mouth in horror. "Oh my god, Nik, I'm so sorry. That was insensitive of me."

He waves me away with a hand. "Don't worry about it. There was no love between me and Veles." He pulls me in front of him, aligning the length of my body with his. "But I thank the gods that he created me. If he hadn't, then I never would have found you." He bends down and presses a kiss to my lips. "And to answer you…even gods will perish if their heart is pierced."

"Oh," is all I eke out. I bite my lip and look down at his chest. Nik's thumb lifts my chin, and we lock eyes. "Don't ever be ashamed of asking questions, Abby. This life, this existence, is all new to you, and I happily volunteer to guide you through it." He smiles at me, revealing his twin, heart-breaking dimples. The air around us slowly picks up until its racing frantically around us. The icy breeze seeps into my clothes, chilling me to the bone. I snuggle against Nik's ever-balmy body, clinging to him as we allow the elements to carry us away.

****

I blink my eyes open and there is a sheet of white ceiling above me. My eyes flick to the right, and I see familiar curtains, fluttering from a gentle breeze blowing through the open window. I recognize where I am. *Home.* I shift just slightly, and realize I'm achy and stiff. I groan, and touch my hand to my forehead.

I look down the length of me. I am covered to my waist with my comforter, and I'm wearing the same tank top I had on under my clothes yesterday. I suddenly recall everything. The evil Sky Sorcerer. Veles, and his ghoulish earth creature. Diva-Dodola. Nik… *Where is he?*

A light gust of wind moves through the room, carrying with it the enchanting scent of honeysuckle and rain. *Nik.* My heart skips, and I search the room for him. He emerges from the hallway, stepping through the doorway. He's holding a plate of steamy food. He pauses, clearly surprised that I'm awake.

He smiles, and says, "Morning sleepy head." He enters my bedroom. His feet are bare, padding lightly as he crosses the floor.

"I made you breakfast." He sits on the edge of the mattress, the bed dipping down with his weight.

I study him. He appears vibrant. Refreshed. His eyes shine with brilliance, and there's an air about him that is placid, not his usual gruff demeanor.

I drag myself backward so that I'm leaning against the pillows. "Everything that happened…really happened, didn't it? I mean, I didn't dream it, did I?"

Nik regards me intently, his face shifting into serious planes and angles. "I wish it were a dream Abby, but it's not."

My chest feels as though stacks of stones have settled upon it, and I grow light-headed.

Nik's hand seeks out mine, and wraps around it tenderly. "Abby, love. Do you remember what I said back at my father's castle?"

I retrace the steps leading to that point, easily drawing up the image of the length of our bodies touching, the feel of his lips pressing sweetly against mine. I nod.

"I told you then, and I'll say it again. I will gladly guide you through this life. We are Polar Mates. You will never be alone."

I reach out and touch his face, tracing my fingers along his full lips. "I love you," I say with a contented sigh.

He places a kiss on the pads of my fingertips, and lays my palm against his cheek. "You have me on my knees, Abby, and I will remain this way forever if you should tell me to do so."

He leans down and I lift my face to meet his. I'm eager to taste him again, still delighting in being able to express my love for him through a kiss. Our mouths merge, working together to create the most tender and blissful display of affection imaginable.

I part my lips to allow him deeper, and he fervently obliges. I wrap my arms around his neck, pulling him closer, moaning against his lips when his chest smothers mine. His strong hand runs along the length of my leg. Even through the thick comforter, it sends a flutter of arousal through me.

We finally part, each panting. Each so on fire for the other, there is no point in denying our needs a moment longer. Nik touches his forehead to mine, and whispers, "If you value your virtue, we better stop now. Another kiss like that, and I will surely tarnish you."

"It would be an honor for you to tarnish me," I say as I tunnel my fingers through his hair.

Nik half-chuckles, half groans. "You shouldn't have said that Abby." He rises off me and sheds his T-shirt. I allow my eyes to wander greedily over the coiled muscles of his biceps, and down to the chiseled etchings of his abs. I lick my lips hungrily. *He belongs to me.* He stands. A sexy smirk spreads across his mouth as he snaps the button loose from his jeans and steps out of them. He wears nothing beneath them. He's impressive, like a Greek god sculpted from exquisite marble. *I can't believe this beautiful being is mine. All mine.* His eyes never stray from mine as he climbs back onto the bed.

I toss the comforter aside. Nik's eye drift across the entire length of my body, a soft growl escaping his lips as he places a hand on my stomach, flattening his palm against my bellybutton. The final shred of my innocence and chastity diminish right beneath his skilled hands. I yearn for him in the most primal of ways. Needing to be touched. Needing to be loved.

"You are so beautiful," he says, his eyes cast down to my abdomen, watching his own hands as he works wide, lazy circles across my skin. As if starting a fire with just kindling, he kneads me expertly until a blooming heat spreads through my core. His fingers tunnel under my tank top, tickling their way up my sternum. I arch into his touch as his hands leisurely roam over me. I let out a gasp as he abruptly removes his hands and yanks me upright by my wrists.

We are nose to nose, and I tremble before him. In one fluid movement, he lifts my tank top over my head and disposes of it over the side of the bed. I sit, exposed and wanton. Anticipating the feel of his mouth against my skin, I'm ready to burst at any moment. Even the cool air is yet another splendid sensation against my bare flesh, and I shiver with ecstasy.

With his eyes still firmly latched onto mine, Nik reaches down and draws my panties down over my thighs, slowly bringing them over my knees and down to my ankles. He fists them into a tight ball and tosses them over his shoulder.

Like the calm before the storm, he observes me for a long moment. He takes care not to touch me, as he stares deeply into my eyes. By now, I'm a writhing ball of need; even just a well-placed blow of air across my ear will surely cause me to explode.

"Please, Nik," I whisper. "I am not opposed to begging."

He quirks an eyebrow, and his smile turns sinful as he crawls over me like a slinking leopard. He places his forearms on either side of my head, sustaining his weight as he settles his apex between my thighs. I clench my legs tightly around him, caging him there.

"For so long, I wished to be the electricity that courses through your blood," he says. "To caress you from the inside out would have been my highest form of salvation. But this…" He pushes into me, stretching me until I turn my head away and scream into pursed lips. "*This*…is heaven in the flesh." He rubs his thumb along the crease of my lips, and I take it into my mouth, biting him as pain plows its way through me.

"Oh Abby," he moans. "I had no idea tarnishing you would feel this damn good." He growls against my ear, and before long, his rhythm has me hypnotized. The agony eventually ebbs and I begin to match him thrust for thrust, as if we are one entity. My blood runs hot through my veins, and the crackle of power sparks deep within my gut. It travels along my bloodstream, warming me as it goes. My throat is on fire as it passes up my neck and builds behind my lips.

Nik looks down at me, his weight pressing me into the mattress. His face and shoulders are framed by the stark white ceiling of my room. I bring my hands to his back and rake my fingernails down his skin. He curses beneath his breath, then fastens his mouth to mine, and I feel the electrical current move like a live wire, leaping from my lips straight into Nik's. It penetrates him, rocking through his body with mind-blowing undulations.

He convulses, but it's not from pain, but from total rapture, and isn't long before we both shatter into each other's arms. We lie there spent, the electricity still charging through our bodies until it eventually subsides and is replaced with a blissful afterglow.

After *literally* sharing the same spark of power that I feared and loathed for so long, I know Nik and I are destined to be more than just lovers. More than just Polar Mates. We are one soul in two separate bodies. Like comets careening through the sky, our lives collided, and the aftermath was far from catastrophic. Instead, it ignited a love so strong, the stars must have aligned our paths themselves.

I nestle into the crook of Nik's arm, and lay my head against his chest. I listen to the gentle drumming of his heart as he skates his fingers up and down the length of my arm.

"You're quiet," he says after a few minutes. "Is everything all right?" He takes my hand and sprinkles feathery kisses across my palm.

"I can't put into words what I'm feeling right now." Beneath my hand, I feel him smile.

"And you call yourself a poet."

I laugh, and raise my head, resting my chin on his chest. "Sometimes the greatest muses leave a poet spellbound, and speechless." I gaze at him, silently wondering if someone had plucked a piece of heaven right out of the sky, and sprinkled it into his eyes somehow. He's perfection in every possible way, as though he was personally handcrafted by the gods. In a way, I guess he was.

A question still remains, and because I can no longer tamp my curiosity, I ask him. "Why are you called a Storm Thief?"

He chuckles. "It's silly really." He hooks a strand of hair behind my ear, his eyes following his movement. "Storm gods expel all of their rage and emotions on creating mighty tempests. A Storm Thief's duty is to evaluate the storm's damage on the mortal world, and when we do…well, humans are so enthralled by us, they tend to overlook any destruction or inconvenience caused by the storm."

"So the Storm gods are upset that you, pardon the pun, steal their thunder?"

"Essentially, yes. We steal their moment of glory, so they gave us that ridiculous name. Unfortunately, it stuck."

I gape at him, and a little giggle bubbles inside me.

He frowns. "I told you it was silly."

I cover my mouth and laugh through my fingers. "It's not just silly, it's utterly absurd."

His mouth twitches into a grin, and he rolls me onto my back playfully. The length of his hard body pins me to the mattress. He's like a massive shield, impenetrable and protective.

"I'll tell you what isn't absurd," he murmurs, smoothing the hair out of my face. His thumbs linger on my cheeks, rubbing calming strokes along my skin.

"Rainbows only exist because of the storm. They

are purely at their mercy. Indulging the whims of the storms, they remain submissive," he says. He traces a finger along my collarbone, and I shiver as a cropping of goose bumps bloom in its wake. "There's a powerful storm within you, Abby. And I will gladly be at your will until the day I die." He sets his mouth upon mine, and we embark on a slow, passionate kiss. I find myself wishing we could stay this way forever. Lost in one another's arms, a tangled display of sweaty, hot flesh as we pass the minutes, hours and days alternating between making love, and resting our spent bodies.

For the next few, glorious hours, we go on to create our own piece of heaven, right here in my bedroom.

Chapter 21

I awaken blissfully sated, but sore. I'm a complete contradiction, as my muscles are loose like jelly, but the ache between my legs is tight as it throbs like a pulse. My eyes slowly adjust to the darkness of the bedroom. I check the clock on the nightstand. Just after two a.m. My backside is warm, and I realize Nik is lying behind me. His arm slung over me, with my back pressed against his chest. His breathing is soft and steady as he's still in a deep sleep.

I snuggle closer, and he stirs. His hand moves, sliding along my hip until it dips down to my inner thigh. There it rests, his fingers splayed wide across my skin. The warmth of his palm radiates through my skin, relaxing me muscle by muscle, trickling into my blood like a sedative. *This feels wonderful.* Just as my eyes flutter closed again, a crack of lightning breaks loose across the ceiling. My eyes jolt open, and I'm shocked into complete silence.

The room floods with an eerie pale glow as a blinding white webbing stretches across the ceiling. It doesn't fade immediately as normal lightning would, instead it lingers, taking the form of slashes and odd symbols I don't recognize.

Nik is on his feet, standing at the foot of the bed. His head is craned upward. His face tense, and scored with harsh angles as he studies the ceiling. "Perun," he explains. "He sent a message."

I shift my gaze to the ceiling. "What does it say?"

The writing fades and another bolt of lightning rings through the air. Again, the network of electricity spells out something in a strange, unknown language. The charge in the air is tangible as the hairs on my arms lift, and a continuous faint crackle snaps from above.

Nik grows rigid. Ever so slowly, he lowers his head and looks down at the floor, his expression dumbstruck.

My chest compresses. "Nik," I say, sitting up. "Nik, what is it?"

Panic seizes me in its unrelenting grip, crushing me as I anxiously wait for him to speak. He remains stone silent, staring at the floor for several moments before he finally opens his mouth, only to close it again. He's clearly struggling with the news, and my mind is a frenzy of possibilities. *Is it about his mother? Is it about Veles? Is he...alive?*

My throat closes, and fear stabs through me. *If Veles is alive, he will surely come for me.* I suddenly feel vulnerable, and too far from Nik. I kick off the blanket and swing my legs off the bed. My feet touch the cold floor, and it sends a shiver up my body.

Nik turns his head to look at me. His eyes somber beneath the fading light of the markings on the ceiling.

I rub his shoulder gently, dividing my gaze between him and the strange script overhead. "What did it say?"

His eyes burn into me and the muscles in his jaw tense when he says, "I'm the new ruler of the Underworld."

Those words still me, my hand instantly freezing in place, resting like a heavy brick atop his shoulder.

"What?" I ask hesitantly.

"I am the only blood descendant of Veles. With him dead...I automatically inherit the throne." He angrily rakes his fingers through his hair. "Damn it!" he cries. "I don't want to take that bastard's place."

"Don't you have a choice in this?" I question.

He stares holes into the floor as he barely gives a shake of his head. My heart sinks at this. *Nik will be the ruler of the Underworld. What does that even entail?*

Another crack of lightning slices through the room, brightening the ceiling with its strange cryptic language. The muscles in Nik's jaw clench as he briefly scans it.

His blue eyes look haunted, as he swings his gaze onto me.

I hold my breath, and wait.

"He's summoning me," he explains. "I must go. Now."

He dresses quickly and moves to walk past me, but I catch his sleeve. "Take me with you."

"No," he says, gently detaching me from him. "Traveling to his realm is dangerous."

I plant my hands firmly on my hips. "If you don't, I will just follow you."

His eyes blaze with a steely fire, but the anger quickly fades and is replaced by quiet resignation. "Perun lives amongst the clouds. The distance will wear on you heavily. It's not like the other Elemental Travel you have done."

"I can handle it," I declare with stubbornness, and I step into a pair of jeans.

A grimace creeps its way across Nik's mouth, but he doesn't say anything. I'm sticking my arms into the sleeves of my sweater when he finally says. "Very well." He takes my hands just as a gust of cold air snakes around us like a coil of invisible chain. It whisks wildly about, pushing our bodies closer and closer until there is not a sliver of space between us. I close my eyes against the whipping winds, as they cut through my clothes and tear at my eyes. Nik wraps me in his arms, shielding me from the biting wind, as it continuously screams like a tortured soul.

We're lifted, and embed within the icy breeze. It carries us away, effortlessly, as if we're nothing more than a waft of a scent.

This travel is indeed different. I am aware of our movement, and the time it takes to travel is noticeably longer. I feel weightless, like a feather caught in a whirlpool, and vertigo quickly sets in. I squeeze my eyes tighter, and hold onto Nik with every last reserve I have within my muscles.

"Almost there," he whispers into my hair.

This gives me hope, but still, my body is ravished by the travel. My head aches from the deafening whine of the wind. The frigid temperatures have me shivering in Nik's embrace. I gnash my teeth together to curb the chattering, but the freezing gales are beginning to numb my fingers and toes.

Just when I think I can't take another second of this, the wind abruptly ceases and we're dropped to the ground. I land with a grunt on top of Nik, my body ungracefully sprawled over his.

"Are you all right?" he asks.

I roll my shoulders, checking for damage, but thankfully there is only slight throbbing from the impact, nothing serious. I nod and lift myself off him, and stand, offering my hand to him.

He takes it, but he's closely scrutinizing me. "Are you sure? That was a difficult trip."

I'm woozy upon my feet, and I desperately need aspirin, but all I say is, "I'm okay."

I help him up, though he seems completely unruffled by the travel. I observe him a moment, noting that while I stand here with wild hair, and a wind-chapped face, wiping my surely frostbitten nose, Nik looks glorious. His eyes are bright, and his cheeks are tinged a healthy pink.

I smile at him, and he gently cups the back of my neck, and draws me closer. "Your courage knows no bounds." He presses a chaste kiss between my eyes, holding it for a beat before pulling away. "Come, Perun waits for no one."

Nik leads me across rolling landscape. Whatever is below my feet is hidden by a thick, low-lying mist. I push away the thought that we are actually walking amongst clouds, because the very idea spikes my heart rate. *How are we not falling through?* I wonder as I watch strands of hazy air swirl around our ankles like a fog. Before us is a grand castle, much different than Veles' dark, dilapidated fortress in the Underworld. This palace is stark white, with glistening turrets that shine like glossy pearls beneath the golden bars of the distant sun. It's breathtaking.

To get to the castle door, we must first climb a series of steep, winding stairs. They are carved out of the massive rockwork that surround the palace, hanging precariously over the edge of a cliff. I take care not to look down as we venture further and further up the staircase. The air is punctuated with a crisp scent, much like the smell that accompanies an impending rain.

"Couldn't we have just been teleported straight into the castle," I pant.

Nik chuckles. "You can't just enter Perun's castle without being properly received first."

"But *he* summoned *you*," I point out. "Isn't he already expecting us? Well, expecting *you*."

"It doesn't work that way Abby," he says with a genuine smile.

"If I'm to be the girlfriend of the future ruler of the Underworld, I guess I need to learn the rules of Elemental Travel."

His grin collapses and he visibly tenses.

I instantly regret my words. It's apparent the idea of ruling in Veles' place terrifies him. I seek out his hand, and pull him to a stop. He turns his back on the wide expanse of empty space behind him. Fleetingly, I assess the drop off that lays just behind his heels, my heart rate spiking at the dizzying height.

"Nik, you're standing right at the edge," I say, my tone wavering as I grow lightheaded. "Come away from there."

He nonchalantly glances over his shoulder. "If it wasn't for you, I'd be tempted to leap off this cliff this very moment." His features are awash with a resoluteness that sends a creeping shiver up my spine. He's on the move again, stalking his way up the staircase with heavy, almost reluctant steps. We don't speak again until we reach the castle's doors. Thick wood so pale it's almost snow white stands tall before us. Studded with polished brass, they are adorned with elaborate scrollwork crafted out of solid gold. A thunderbolt made of some sort of shiny metal serves as a doorknocker.

Nik raises his hand to lift the thunderbolt, but before he can touch it, the doors swing open. We step into a grand vestibule. The floor shines like a slate of glistening opal beneath a beautiful golden chandelier. The walls are slabs of white rock, resembling polished oysters. Towering marble columns are posted in each corner of the room. A golden cord hangs to the right, and Nik pulls it. A beautiful melody of ringing bells, like a beautiful church hymn plays through the room.

A tiny creature scurries from an adjoining hallway and scampers across the floor. It stops before us, and rears up on its back feet. Standing no more than a foot tall, the little figure cocks its head at us. It's a peculiar looking thing, as it seems to be some sort of a nymph, but it moves much like a rabbit.

Its skin is a beautiful jewel-green, and its eyes are huge, taking up most of the space on its small face. It doesn't speak, but it makes a series of clicks and squeaks before again hunching back onto all four legs, and turning around. It glances over its shoulder, its wide eyes expectant as it waits for our understanding.

Nik seems to know immediately what it wants, as he simply begins to follow the nymph through the room. I hesitate a moment, lost in the surrealism of it all. Being in this exquisite palace with Nik, my Polar Mate, a Storm Thief, watching his towering frame follow behind a tiny, supposedly-mythical creature is suddenly too much for me. My ribcage tightens like a contracting corset, and I have to concentrate on my measured intakes of breath.

Nik looks back at me, his brows pinching in question.

"Abby? Are you all right?" In several long strides, he's at my side, touching my wrist.

I nod feebly, and draw in a deep drag of air through my nose.

The nymph flits toward us, squeaking in its high-pitched language that we clearly do not understand. Nik casts his eyes down at the creature, and acknowledges it with a curt nod.

We follow it through the room, and I'm amazed at how speedily and soundlessly it moves. The castle has several wings, and as we make our way deeper into its belly, I steal quick peeks into each room. All are expansive and richly decorated with ivory carvings, clay sculptures, and gold-plated furniture. We enter a large stateroom, and by the plush furnishings, and expensive tapestries lining the walls, it's obvious that it's Perun's throne room.

The nymph stops here. Nik thanks it, and together we go further, passing a rushing fountain. The water flowing over the tiered bowls is an unnatural sea-foam green. A statue of a lovely woman is centered at the top. Her hands are pressed in prayer and water pours out at her feet. It's handsomely carved, and the details are impressive. There are three thrones stationed at the head of the room. The largest is well worn, with its velvet upholstery crushed at the armrests and seat. The other two appear to be completely abandoned and neglected. A fine coat of dust has settled upon them and the cushions are still plump, as though no one has sat in them, nor touched them for years.

I scan the area, searching for Perun, but it's empty. "Where is he?" I ask quietly.

"He's here," Nik answers. "He just hasn't made

himself visible to you yet."

Oh. I sharply look left, then right. Nothing. Then I catch it. There in the distance, near the throne is a gentle waver in the air. It's faint, but it vibrates just enough for me to notice the difference.

"There," I breathe, shocked that I was able to find him.

Nik sweeps his gaze sideways, and gives me a small, but proud smile. "Well done."

I want to return the smile, but all I can do is swallow back my nervousness. The lump of dryness stubbornly remains, sticking uncomfortably to the roof of my mouth. My stomach churns bitterly, and it's almost impossible to ignore the nausea that is climbing its way through me.

The sphere of pulsing air begins to warp and shimmer, and Perun materializes from it. He steps forward as if he just exited an invisible portal, and perhaps he did. I know nothing of these mighty Gods, so dimension travel seems totally plausible. He wears a chest-plate that bears the image of crossed hammers. His boots ride high, covering most of his calf and his wrists are bound in broad, hammered metal cuffs.

He walks with heavy, but purposeful steps toward his throne. I am in awe of him. Veles was grossly terrifying, but Perun is a completely different entity. Everything about him is big, glaring, bold, and overpowering. If he were a force of nature, he'd be a thunderbolt.

He settles into his throne and casts his steely gaze out like a capture net. He snares me with a blazing stare, and I am frozen. His presence is intimidating, and I feel like a tiny minnow alone in a shark tank.

Nik's hand reaches for me, and like a fool, I jump at the contact.

"It's okay," he whispers. "It's only me."

I nod, but refuse to take my eyes off Perun. When I read about him that day in the library, it was said that he's a fair and compassionate God, but still, the mere presence of him unsettles me.

"You summoned me, Father?"

Perun's eyes shift to Nik, and I expel a little sigh as the weight of his stare is removed from me. I focus on Nik, and find comfort in his hand being in mine. I squeeze tighter, and his gaze flickers fleetingly to me in response. He turns his attention back to his father, and I follow suit.

Perun's eyes travel to our joined hands. "Yes. And I see you brought a companion." He looks back at me, and through his thick beard, I sense a slight smile. "Abby Cox I presume?"

My mouth pops open in surprise. He waits for me to speak. I'm not sure if I should curtsey or bow, though I'm sure I'd feel silly if I did either. The word bubbles at the back of my throat, then finally I say, "Yes." He regards me with keen interest. "Sir," I add. My palm feels wet in Nik's grasp and I groan inwardly.

"Do not fear me Child," Perun says with a gentle tone. "I wish to speak freely and forthrightly in your presence, so please do not judge me based on the outcome of this interchange." He shifts in his chair slightly, drawing all his attention to Nik.

"Nikolas, I have learned of Veles' untimely, though justifiable demise," he begins. "I wish to allow you an adequate grieving allowance, but unfortunately this matter won't allow that. It must be dealt with a swift hand."

"Grieving allowance?" Nik's tone drips with disgust. "You think I need a grieving allowance for that man?"

Perun's eyes tighten, as do both fists as they squeeze the armrests. "Forgive me, but I assumed the loss of your blood father would still affect you."

"I felt nothing for him except hatred. After what he did to my mother…" He pauses, his jaw clenching as he breaths deeply through his nose. He closes his eyes for a beat, then continues. "And as if that isn't enough, he had the *audacity* to interfere with my life. As if he had a stake in it." His voice is stronger now. Not a hint of falter in it as he says with a somber expression, "His death is my greatest joy."

"Indeed," Perun says, arching a thick brow. "Well then, expediting to the issue at hand. Without Veles, the Underworld is without a ruler. As the only blood heir, you are expected to ascend to the throne."

No, I think. *Please don't take him away from me.*

"I won't do it," Nik replies with a fierceness that startles me. "Take the damn throne and burn it the ground for all I care. I will *never* reign in my father's place."

Perun stands and slowly descends the steps toward us. That's when I notice the mighty axe strapped to his broad back. His auburn hair is long, and drawn into a ponytail at the nape of his neck. He stands before us, and his massive size crowds our space. The crown he wears is simple. The gold gleams in the light, but there are dents and nicks throughout the precious metal. It's seen many battles, and yet still it sits squarely on Perun's head with quiet pride.

"Son." He places a hand on Nik's shoulder. "Do not allow your hate to decide your future."

Nik looks up, and they hold each other's gaze for a moment. Perun's powerful green eyes match the intensity in Nik's beautiful blue ones. Their exchange is tense, but touching. Nik finally says, "I'm not." He turns to me. "I am allowing my love to decide." He smiles, and for a single scrap of time, everything else fades, and all that exists is *us*. He pulls me close, and wraps me in a tender embrace. "My place is beside her." He dips his head and places a kiss to my lips. My heart bursts with happiness, knowing that he is still mine.

"Very well," Perun says as he spins his back to us.

Still coiled within one another's arms, we turn our gazes to Perun. He mounts the steps and climbs them one by one until he is back at his throne. He sinks into it with an exhausted sigh. "Somehow I knew you would not be swayed." His gaze swings to me, and he offers a kind smile. "And I understand why. Love typically trumps all. You have chosen well, son, and I honor your decision." He nods once in acknowledgement.

I let out a relieved laugh, and gaze up at Nik's handsome face. *He's mine. All mine.* He smiles down at me, and his sweet dimples surface. I want nothing more than to place kisses to each of them. The air in the room turns crisp, like we were upon the cusp of winter season. Diva-Dodola emerges from a gust of blustery wind, and stands at the foot of the throne. Her hair is disheveled, but her face is bright with renewed hope. Her eyes shine, and there is a peaceful smile on her lips.

"Diva-Dodola," Perun says in shock. His eyes are wide, and they cling to her as if her image supplies his very breath. For the first time, his overpowering demeanor reveals a weakness. A chink in his thick armor of muscle and brute size. His love for Diva-Dodola is apparent in his reaction to her appearance. A confused, but elated smile plays at his thin lips. "My darling. You have returned." He rises and reaches out for her. "You have returned." She flinches, but doesn't flee as I feared she would. He registers her recoil, but doesn't press the contact further. He simply lowers his hand with a look of defeat before bringing it to rest on his knee.

Diva-Dodola's eyes are cast down at her feet when she finally speaks. "The restraint of the past is broken." She chokes back a quiet sob, and looks up at Perun. Tears glisten around her eyes, and her cheeks are tinged pink. "Even still, I am not the same as when you married me, Perun. Veles slayed that woman years ago."

"Darling," he says, gently stretching his fingers out to caress her cheek. "Veles' touch did not desecrate you. When snowflakes land upon mud, they do not simply dissolve. They cleanse it from the inside out."

Diva-Dodola begins to weep openly. The tears run down her dirty face, leaving clean trails in their wake.

Perun embraces her, and she leans her head against his chest. I feel that we are intruding on their tender moment, so I turn to Nik, and whisper, "Perhaps we should go." He nods once and conjures the elements to take us home.

As the wind picks up, Perun lifts his head, and says, "I shall oversee the Underworld in your absence, my son. Should you decide to someday take the throne, it will be awaiting you."

Diva-Dodola gently extracts herself from Perun's arms and crosses the floor toward us. Her bare feet pad softly as she moves. She places a small hand against Nik's cheek, and says, "I mothered you from the shadows. I should have been stronger for you." Her face tightens as she fights back emotions.

Nik releases me, and takes his mother's hands. "You are strong," he says. "Your strength *saved* me. Saved Abby. Mother, you guaranteed the safety of the only thing I find precious, and that's Abby."

Her gaze slowly shifts to me, and she attempts to smile, but she ends up exhaling a relieved sob instead. She looks back at Nik, and suddenly pulls him close. He hugs her back, and allows her to place a kiss to his forehead.

"Diva-Dodola," Perun says with his booming voice. "It is time you take your rightful place." She straightens her spine, and pushes her shoulders back as she turns to him. We watch her as she makes her way across the shimmering white floor. She climbs the dais's steps, the train of her tattered gown dragging behind her. She stands before the throne, staring at it for a moment before finally turning around. She lowers herself into the cushion and perches herself on the edge. She wipes the armrests clean, and curls her fingers around them tightly. With a stiff back, she rotates slightly and faces Perun.

"Welcome home darling," he says with a smile.

Nik summons the wind again, and the cold wind carries us away just as Perun reaches out to take Diva-Dodola's hand.

****

The wind dissipates and leaves us standing in the

middle of my bedroom. Jack is whistling happily in the other room, and the familiar sound of him is comforting. Nik's hands rest on my hips, and for a long while I remain quiet, simply staring into his face, absorbing the gentle curve of his chin and the chiseled arch of his nose.

"Penny for your thoughts?" he asks, kneading gentle circles into my skin.

I run my fingers through his hair, sending it into a wild disarray of golden spikes. "You gave up a *throne* for me. Are you sure that's what you want?"

He leans back, and regards me sharply. "When it comes to you, never question my decisions. I will *always* choose you, Abby. I cherish you more than my own life. My last breath will be used speaking your name."

My heart squeezes with joy. *Finally*, I think. *Finally, I have found love.* I have someone who finds my kisses tender, not terrible. Overwhelmed with love, I press my lips to his and he quickly stokes our kiss deeper, hotter, and more eager. The temperature in the room becomes stifling, and soon the windows fog and the fire alarm goes off. We break our kiss abruptly and I frantically search for smoke or fire.

Nik laughs, and takes my face into his hands. "Little Sorceress, you still need to learn to control your emotions."

Realizing I was the reason for the temperature spike, I chuckle shyly, feeling a slight blush spread across my cheeks. "It's impossible when you're around. Especially when you kiss me like that." I cover his fingers with my own, nestling my cheeks further into his warm palms. Gazing up into his sky-blue eyes, I see myself in their reflection.

"Well," he says, brushing his lips across the bridge of my nose. "Then I guess the world just better get used to hot weather." He plants a heated kiss to my mouth, and I melt into the splendidness of it, forgetting about everything else, except the two of us, and our connected lips. With the fire alarm still ringing, a gentle rain begins to pitter across the windowpanes. Nik smiles against my mouth, and we continue to kiss through the contrasting extremes.

Polar Mates. Two completely opposite beings, destined to create harmony as one. That's us. The Storm Sorceress and the Storm Thief. I will continue to create the madness, and Nik will continue to be the beauty that comes after the storm....

~ The End

Epilogue

Perun held true to his word. With his tight reign over the Underworld, as well as the sky, harmony, though fragile, exists amongst the two worlds. For now, Perun remains unchallenged, but in time, the creatures of the Underworld will grow restless, and they'll seek a new ruler. A ruler who bears the blood of Veles.

Nik remains adamant he will never take the throne, but the lure of sovereignty is bred into him. I worry the harder he tries to outrun it, the weaker his defenses will be against it. He could have the entire Underworld at his mercy, to do his bidding should he ever want it, and I can't help but wonder, can Nik truly turn his back on what's rightfully his?

As I gaze at him from the window, his tall frame settled back against the ropes of the hammock, I can almost forget he's the heir of the Underworld. With a contented smile, and that handsome face framed in his upturned hood, I can *almost* forget he's a powerful Storm Thief, capable of commanding fire bolts at his whim.

Jack chirps happily in the living room, and the simple normalcy of the day makes me smile. I open the backdoor, and cross the lawn, realizing it's still dewy from the morning's rain. A squirrel dashes across the branches overhead, jostling the wet leaves. Cold rainwater is shaken loose, briskly showering over me. I shriek with laughter and climb onto the hammock with Nik. The hammock creaks, tilting, and swinging back and forth, as I work to straddle his waist. He watches me, his lips turned up into a heart-melting smile. *God, he's beautiful.*

I brace myself over him by twining my fingers into the fibers of the hammock's rope. Nik's scent is intoxicating. Honeysuckle, and rain. It draws me closer, my hair tumbling forward as I lean in. My heartbeat flutters against my ribcage like a panicked butterfly trapped in a cobweb. It's still hard to believe he's mine. *All mine.*

Nik tenderly brushes my hair back over my shoulders, letting his fingers travel suggestively over my skin. His touch is so gentle it's hard to believe he is capable of creating havoc with just one sweep of his hand. I take his wrists, and press a kiss on the center of each palm, before gathering his hands to my chest.

"Are you nervous?" I ask.

He scoffs. "Please," he says with a playful arrogance. "I'm not afraid of your cousin."

"You should be," I warn with a laugh. "I'm telling you, once he sees your hair, he's going to drag you to every gay pride parade across the entire state. Seriously. You'll become his personal mascot."

Nik chuckles. "A small price to pay to be with you," he says, pulling me down into a kiss. I am instantly lost in him, which is easy to do. Nik is overwhelming. Being near him is like being trapped in the middle of a downpour with no shelter. There is simply nothing you can do but endure it.

"Gross!" exclaims a voice. "Hetero foreplay! Get a room."

We untangle ourselves, and turn to find Mo walking toward us. His dark hair is swept into a slick pompadour, and his lips, noticeably plumper, are curved in a wide, endearing grin that reaches all the way to his chestnut eyes. *Did he seriously get lip injections?*

"Mo," I say, a little flustered, and breathless from Nik's kiss.

He pops the collar of his polo shirt, and struts like a proud peacock in his electric green capris. "The one and only." In true Mo fashion, he's impeccably dressed, although the lace socks and loafers seem a bit pretentious.

I slip off Nik, and smooth my sundress back into place, distinctly aware of my flushed face. "Hey," I greet, reaching my arms out for a hug. Mo embraces me while simultaneously pecking me on the cheek. I'm surprised by his choice of perfume. It's rather tame today, sweet, and dainty, not the usual overbearing spice that chokes you from across the room. When he pulls back, he regards me closely, and unapologetically. When he finally gives me a wink of approval, I exhale a breath of relief. It's strange for me to be nervous of Mo's reaction to Nik, but having his support is important to me. Now that Dad is gone, Mo is the second most important man in my life. Nik being the first, of course.

"Looking good girl," Mo says with a flourish only he can pull off. "Love looks good on you."

Nik strolls over to us, reaching past me to offer his hand out to Mo. "Nice to finally meet you."

Mo lifts an artfully shaped eyebrow, but he takes Nik's hand, and the two men shake. "So this is the famous Nik," he says, his eyes firmly set on Nik's. *He's being protective*, I think to myself, my heart expanding at the notion. It's an odd quality to see in action. Mo normally is desperate to push me out on dates, or into awkward conversations with strangers.

The two release their grip, and Nik brings his hands to my shoulders. The innocent touch warms my Marks, and they darken, as if they're blushing. Mo doesn't miss this, and his brows dart into his hairline. I purse my lips, wondering if I should have opted for a more discreet outfit, but Nik likes my strapless sundress. That morning, as I dressed, he traced a finger down my scars, and said, "Your Marks drive me crazy. Don't cover them up." Right then and there, I swore to wear less turtlenecks, and more spaghetti straps.

Mo cuts his gaze to me, his expression aghast. "What the hell was that?"

I knot my fingers at my stomach, clenching them tightly to ground myself to this moment. The moment I tell Mo everything. "Mo," I start. "I need to tell you something." Nik squeezes my shoulders, silently reassuring me of his presence, and unwavering support.

I tell Mo everything. Sky Sorcerers, Storm Thieves, Perun, Veles…I don't leave anything out. Not even my father being cast into the cosmos with my mother. Mo's eyes grow round, and his brows pinch sharply as I speak, but otherwise he seems to be taking everything in with cool composure. When I'm finished, I bite my lip nervously, waiting for his reaction.

Mo takes in a measured breath, then crosses his thin arms. The seconds tick by, and with them, my knees grow weaker, and my stomach twists tighter.

"Well," he finally says. "Shut my mouth, and slap

my hiney red." A smirk forms on his lips. "Abby, when you finally land a man, you go out and claim the hottest one around."

"What?" My head spins. *Did he not hear anything I just said?* I stand here, gaping at him like an idiot, not sure what exactly is going on. "Mo, were you even listening to me?"

He rolls his eyes. "Of course I heard you. You both belong to some weirdo fandom, and you think I'm going to judge you for it." He flicks his wrist flippantly. "But it's okay by me. Everybody needs love. Even fan boys and fan girls. You two do your thang."

I'm speechless for a long moment. *What?* I stare at him, part of me compelled to slap him, but part of me wanting to laugh. *He thinks Nik and I are part of a fandom? We're two people extremely obsessed by what? The weather?*

"Morrison," Nik says in a calm, soothing voice. Mo starts, and his cheeks flush pink at his full name. "Abby and I are part of a rare population of beings that thrive amongst nature's elements. I am not a mortal, and Abby is what's known as a Bearer. She has the Mark of Light, which gives her the ability to bend the elements at her will."

I touch my Marks to drive Nik's explanation home. Mo's questioning eyes track my movement, and a dawning starts to spread across his face. I offer him a sympathetic smile. *His mind must be spinning*, I think, remembering how overwhelming this discovery was to me when I first heard it, and how completely implausible it all seemed. Sometimes I *still* find it far too fantastical, and surreal to be reality.

Nik casts his gaze to the sky. A light mist lingers in

the air from the morning's storm, and the scent of rain still clings to everything. The grass, the trees, the breeze. The muscles in Nik's jaw work, and his eyes, though pensive are like cut ice. I tense, suddenly realizing what he's going to do. He swallows, and then lifts a hand to his hood.

My breath hitches as he slowly draws the hood back from his head, letting it pool between his shoulder blades. Mo watches suspiciously at first, but as soon as the sunlight catches Nik's golden hair, his mouth hangs open wide.

"*Holy Cher*," Mo exhales in a shaky voice, his eyes transfixed to the watery rainbow undulating from atop Nik's head. The sight of it still causes me to pause, so I gaze at it as well, lost in its beauty. The transparent colors wave gently in the breeze, warbling, and dissipating like an actual rainbow after a storm.

Mo is noticeably paler, but he only says, "You're a walking, talking gay pride flag." He raises his hand over Nik's head, running his palm through the rippling colors. "Amazing. If we could bottle this, we could make a fortune! Do you know how many gay men would die for this hairdo?"

The seriousness in Nik's face breaks into a charming grin, and he drops his gaze to me. I turn to Mo. "You're not freaked out by this?"

"Freaked out by this?" He jabs a thumb toward Nik's head. "I admit I don't quite understand what this all means, but honey, let me tell you. I know a few men with stranger lifestyles than this, *trust* me."

I snatch Mo into a fierce hug. He hesitates a beat, then wraps his arms around me. The weight of this secret was a heavy burden to bear, and I'm so relieved to finally share it with him.

"Have you told any of this to Lora?" Mo asks against my hair.

Lora. Sweet, breakable, on the verge of collapse, Lora. I bite my lip, and lean back. "No," I answer quietly. "She's met Nik, but she doesn't know the truth about him. Or me."

Mo nods in understanding. Lora is still too fragile from Tony's death. The adjustment of being a single mom has been straining and incredibly exhausting for her. This revelation could send her straight over the steep edge she's currently treading. In time, I'll tell her, but first she needs to heal. To become herself again.

Before the pause in conversation becomes uncomfortable, Mo tugs me into a hug again, and whispers in my ear. "If he has any bi-curious brothers, you'd tell me, right?"

I laugh, and elbow him in the rib. "Of course I would."

We break apart. "So does he?" Mo persists. "Please say yes." He presses his palms together as if in prayer.

"No." I shake my head. "I'm sorry."

He frowns, and snaps his fingers. "Damn." He casts his eyes back to Nik again, and I follow his gaze. My heart kicks with pleasure. Nik is a picture of absolute perfection with his chiseled good looks, and muscular physique. He gives us both a smile, and pulls his hood back into place, extinguishing the rainbow halo over his head.

"Listen, girl," Mo says. "I'm going to run."

My gaze snaps back to Mo. "What? Why?"

"Girl, please. If *I* had all of *that* wanting my attention, I'd damn sure wouldn't make him wait." His lips curve into that mischievous grin of his, and he gives me a playful wink. "Give me a call later, and give me all the juicy deets." He mock kisses each of my cheeks, and turns to Nik, and waves at him like a beauty queen on a parade float. "*So* great to meet you, Nik, but I've got to go. Wax appointment. If I miss it, it will look like Tom Selleck's moustache migrated to my forehead."

The corner of Nik's mouth quirks, and he sort of salutes, but chooses to hang back, giving Mo, and I privacy.

"I love you Mo," I say, hoping he knows how sincerely I mean it.

"I know," he says, tapping the tip of my nose. "And I love you too, baby girl." His fond smile causes my heart to swell. Though Mo is constantly pissing me off, our connection has always ran deep. "Now go climb that mountain of a man you got, and stake your claim on that…" He rakes his gaze up, and down the length of Nik. "Luscious piece of property." He makes a silly growling noise, and we both break out in laughter.

He gives me one more hug, then walks away. Just before he's out of sight, he turns and blows me a kiss. I smile, and wave before glancing over my shoulder at Nik. He's back on the hammock. His frame draped out lithely, like a tomcat slinking his way into a comfortable stretch. His eyes move to mine, and they clearly read, *come join me.*

I'm all too eager to oblige, hurrying over to him, and carefully arranging myself beside him. I nestle close, resting my head against his neck. He wraps an arm around me, fitting me snug against his body, and I relax in his embrace. The hammock sways, rocking us hypnotically, lulling me into a calm, and blissful state. I've never been so at peace with myself, and my existence in my entire life.

"I love you," I whisper, the words packed with so much emotion, and truth, it almost hurts to say it out loud.

Nik finds my hand, and brings it to his mouth. "I love you, Abby. More than life itself," he murmurs against my palm. His breath is hot, and it sends sweet tingles along my skin. I lift my gaze to his face, and he's staring up at the sky. His features are contemplative, but serene. I look up at the wispy clouds as they meander their way across the canvas of brilliant blue sky.

"They're watching over us," he says.

I search the depths of the sky, as if I could see Perun sitting at his mighty throne, overseeing his realm with Diva-Dodola stationed obediently at his side. I know they are there, somewhere, keeping a watchful eye on Nik.

"Your parents love you," I reply. "They want to make sure you're happy."

"They know I am. Don't ever doubt that, Abby." He lays my hand flat over his chest. I can feel his strong heartbeat beneath my palm. "But I wasn't talking about Perun. I was talking about *your* parents."

My chest tightens, and heat prickles the space behind my eyes. I struggle to keep the tears at bay, but as I look up at the sky over us, my heart is overwhelmed with far too many emotions to contain. Nik, my Polar Mate is here, on earth with me, forever within my arms. And overhead...my parents, enjoying eternity amongst the stars together.

Nik's fingers slide under my chin, and tilts my face upward. "When the eons turn to eternity, I will still be struck by you. Love struck, and completely lost to you. You don't just have my heart, Abby, you own my very spirit."

I smile, and press a tender kiss to his lips. The familiar spark rushes like a tidal wave through my blood, and spills through Nik, eliciting a moan from him. A kiss is more powerful than any words I can create. Stronger, and more telling than anything I could ever write on paper. It evokes everything I feel inside, and can't seem to properly convey into mere words. Withheld from me for so many years, my kiss is now a language of its own, and as long as Nik understands it, then my words will never be lost.

A word from the author...

I work full-time as a zoo curator, so when I'm not running a zoo, I'm trying to tame the one I live in! I have two kids, and a husband who sometimes acts their ages.

I can usually be found jamming to Elvis Presley tunes, or diligently chipping away at my never-ending "to be read" pile.

I tend to gravitate toward anything paranormal. I love creatures who fly and characters who sprout fur or fangs. Sprinkle some romance and magic into the mix, and I'm a happy girl!

Thank you for purchasing
this publication of The Wild Rose Press, Inc.

If you enjoyed the story, we would appreciate your
letting others know by leaving a review.

For other wonderful stories,
please visit our on-line bookstore at
www.thewildrosepress.com.

For questions or more information
contact us at
info@thewildrosepress.com.

The Wild Rose Press, Inc.
www.thewildrosepress.com

Stay current with The Wild Rose Press, Inc.

Like us on Facebook

https://www.facebook.com/TheWildRosePress

And Follow us on Twitter
https://twitter.com/WildRosePress